D0800991

Of Blood and Brothers: Book Two
by E. Michael Helms

ISBN 978-1-938467-50-9

Published by

köhlerbooks™

210 60th Street, Virginia Beach, VA 23451
212-574-7939
www.koehlerbooks.com

Publisher
John Köhler

Executive Editor
Joe Coccaro

Also by E. Michael Helms

The Proud Bastards

Of Blood and Brothers: Book One

Deadly Catch: A Mac McClellan Mystery

The Private War of Corporal Henson

For my grandsons, Liam and Levi:
may you never have to experience
the bitter taste of war.

OF BLOOD AND BROTHERS

BOOK TWO

E. MICHAEL HELMS

VIRGINIA BEACH
CAPE CHARLES

We few, we happy few, we band of brothers;

For he today that sheds his blood with me

Shall be my brother...

SHAKESPEARE, HENRY V, ACT IV, SCENE 3

Acknowledgments

Thanks to Fred Tribuzzo of The Rudy Agency for your steadfast help and support.

Also, to those two elderly brothers whose names have escaped me over the years. As a child I listened mesmerized to the stories about your Confederate veteran father. It was your voices that gave rise to the voices of Daniel and Elijah Malburn.

May you rest in peace.

—E. Michael Helms

Calvin Hogue
October 1927

ONE

THE DOOR TO DANIEL MALBURN'S cabin swung open, and there stood the Confederate veteran, "grinning like a suckling shoat," to borrow a phrase from the venerable old gent's own repertoire.

"Welcome back, Calvin," he said, stepping aside and motioning me inside. "Thought I might never lay eyes on you again in this here life. Here, let me get shed of that hat and coat for you. Pull that chair yonder over to the stove and I'll go pour us a little snort to limber up your writing hand, heh-heh," Daniel said with a wink of his good eye, the other being clouded by a cataract. "It's right nippy today, ain't it? Yes, sir, nothing like a good wood fire and a sip of corn squeezings to warm up the old bones."

I agreed and moved the straight-backed chair near the pot-bellied stove. I waited while Daniel ambled to the kitchen to pour the "little snort" that I knew would be a hefty glassful of moonshine. One of his nephews made the fiery concoction, reputed to be the best corn whiskey available in three counties.

Five-thirty on a Friday afternoon was a little early in the day for me to imbibe, but I didn't want to chance offending the Malburn family patriarch.

It had been over three weeks since I'd traveled by train to my hometown of Carlisle, Pennsylvania to bury my father, who had passed away suddenly and unexpectedly at age forty-eight. Two days ago, I'd returned to the Florida panhandle town of Harrison and my job as a reporter for my uncle Hawley Wells' newspaper, the *St. Andrew Pilot*.

When I met Uncle Hawley in his office upon my return, he'd handed me a stack of letters. "All these arrived from our readers since you've been gone, boy. Nearly every one of them is complaining about how much they miss your story on the Malburns, and wondering when it's going to continue. You'd best get to it. Disappointing our readership is the last thing we need."

"Right away, sir," I said, itching to get back to work. Back in May I'd begun a weekly serial about the exploits of Daniel Malburn and his younger brother, Elijah. The weekly feature was an unexpected result that sprang from a routine assignment covering the Malburn Reunion along the Econfina River, one of the longest continuing family gatherings in the nation. I became intrigued upon learning the brothers, as had my own grandfathers, fought on opposing sides during the Civil War, or the War of Northern Aggression, as Daniel was fond of putting it. Daniel had been a nineteen-year-old volunteer serving with Company K of the Sixth Florida Infantry in the Confederate Army of Tennessee.

Elijah, four years Daniel's junior, had wanted no part of the war. He was working at John Anderson's salt works on the shores of St. Andrew Bay when he and family slave, Jefferson, were taken prisoner during a raid by Union forces. Elijah and Jefferson had grown up together and were more like brothers than master and slave. When Jefferson was conscripted into the

Second U.S. Colored Infantry, Elijah faced being sent to a Union prison camp or joining the Second U.S. Florida Cavalry Regiment as a scout and courier. Feeling responsible for Jefferson's well-being, Elijah had reluctantly agreed to become a Union soldier.

In a few minutes Daniel returned carrying two glasses filled to the brim with clear liquid. I could almost feel my taste buds and sinuses cringe as he handed one to me. Daniel eased himself into his padded rocker opposite my chair and held his glass aloft. "Here's to what ails you, heh-heh," he said and downed a hefty swallow. He looked admiringly at the glass. "Ah, even better'n it was this morning."

I lifted my glass in return and took a sip, trying my best not to squint as the liquid fire trickled down my throat. "Thank you, sir," I managed after catching my breath, "that is mighty fine whiskey."

Daniel settled back in his chair and rocked contentedly for a moment and then stopped. "Forgetting my manners, Calvin. You hungry? I got some of Alma's fried chicken in the icebox."

"No, sir, I'm fine," I assured him. "In fact, I stopped in Bennet and had an early supper at Alma's on the drive over."

Alma Hutchins, daughter of Elijah and niece of Daniel, served as my invaluable and trusted go-between in my dealings with the Malburn brothers. She arranged our meetings and did her best to insure the sometimes ornery and obstinate siblings minded their respective manners with me.

Daniel nodded. "Well, sir, you let me know if you get a hankering for something later on. Now, where was we when we left off?"

I found the marker in my notebook and scanned down the page. "You were home on furlough and had just given Annie the ring while the two of you were sitting by the big spring," I said, reading from my notes. "Annie had said she'd couldn't marry you until the war was over, but that she would wear the ring for the rest of her days."

Annabelle Gainer had been engaged to Daniel since he'd ridden off to war in March of eighteen sixty-two. Not wanting their daughter to end up a teenaged widow, her parents had disapproved of the two marrying until the war was resolved. To further complicate matters, Elijah was secretly in love with Annie, and was determined to somehow win her from his brother.

Daniel's face seemed to light up at the remembrance. He took another hearty sip of whiskey. "Yes, sir, that was a mighty fine time, all right. Didn't have a clue then that things was fixing to turn upside down for me."

Daniel Malburn
Spring 1864
Dalton to Dallas

TWO

WELL, SIR, THE REST OF my furlough flew by like a hawk on the hunt. I courted Annie nearbout ever day, even tried to get her to change her mind about marrying up a time or two. But it weren't to be, so me and Joe Porter made it back to our winter quarters up at Dalton with my bachelorhood still untarnished.

It was the coldest winter any of us Florida boys could ever remember. Got down around zero now and again, and snowed to beat all hell. It was miserable weather, but it weren't all bad. Ever now and then some of the fellers would commence tossing snowballs at each other till it growed into a full-blown fracas betwixt whole regiments. That was fun times for them of us had never seen much snow.

By early spring the cold weather broke. Some Kentucky boys taught us a game, name of town ball, they'd learnt from Yankee prisoners whilst we was up at Cumberland Gap in late '62. It was sort of like the game of baseball is today, but ever team had a heap of players. And to get a feller out you had to strike him with the ball, which could hurt some, seeing the balls we made had a rock in the center wound tight with strips of cloth and sewed inside a scrap of cowhide. Shames me to admit it, but them Kentucky boys give us a thrashing ever game we played 'em.

I reckon the biggest thing to happen that winter was the revival that swept through the Army of Tennessee. Makeshift churches sprung up all over camp, and there weren't a day went by that services weren't held one place or another. Over a hundred-fifty Florida boys got converted or rededicated their lives to the Lord. I weren't amongst 'em, sad to say, though my folks had raised me up in the Christian way. Since Chickamauga and what had befell poor Hamp Watts, I'd become a wayfaring soul of sorts.

But you couldn't keep Joe Porter out of them meetings, no, sir. Ever night, if he weren't on picket or other such duty, you could bet your last grayback he'd be somewheres amongst the worshipers seeking the Lord's will and guidance. Joe's folks was godly people, and it was a rare Sunday back home before the war that he weren't sitting with 'em on their pew in the First Baptist Church of Bennet. But in them days Joe had a touch of the devil in him, same as me, and it was nearbout torture for him to sit still for a hour listening to the preacher spout hellfire and brimstone. I reckon seeing hellfire and brimstone firsthand had put the fear of God in him. From that first day of preaching at camp on, Joe Porter weren't ever without the Testament they give him and the others that found the Lord at them meetings.

The Yankees had mostly behaved theirselves over the winter. Ever now and again our pickets and theirs would get in a little scrap, but it weren't nothing to write home about. Then one day in early May they went and spoilt our winter jubilee.

That goldamn devil General Sherman was bound and determined to capture Atlanta and destroy the railhead that run from there to divers points throughout the Confederacy. If Sherman could do that, the Confederate armies would starve from want of food and supplies. So Ol' Joe Johnston was ever bit bound and determined to stop him from doing just that. Now word come down that our cavalry had spotted the bluebellies advancing in force towards Rocky Face Ridge. Sherman was on the move, and our town ball days was done. We swapped bats for rifles and took up our position in the works which stretched along the length of the ridge and waited for the Yanks to show.

Weren't much of a wait either. Early the next morning, them Federals come marching up in column after column which looked like long blue snakes slithering through the hills. They was doing it up right, too. Everwhere you looked flags was waving and bands was playing music fit to stir the soul. Almost made a body anxious to get on with the war after a long winter's slacking.

Well, sir, I'd of never believed them bluebellies would attack us straight up the ridge, but that's just what they done. Which was jim-dandy by me. If they was fool enough to walk into a meat grinder, then we was more'n game to do the grinding. And we did a heap of grinding too, that's the gospel. Them boys in blue had plenty of grit in their craw, I'll give 'em that. We shot 'em down till our barrels growed too hot to reload, then commenced throwing rocks whilst waiting for our rifles to cool, but they kept on coming. Like on Missionary Ridge, some of the boys took to prying boulders loose, sending them tumbling down on the Yanks like wrecking balls. The bluebelly artillery firing on our position loosened up a heap more rocks that come raining down on them poor souls. Rocky Face Ridge come by its name honest, gospel truth.

For two days, the Yankees kept at it hot and heavy, then things slacked off a mite. Two or three days later, our cavalry reported that the bluebellies was on the move. Two wings of their army was on the march, trying to flank us around the south side of Rocky Face. Seems downright shameful, but that goldamn Sherman had sent the center of his army agin us like sheep to the slaughter to hold our attention and keep us occupied whilst the others commenced the flanking movement. So Ol' Joe Johnston figured it was time to leave our perch on Rocky Face and hightail it south towards Resaca.

During the night, General Johnston set the Army of Tennessee on the march towards the railhead at Dalton and on to Resaca, where defense works was already being prepared. Being part of Hardee's Corps at the time, the Sixth Florida was amongst the last to pull out of our positions on Rocky Face. For the next two days we fought a delaying action to slow the Yanks' march to give our boys time to strengthen up the works around Resaca. Ol' Joe aimed to make a stand there, if Sherman had the gumption to fight. Around mid-afternoon of the third day we made Resaca and took up our place in the lines and waited.

Here and yonder light skirmishing commenced out front along the lines, but mostly we spent the rest of the day shoring up our works and watching the Yankees march up and take position on the hills across the valley from us. There was a heap of them bluebellies, too. Sherman had hisself upwards of a hundred thousand troops, whilst General Johnston had a mite over forty thousand.

Our works was on a line of hills which formed a rough half-circle just north of the village of Resaca. Our lines stretched from the Oostanaula River south of town, then run northward and eastward to the Connesauga River north of town. Hardee's Corps was in the middle, General Hood's boys was to our right, and General Polk's was holding our left. Us Florida boys was tied in with the left of Hood's Corps, where the line took a sharp angle east towards the Connesauga.

Betwixt the two armies was a rough valley, maybe four or five hundred yards wide. Through it run a creek bordered by a thick tangle of trees and bushes and brambles. If the Yanks did mean to fight us here, they would have theirselves a hard row to hoe just getting to us.

By dark, the skirmishing had mostly petered out, but the artillery kept swapping fire across the valley through the night. I lit a small cook fire in the bottom of our trench from the wood Billy Yon had gathered, then boiled coffee and fried up some fatback and cornbread. When it was done, Joe and Billy commenced to eat whilst I carried supper to Orv Cowart and Goose Hutchins who was standing first watch.

"Much obliged, Danny," says Orv when I give him his share. "I'm near hungry enough to eat a mule."

"Sorry, but this'll have to do," I says, pointing to the fatback. "Their ain't a mule in the whole Confederate Army got this much fat on it."

Goose was staring through the head log out across the valley towards the Yankee lines. He had a solemn look on his face and didn't say a thing when I give him his coffee and food. That weren't like Goose Hutchins, who was nearbout the biggest jokester in the Army of Tennessee.

He flinched and ducked when a shell whistled overhead and exploded a ways behind the lines. That weren't like him either. Goose was usually cool as spring water under fire. "What you reckon they's up to?" he says after a spell.

I looked out across the valley into the dark. "Way I see it, come morning I figure them Yanks to come walking up here asking would we like to join their tea party."

Seems ol' Goose weren't up to no humor. "I got me a bad feeling about this, Danny. Mighty bad." It weren't the first time I'd heard such talk before a fight. Most times it come to nothing, but Earl Hayes had said nearbout the same the night before the Yanks kicked us off Missionary Ridge, and the next day he was dead.

"Goose," I says, "you're too goldamn homely for any Yankee ball. Why, I know for a fact they change directions just to miss you."

Goose looked at me and give a half grin. "Reckon that's a

fact, ain't it? We been in a mess of fights and I ain't got so much as a scratch yet." Then the grin faded. "All the same, you'll write my folks if something happens?"

"I'll see to it," I says, "but you best get to eating. It ain't polite to go to a tea party on a empty belly."

Next morning the Yankees didn't waste no time getting down to business. Their bands struck up that stirring music they was so fond of playing, and we watched as the bluebellies come down them hills at us stretched out in four long lines of battle, one after the other, flags a-waving. Their artillery commenced firing on our works, but we just hunkered down and waited. On they come across the valley till the first line hit the creek. It took 'em a spell to worm through them trees, wade the creek and pull theirselves up the steep bank and regroup. They was nearbout in range then, but we still held our fire. When they come within two hundred yards our cannons opened up and we give 'em two or three volleys that sent that first line of Yanks scrambling back to the safety of the creek.

There was maybe a hundred or so dead and wounded bluebellies littering the ground, but after a few minutes, here the others come again at double-quick. This time we let 'em get closer, maybe a hundred yards away, then our cannons opened up with double loads of canister and them poor boys in blue went down like hay before a scythe. A few brave souls that was still alive managed to crawl their way back to the creek, whilst others hunkered down amongst their dead.

On my left Joe commenced to reload his Enfield. "Lord a'mighty," he says, "this is worser than butchering day."

A Yankee shell come screeching in. Me and Joe ducked. It blowed up a few feet in front of our works, giving us a dirt shower. When the smoke and dust cleared I seen the head log had been shoved back a few inches. "See what you done, Joe Porter? You ought not be taking the Lord's name in vain thataway."

Joe dug at the dirt that had splattered his eyes. "I ain't done no such a thing. He is the Lord God Almighty. That ain't cussing."

"Well you best get to praying then," I says, looking through the head log, "cause here they come again."

And come they did. Three more times them brave bluebellies come across that creek and charged up our hill. We commenced firing and reloading and firing and reloading till the air was choked thick with burnt powder. My ears was ringing to beat all hell and my head ached from all the musket and cannon fire and the concussion of Yankee shells exploding nearby.

I was ramming a load down my barrel just as the smoke cleared enough that I seen a passel of Yanks just yards from our works. Before I could finish loading, a Yank jumped into our trench. I grabbed my Enfield by the barrel and knocked the bluecoat backwards agin the wall of the trench. Raised the rifle over my head and was fixing to bash his brains out when I froze. Hamp Watts stared up at me, wide-eyed and scared as a trapped rabbit. I reached down to help him up when of a sudden his chest exploded into red spray.

"Lord a'mighty!" Joe says, smoke still rolling out the barrel of his rifle. "You trying to get us kilt? That Yank was fixing to shoot you!"

Well, sir, I was stunned. Wondered if I weren't losing what little scrap of sanity I had left. I looked down at the Yank Joe had shot dead. His dark eyes was open and staring at me. Didn't look nothing like Hamp. This poor soul had hair black as coal and whiskers to boot. Blood was pouring out of his chest like a red spring where Joe's ball had struck.

I shook my head to clear it and grinned at Joe. "There you go cussing again," I says. "You'll be the death of me yet."

It was midafternoon before the bluebelly infantry got their

fill of fighting, but when they retreated for the last time, the party was just getting started. Then the Yank artillery opened up with a barrage the likes of which we ain't never seen. The shells rained down on us like exploding hail. The head log in front of me and Joe got blowed loose but the support logs over the trench saved us. There was so much falling dirt and thick dust and smoke we couldn't see how Goose and Orv and Billy was faring to our right. It looked like our works was going to cave in and bury us, so me and Joe commenced tunneling into the back wall like gophers.

The shelling went on for hours. All up and down the lines poor souls was crying out for help. We had kilt a heap of Yanks that day, but they was giving us a eye for a eye now. Seemed like a week before the barrage finally petered out. I crawled out of my burrow and brushed what dirt I could off my rifle.

My eyes adjusted to the dark enough to see Joe crawl out beside me. The shelling had stopped but my head was still pounding. I looked around, trying to make sense of things. Our position was spared, but from what little I could make out the trench had caved-in on both sides of me and Joe. The dead Yankee Joe had shot was buried. "We best get looking for the boys," I says to Joe. "The works has caved-in."

We laid our rifles agin the trench wall and scrambled out. Walked over a few yards to where we figured Goose and the others was, and seen the whole shebang had come down on 'em.

Me and Joe commenced digging at the dirt and timbers fast as we could, stopping ever now and again to call out our pards' names and listen. It was a spell till we heard so much as a whisper.

"Over here, Danny!" says Joe. "Help me get this log off."

Must've took us another half hour or so to get to him, but finally Goose Hutchins poked his head out betwixt two logs that had fell over him. He was covered with dirt from head to foot, but he was still amongst the living. Joe commenced spouting

Bible verses and praising the Lord, whilst Goose commenced spitting dirt and cussing up a storm.

"Get this goddamn log off'n me," he says. "We got to get to Billy."

"Where's Orv?" I says.

"Dead," says Goose, "shot through the neck. But Billy was still alive when this goddamn trench come down on us."

The three of us commenced digging till we was plumb tuckered. My back and shoulders ached something fierce, and my hands was bleeding from digging like a dog. Goose hadn't heard nothing from Billy, he told us, but his ears was packed full of dirt so Billy might still be breathing. More'n once I wanted to quit, but I figured it could've been me buried under them logs and dirt so I kept at it.

It was daylight before we finally found poor Billy Yon. He was stone cold, his neck and chest crushed beneath a head log that got blowed into the trench. When we got most the dirt off him his face was peaceful enough, so we figured he didn't suffer none.

We laid out poor Orv and Billy a few yards back of our trench till we could give 'em a proper burial. Joe took out his Testament and read a few verses over them, then offered up a prayer. When Joe was done with his new-found duties, I hunted up some wood and built a fire for coffee whilst Goose went looking for the engineers to borrow some shovels so we could repair our works.

Goose was back with two shovels before the coffee was good and boiled. The three of us sat around the cook fire drinking coffee and looking out across the valley where so many Yankees had gone to meet their Maker. Here and yonder, vultures was already circling, waiting for their feast to get good and ripe. It seemed them feathered devils had took to following the armies around of late, knowing a good feed couldn't be too far away.

After a spell Goose says, "Here I was thinking I was gone up for sure. And now Orv and Billy is done in."

"Reckon it's the Lord's will," says Joe. "No man knows the minute or the hour, the Good Book says."

I swallowed the last of my coffee, reached for the pot and poured me another cup. Looked over at Goose and grinned. "Told you you was too damn homely to die."

THREE

AROUND NOON THAT DAY, THE Yanks launched a spirited attack agin General Hood's Corps on our right, and later in the afternoon, they struck General Polk's Corps on our left. Neither attack come to much, but when it was done a heap more souls on both sides had breathed their last. Mercifully for us Hardee boys, the Yanks let our center be except for some light shelling. Reckon the bluebellies weren't antsy for a repeat of yesterday's slaughter.

Midafternoon Tom Gainer come by our position and told us to get ready to pull out after dark. Our cavalry had spotted a passel of Yanks crossing the Oostanaula at some ferry downriver of town, so General Johnston decided it was time to abandon Resaca for points south. We commenced the sad business of burying our dead in mass graves, Orville Cowart and young Billy Yon amongst them. That grim duty done, we turned to readying for the retreat.

That night we pulled out of our works and marched through the village of Resaca. We crossed the Oostanaula River over pontoon bridges and the covered railroad bridge me and Joe Porter had rode across back in January. When all the troops was safely across, the engineers set fire to the railroad and pontoon bridges to delay the Yanks whilst we made good our escape.

———— •◆• ————

Well, sir, it's been a goodly number of years since this all come to pass, and time has fogged over my memories some, but I'll tell the story of our retreat towards Atlanta the best I can recollect. Keep in mind how I'm obliged to them army guides at the Chickamauga dedication that give us the particulars for much of what I recall.

It seems Ol' Joe Johnston had growed right fond of using General Hardee's Corps to cover his retreats, because that's just what we found ourselves doing again. Whilst the rest of the army marched south towards Adairsville, us Florida boys and the rest of Hardee's troops took up positions near Calhoun at a place called Rome Crossroads. Weren't long before the bluebellies showed up and we commenced to do battle whilst our army moved south to find better ground to make a stand. A right lively fight went on for the next day or so, then General Hardee put us on the march to Adairsville to join up with the rest of our boys.

Johnston had figured on fighting Sherman at Adairsville, but for some reason or other, the terrain weren't to his liking. So the next day he sent Hardee's Corps with the wagon train and cavalry heading south on the main road towards Kingston. Our job was to raise as much dust and ruckus as we could so the Yanks would think we was the main body of the army. It was ten miles or so, but the road was good and we had ourselves a easy march for a change. General Johnston moved the rest of the army over back roads southeast to Cassville, where he figured to spring a trap on the wing of Sherman's army our scouts had reported was headed there.

Our cavalry had also reported there was a line of ridges just north of Cassville that would make a strong defensive position. Ol' Joe figured on placing Hood's Corps on a ridge a ways east, whilst Polk would hold the center in front of the town. General Hardee would fight another delaying action agin Sherman's other two wings, tearing up the tracks and blocking the roads that led from Kingston to Cassville, then hurry on to join the rest of Johnston's army. Whilst Sherman stumbled towards Cassville to join up with his flanking army, our boys would come at the bluebellies from three sides.

It was a right sound plan. It most likely would've worked too, causing Sherman to retreat back north after losing a whole third of his army to a crushing defeat. Only thing was, it seems General Hood had growed hisself a yellow streak of sorts. He failed to launch the attack as Ol' Joe had planned it, which went and spoilt the whole kettle of fish. That give General Sherman time to reunite his whole army in front of Cassville. Weren't nothing Johnston could do then but retreat to another line of works on a high ridge line south of town. We sat there for a spell whilst our artillery and skirmishers swapped fire with theirs. We was a mite tired of retreating and was itching to stand and fight.

This place seemed a mighty fit place for a fight too, even better than our strong position atop Rocky Face Ridge at Dalton. The ridge was nearbout a hundred and fifty foot high in places, with a fine view of the valley below. If Sherman wanted to attack us here, he'd have to come across the open valley floor that stretched before us. Our cannon and rifle fire was bound to chew them bluebellies to pieces before they ever stepped foot on our ridge. Our mouth was nearbout watering at the thought of it.

But it weren't to be. During the night orders come down to move out again. There was a ripsnorting heap of cussing and bellyaching and such being spouted as we give up them strong works without a fight. We marched on south through the dark, crossed the Etowah River and burnt the bridges behind us.

FOUR

IT WAS SOMETIME NEAR THE last week of May when we crossed the Etowah River. General Johnston left some cavalry and a small infantry force in the works on the south bank to keep a eye on the Yankees, then moved the rest of the army on south to Altoona Pass. That was some rough country, gospel truth. Them Altoona Mountains was steep and rose nearbout a thousand foot above the surrounding countryside. The gap at Altoona was sixty-some foot deep. The railroad and main road run through it on towards Marietta and Atlanta. It was a mighty strong position, and Ol' Joe was hoping Sherman would be fool enough to attack us there. Three days later, our cavalry reported the bluebellies had crossed the Etowah in force and was on the move southwest to try to outflank us.

General Johnston weren't about to let the moss grow under his boots whilst deciding what to do. Right quick, he left enough troops to protect Altoona Pass and commenced marching the main army southwest towards the little towns of New Hope and Dallas.

We hoofed it hard all that day under a hot sun and on into the night. Finally we halted to rest a spell, but the weather weren't about to cooperate. It commenced to rain a gullywasher, making things even more miserable. We hunkered down in the mud and done our best to catch a couple of hours of sleep, then before dawn, we took up the march again.

We made Dallas that afternoon, nearbout tuckered from the heat and lack of sleep. Weary as we was, there weren't no time to rest. The Yanks was expected at any time, so we commenced digging rifle pits on a low ridge a quarter mile east of town.

The land thereabouts was some of the most rugged and inhospitable country I ever laid eyes on, gospel. Them hills was covered with trees and tangled brush so thick a boar hog would've had a time rooting through it. It was plumb full of crisscrossing ridges and deep ravines with briars and brambles that would rip the clothes slap off a body. If all that weren't bad enough, there was deep swamps and quicksand bogs to boot.

We weren't no sooner dug in when the bluebellies come marching up without a goldamn clue that we was waiting there for 'em. They come busting through the brush into a open field to our front. We kept hunkered down in our works till they was close enough to where we could hear 'em cussing to beat all hell about the weather and the countryside and their officers and such. Then we raised up and give 'em a volley that sent them that didn't drop skedaddling back into the brush.

For the next two hours, we kept at it. Them Yanks would mount up a charge, and we'd send 'em scurrying back into the woods with their tails tucked betwixt their legs. Near sundown, there come the booming of artillery and crashing of musket fire to our right. That happened to be General Hood's boys over by New Hope Church giving the bluebellies a sound thrashing. Weren't long before clouds rolled in and a cold rain come pelting down to beat back the heat. Thunder boomed and lightning flashed to beat all hell till it was nearbout impossible to tell the storm from the sound and flashing of the guns.

It was long after dark when things finally quieted down to where we figured the bluebellies had had their fill of fighting for the day. The rain had slacked off considerable, and me and Joe and Goose had just broke out our cold rations when Tom Gainer stopped by our rifle pit.

"You boys have got picket duty. See that ditch yonder, maybe a hundred yards out?"

"I cain't see a goldamn thing," I says without looking. I knowed the ditch he was talking about, but I was more'n a mite irritated. "The Yanks ain't fool enough to come stumbling at us in this dark."

"Reckon they're not," Tom says. "All the same, the captain wants pickets out front of every squad, and you boys are it."

"This is a jim-dandy way to treat family," I says to Tom as he took off to check on the next rifle pit.

"We best get at it, boys," I says to Joe and Goose whilst I reached for my poncho. It had started raining again. "Rifles and ponchos. We don't want nothing rattling around out yonder."

Joe fumbled around in his haversack and fetched his Testament and stuffed it inside his shirt. "You cain't read in the dark," I says, "and you sure ain't lighting no fire."

Joe grinned and patted his shirt. "The Lord is my shepherd, and I aim to keep Him close by."

"Goddamn rain," says Goose.

———————

Well, sir, that was one miserable night. We wrapped up in our ponchos and done our best to keep dry, but it weren't no use. We was soaked head to foot. The night growed cold, so we was shivering to boot. A good foot of water had settled in that shallow ditch we was sitting in, so we finally give it up and climbed out. We found a tree that had been blowed down by cannon fire and hunkered down behind it for the rest of the night. When the sky give the first hint of gray, we snuck back to our lines, making sure to halloo our boys with the password so they wouldn't take us for Yanks.

Well, sir, that day weren't much to write home about. Ever now and again we'd fire a volley at the bluebellies to keep 'em honest, but mostly we stayed hunkered down in our works, and the Yanks done the same. We suffered the heat all day, then long about dark it commenced to rain and we commenced shivering again. Good thing was, our mess didn't have picket duty that night, so we got to stay in our own rifle pit and be miserable.

The third day at Dallas, General Hardee sent one of his divisions, commanded by General Cleburne, to reinforce Polk's Corps defending the Confederate right. Seems the Yanks was hankering to attack our boys along Pickett's Mill Creek, which would put a goodly part of Sherman's troops in our rear if the Yanks was to carry the day.

Late that afternoon the bluebellies struck our boys at Pickett's Mill and a battle commenced to beat all hell. It was maybe five miles away as the crow flies, but from the ruckus them boys was raising you'd of swore it weren't more'n five hundred yards. It went on till well after dark, maybe two or three hours, then things petered out for a spell.

Goose Hutchins was taking first watch. Me and Joe had just rolled up in our blankets when of a sudden a volley of musket fire tore through the night. Seems General Cleburne's boys had took offense at some stubborn Yanks that hadn't yet skedaddled, so they commenced a night attack and drove 'em from the field of battle.

Me and Joe sat up with Goose and listened to the fight until it played out and crickets took up the offensive, then we turned in.

That's when I had the dream.

FIVE

MY ANNIE WAS DRESSED ALL in black, head to foot. She was wearing a long black dress of fancy cloth, with silk gloves and hat to match, and black leather shoes. Even the kerchief she slipped underneath the veil to dab at her swollen eyes now and again was black.

Weren't long till she broke out sobbing again. From across our parlor where I was sitting cleaning my rifle, I seen her shoulders heave in sorrow. Mama was standing beside Annie, dressed in black too, the same dress she'd wore for months after my daddy fell off the barn roof and died.

I watched as Mama turned to Annie and give her a hug and patted her back to comfort her. That's when I noticed my brother Eli, standing by Annie's other side. He was all gussied up in his best Sunday go-to-meeting suit, with starched collars and necktie. His shoes was freshly blackened and his hair was combed proper. When he turned towards Annie, I seen his face was stricken. It dawned on me then that somebody must have up and died.

It's always a sad affair when some poor soul goes to meet his Maker, but I had seen such a heap of death in the war that one more didn't seem such a grievous thing, not to carry on such as them three was. Figured I'd best see what all the ruckus was about and pay my respects. I draped the cleaning rag over the barrel of my Enfield, leaned it agin the wall and walked across the parlor to join the mourners.

My skin crawled with gooseflesh when I got close enough to see that the recent deceased was wearing a fancy new gray Confederate uniform. Then it struck me—poor Tom Gainer! I nearbout strained my brain trying to recollect when and how Tom had been kilt, but try as I might I just couldn't.

Poor Sara, I thought, my dear sister a widow, and so young! Where was Sara, anyhow? Pitiful thing was probably bedridden, I figured, overcome with grief for her beloved Tom.

I moved closer to Annie, hoping to comfort her agin the loss of her poor dead brother. She didn't seem to notice I was even there when I put my arm around her. "Annie," I says, "I'm powerful sorry about Tom. He didn't suffer none, I thought you'd want to know that."

Now that's a mite queer, I thought, when Annie didn't pay no mind to what I said. Instead, she reached out for brother Eli. Laid her pale cheek agin his chest and busted out crying again.

Whilst them two was comforting each other I chanced to look down at the body. It was laid out in a pine casket much like the one me and Eli had helped Uncle Nate build for our daddy. Of a sudden, a cold fist grabbed my gut and squeezed the very life out of me. It weren't Tom Gainer laying there at all, no, sir. Staring up at me was the face of one Daniel Malburn!

———•———

I woke up with a start, temples throbbing and my heart nearbout to pound out of my chest. It weren't raining, but I was drenched through and shaking like I'd been laying in a cold winter rain. It took a minute or so till I realized where I was, and that I weren't laying dead in that casket back home.

I sat up and took some deep breaths till I calmed down a mite. Goose Hutchins was wrapped up in his blanket at the other end of the rifle pit, sawing logs. Joe was staring out into the dark towards the Yankee lines, doing his best to keep awake. Ever now and again he'd start to nod off, then give hisself a slap upside the face.

I looked to the sky to get a sense of what time it was. Found the quarter moon just as it was rising above the trees in the east, its faint shine bleeding through a thin blanket of clouds. It would be daylight in a hour or so, I figured. I had already stood my watch but there weren't no way I was going back to sleep this night. Truth be told, the very thought of sleeping spooked me.

I crawled over to the front of our pit and shook Joe awake. "You go catch some sleep," I says. "I'm up, cain't sleep nohow."

Joe give a big yawn and looked at me. "You mean it?"

"Yep. Best get before I change my mind."

Well, sir, I sat there till daylight playing it all out in my mind over and over. Try as I might, there weren't no denying it. That dream had been a sign, sure as the sun would chase that moon up the sky. It had only been a few days before that Joe had read me a passage from the Bible saying the Lord sometimes spoke through dreams and visions. And I ain't never had such a real and terrible dream in all my born days. And weren't there something else Joe had read me, something about mockers or such? I had been mocking Joe ever since he'd got religion at the revival back at Dalton, and now God would have his revenge.

Yes, sir, I was a goner for sure. I would've bet my last grayback on it.

SIX

THAT MORNING WHILST GOOSE HUTCHINS was busy cooking our rations I took Joe aside and told him about my dream. "It weren't just no ordinary dream," I says when I was done, "it was a vision. I seen myself laid out in that pine box clear as I'm looking at you this very minute."

"Now Danny, don't go fretting about it. Why, it weren't but a few days ago Goose was saying the same thing. Who you reckon that is over there cooking up our breakfast?" he says, nodding his head towards Goose.

I shook my head. "It ain't the same, it ain't the same at all. What Goose said was he had hisself a bad feeling, is all."

"That's so," says Joe. "But all the same, Goose is alive, same as you and me and them crows squawking back in the woods."

"What I seen weren't no feeling. Weren't no dream, either. It was a vision, Joe Porter, sure as we stand here. Orv Cowart is dead. So is Billy Yon," I says. "Goose went and had his bad feeling, and them two was kilt just hours afterwards. And don't go forgetting Earl Hayes, either. He seen his death coming."

Joe stared down at his feet for a spell, then out towards the Yankee lines. "You're scaring me a mite, Danny boy. I wish you would hush up all this nonsense." He patted his breeches pocket where his Testament was. "I aim to do some reading, see if I cain't find some words from the Lord to ease your mind about all this."

"I'm obliged to you for it," I says, just as Goose called out saying our breakfast was done, "but I don't reckon it'll help none. God give me the vision, Joe. I'm done for."

———•———

Us and the Yanks passed most of the morning swapping light fire just to keep each other honest. Neither side seemed antsy to make much of a show of things. True to his word, Joe spent the quiet spells reading his Testament, searching for a verse or two that might give me comfort over my vision. If he'd found any, he was keeping them to hisself for the time being.

By early afternoon clouds rolled in and swallowed up the high sun. Thunder commenced rumbling like distant cannon, but the rain held off. Things had growed right quiet up and down the lines when Tom Gainer stopped by our works.

"Our cavalry reports the Yankees are moving east towards Acworth." Tom hunkered down in our pit as the Yanks cut loose a sudden volley. "General Johnston believes they're trying to gain the railroad and move on Marietta."

Muskets barked off another volley. "Looks like somebody forgot to tell them boys," I says, pointing towards the bluebelly lines as another passel of balls whistled overhead.

"That's what headquarters wants us to find out," says Tom. "In a hour we're moving forward to test the enemy's strength. Word is, most of the Federals have quit our front." He pointed towards the Yankees. "That's believed to only be a line of skirmishers in those works, left behind to keep us occupied."

"Just when was they supposed to have done this

skedaddling?" says Joe. "We ain't seen or heard nothing of the sort. I say there's Yanks aplenty yonder."

Goose Hutchins snorted and let fly a stream of tobacco juice. "I believe them smart gen'rals ought to mosey on over there and count 'em their own selves."

"Just who is going with us on this little picnic?" I says.

"We'll have the Tennessee Brigade plus a whole brigade of dismounted cavalry on our left," says Tom, "and the Kentucky boys on our right. Near ten thousand in all. That should do."

I felt a mite better hearing the Kentuckians would be with us. Them boys had proved to be fine fighters. Still, it weren't enough to shake the dread I had from my vision. The way I seen it, a hundred thousand troops weren't enough to turn the hand of God.

"Leave your haversacks and blanket rolls behind," says Tom. "We'll be moving fast. You boys be ready when I give the word."

———— • ————

The next hour crawled by slower than a three-legged gopher. We kept hunkered down in our works. Joe read his Testament. Goose commenced scribbling a letter to his sweetheart back home. I made a show of cleaning my rifle, but mostly just fretted. Rain come spitting down long enough for Goose to put away his writing paper, then stopped. Before he could fish it out of his haversack orders come down the line to move out at the word.

I grabbed my Enfield and give my cartridges and caps another check. Looked back to where I'd left my haversack and blanket wrapped in my poncho laying agin the backside of our pit. My heart ached to gaze at Annie's sweet face once more, but there weren't time. I grabbed Joe's shoulder. "Look," I says, above the racket of soldiers making ready for battle, "I know you don't put much store in my vision, but I'm counting on you to see to my belongings."

I was expecting Joe to commence spouting a verse or two

about how the Lord would shield and protect me and such, but all he done was give a quick nod and look out towards the Yanks. Well, sir, that spooked me a mite, but then I figured Joe's own gut was quivering some at the thought of the coming fight.

Of a sudden Tom Gainer and the other lieutenants was out front of the works strutting around like banty roosters, shouting orders for us to form up and dress our line. I made sure the Colt's revolver was tight inside my belt as we scrambled out of our rifle pit. My legs felt wobbly as a newborn calf. Tom stood tall with his back to the Yankees, eyeballing the rest of us scarecrows. That boy had nerves of steel, gospel truth.

"Keep it straight now boys," he says, looking this way and that, checking to see his squad was aligned proper. Then he turned towards the bluebellies, waved his pistol in a circle over his head. "Quickstep... forward!"

We ain't made fifty yards when heavy firing broke out on the far left where the brigade of dismounted cavalry was making their advance. From all the ruckus, them boys had found a heap more than skirmishers to their front.

Weren't a minute later the bluebellies cut loose a volley our way. "At the double-quick, boys!" Tom shouts. Balls whizzed overhead and we commenced trotting forward. Blue gunsmoke was rising all along the Yankee works far as eye could see. Then come the belching of artillery and the horrible *thunk!* of metal tearing bone and flesh as canister cut a bloody swath through our ranks.

We went sprawling to ground, hugging earth. "Skirmishers, my granny's ass!" Goose shouts. I looked over at Joe. He was grim-faced, mouthing a prayer or some such to hisself. Of a sudden, on our left the Rebel Yell rose up from a thousand throats. The stirring sound of them cavalry boys on the attack give us Floridians grit. We was up and charging forward, screaming at the top of our lungs to beat all hell.

Before I knowed what was happening, we was on the Yanks

and jumping into their works. Most of the bluebellies that weren't kilt or wounded had skedaddled back to a second line some hundred yards away. We hunkered down a few minutes to catch our wind, then the boys was up and charging forward again.

The battle was raging all around, but blood was pounding my ears so fierce that I barely heard the crashing muskets and booming cannons. Then it come to me that I was still inside the Yankee works, shaking all over. I knowed I had to get out of there and join the charge. Couldn't let my pards down. But when I tried to scramble out of that trench my legs weren't of a mind to follow.

Well, sir, I had been in a fair number of scraps whilst soldiering with the Army of Tennessee. I weren't always the bravest soul in battle, but I sure weren't no coward or shirker either. I commenced cussing at myself to beat all hell. Weren't no oath ever uttered at man or beast that I spared myself. Somehow I leapt out of the works and run forward. If I was bound to die, I aimed to do so facing the enemy, not cowered down in some ditch like a whipped pup.

Yankee rifles spit smoke and cannons belched fire, but I kept running through the deadly hail buzzing all around me. Here and yonder poor souls was laying dead or wounded, but I kept on. I had to catch up to Joe and the boys or die trying.

Of a sudden my rifle flew out of my hands and I tumbled backwards like somebody had whopped me with a axe handle. Laid still a minute or so, taking stock of things. I was a mite stunned, but there weren't no pain, no blood that I could tell. The battle sounded far away, but I knowed that couldn't be.

Figured I'd best be getting back to it, so I looked around for my rifle. I spied it, maybe ten foot away. The stock was shattered and the barrel was bent where a ball had struck it. I crawled over and picked it up. Weren't no way it would fire, but it would make a dandy club if it come to it. And I still had the Colt's stuffed under my belt. I scrambled to my feet and started forward.

Then everthing went black.

———•———

Weren't no way of knowing how long I was out. When I finally come to Joe Porter was staring down at me, muddy tears streaking his face. "Oh Lord!" he says. "Oh Lord A'mighty, Goose, they done kilt Danny!"

I could barely hear him, my ears was ringing so. A pool of sticky blood clouded my left eye, and the taste of it laid heavy on my tongue. I stared back at Joe with my good eye, wanting to tell him to shut his trap and help me up, but my tongue wouldn't work. Truth be told, weren't nothing worked except that one eye. They was both open, and I could see some. That *was* Joe Porter I was staring at, sure enough, and Goose Hutchins looking down at me over Joe's shoulder. I tried moving this part or that to let 'em know I was still amongst the living, but it weren't no use. I couldn't wiggle so much as a finger. Couldn't even manage a blink, try as I might. I was stiff as a day-old corpse.

"We got to get," says Goose, "the Yanks is on our ass!"

"We cain't leave him here," Joe chokes out. "Help me get him up."

"Goddamnit Joe, he's dead!" Goose hollers. "He's shot through the eye. Look how his skull is laid open. Now let's get before they kill us too!" Then they was gone, but not before I felt Joe pull the pistol out of my belt.

Well, sir, them was some right comforting words Goose had spouted. Reckoned then I must really *be* dead. Ain't no way Joe would've left me laying there if it weren't so. I weren't in no pain. The way I figured it, my body was a goner but my spirit was still hanging around, not wanting to give it up just yet.

So I laid there, staring up at the gray sky, listening to the balls whistling overhead, smelling burnt gunpowder, biding my time till my soul took flight. Upwards, I hoped.

Towards dusk the skies opened and a gentle rain come down. The heavens was weeping for me and the other poor souls that had died that day, I reckoned. Then mercifully, everthing faded away.

Calvin Hogue
October 1927

SEVEN

"IT'S TRUE, SUGAR," ALMA HUTCHINS said as she poured me a glass of sweet tea. "Everybody thought that Uncle Dan had been killed in that battle at Dallas."

The old Confederate, who had suffered a relapse from his bout with pneumonia, had retired to his room after recounting the Battle of Dallas and his supposed death trance. I'd found the ending a bit hard to swallow, though I was careful not to convey my suspicions to Daniel Malburn. How could a person be so grievously wounded that he couldn't manage to blink an eye, yet be so alert to his surroundings? I'd posed that question to Alma, as discreetly as possible.

Despite her answer, the whole thing sounded more like an embellished tall tale rather than sound family history that I was determined to report. Not wishing to offend my gracious hostess, I quickly changed the subject and resorted to small talk while finishing my tea. As I bid Alma goodbye, I made a mental note to research the matter.

I had just climbed into my roadster when Alma hurried out

onto the porch. "Look in that box I give you a spell back, Sugar," she called. "The letter Joe Porter wrote to Grandma Malburn ought to be in there."

As soon as I returned home that evening, I began sorting through the box of letters and memorabilia Alma Hutchins had loaned me. I'd had scant opportunity to peruse its contents. A spate of beach drownings and the unsolved grisly murder of a prominent local businessman had kept me hopping the past few weeks.

There were several bundles of letters bound by faded ribbon. I chose a small bundle and untied the ribbon, taking care not to tear any of the fragile yellowing envelopes or loose pages. I browsed through a few of the letters, finding they were written by Daniel to his mother at various times during the war.

A second bundle proved to be from Missus Malburn to Daniel. Yet another, written in a particularly fine hand, were penned to Daniel by Miss Annabelle Gainer.

I untied a fourth bundle written by a number of individuals, some to Daniel, others to friends or family members. It was among these that I found the poignant letter that Joseph Porter had written in his crude hand to Missus Malburn so many years before:

2 June 1864
Dear Missus Malburn:

It is with heavy hand and heart that I write to you of the sad news regards the death of your dear son Daniel. We was attacking the Yankees on the 28th of May near the town of Dallas Georgia when Daniel was struck down and kilt. He passed from this life quick and did not suffer none, so be comforted knowing that.

Of late me and Daniel had many talks and Bible readings, and I know that his soul went up to be with the Lord soon as it left his mortal body. So be comforted in knowing that too.

I have retrieved Daniel's few belongings and have passed such things as he had on to Tom Gainer who will see they get sent to you forthwith. I have kept his pistol, as Danny had told me he wanted me to have it in a previous talk we had.

I know you have suffered a great loss and believe me when I tell you so have I. Danny was my best pard, and I share in your grief.

Regards and blessings to your household.

Respectfully,

Joseph Porter

The following Tuesday I met with Doctor Duell Adams for a brief interview. I relayed the account of Daniel's wounding as he had described it to me.

"It's certainly rare, but not unheard of," the doctor said after I'd finished. "A traumatic head injury such as Mister Malburn suffered could very well result in a catatonic state. Such an individual might appear unresponsive, even to the point of death to the untrained eye, but still be aware of his surroundings. There are a few documented accounts of unfortunate victims being buried alive while in such a state."

I left Doctor Adams' office a chastened man. I had doubted Daniel Malburn's word, and thus his honor. As I drove back to the office I again recalled the words the old veteran had spoken the night he'd agreed to finally tell his story after so many years:

"If you're willing to sit still and listen," Daniel had said to me, *"I reckon it's time I talked it out."*

I vowed never to doubt him again.

Elijah Malburn
Natural Bridge
March 1865

EIGHT

IT WAS A HOT DAY in late July of 'sixty-four when the letter arrived from my mama saying brother Daniel had been kilt somewheres up in Georgia. I ain't ashamed to admit I cried a mite. That senseless damn war had done took my best friend, and now my only brother. A day later I rode to Station Four where Company A of the Colored Troops was on guard duty and broke the sad news to Jefferson. He went to bawling like his own brother had died, which in a way weren't far from the truth.

When I got back from seeing Jeff I asked Major Weeks for a furlough to visit my grieving family. Know what he said, sonny? I'll tell you. He put a hand on my shoulder all fatherly like, said, "I'm sorry about your brother, Malburn, but the timing is most unfortunate." Reckon it was just as well the major turned me down. If I'd of went home, I might not have come back anyways.

Turns out the Confederate cow hunters on the mainland was on the move again, driving cattle north towards the railroad. Major Weeks aimed to see them beeves didn't make it on up to Virginia where General Lee's hungry army was holed up around

Richmond. General Grant hadn't whipped Lee's army in battle yet, so he figured to starve him out.

Confederate cavalry under Captain John J. Dickison had been raising cain up and down the Florida Railroad, raiding one Union outpost after another to keep the Yankees off the trail of them cattle drivers. It weren't for nothing they called Dickison the "Swamp Fox." He was one sly devil, that's a fact.

So, in early August we took up the march heading northeast, following the general direction of the railroad. That road stretched all the way across the state, from Fernandina on the Atlantic coast to Cedar Keys on the gulf. There was fighting somewheres along them tracks for near the whole war. Both sides was bent on controlling that railroad to move troops and supplies and other whatnot of war.

We spent what was left of summer and all that fall chasing Dickison and his boys across dern near half of Florida. Ever time Major Weeks figured he had that wily Reb cornered, Captain Dickison would give us the slip. He was slick as a larded eel, that's a fact. Had a bite, too. More'n once we limped away after a fight, licking our wounds like a whipped cur.

We kept at it till the winter rains come and cold set in, then we give it up and marched back to Cedar Keys to wait for spring. Me and Jeff spent another Christmas best we could away from home and family. The new year finally rolled around. Spring weren't far off now, and I was dern sure itching to get to it. I'd had a craw full of sitting on my hind side waiting out the winter.

If I had knowed what was coming I'd of been tickled to do a heap more scratching, that's a fact.

NINE

TOWARDS THE END OF FEBRUARY, Major Weeks called his officers and staff together for a little powwow. Me and the other scouts and couriers from the Second Cavalry and the Second Colored Troops waited outside on the covered porch while the highfalutin officers did their palavering inside the big house.

I went to jawing with some of the Second Cavalry boys I knowed. Learnt that another regiment of Colored Infantry, the Ninety-ninth, had arrived during the night aboard steamers from Key West. Figured right then and there something big was stewing in the pot. Weren't long before First Sergeant Graham, who had replaced kindly Sergeant Bullard after the Econfina raid, stepped out on the porch to give us flunkies the particulars. He was a Yankee, born and bred. Seemed to be a educated sort from the proper way he talked and such.

Turns out there was a big expedition in the works, so big that the commander of all Union troops in Florida, General John Newton, had sailed up with the Ninety-ninth to lead it hisself.

The whole Ninety-ninth Colored Infantry was going, plus most of the Second Cavalry and the Second Colored Infantry, including Company A.

"We'll be boarding vessels within the week and sailing to the vicinity of St. Marks," Sergeant Graham said, pointing at a rough map that looked like he had drawed it hisself. "Staff, scouts and couriers will be mounted once the horses are landed. The rest of the Second Cavalry will be dismounted and serve as infantry."

That news tickled my ear. Least I wouldn't be hoofing it like most of the boys in the regiment. I held up a hand till I got the sergeant's attention, said, "Whereabouts we headed once we get ashore?"

It weren't a foolish question, but First Sergeant Graham give me a look like I had went and insulted his saintly mother or kicked his favorite dog. He weren't a big man, maybe five foot six in his boots, but he was wiry and hard and was said to carry a mean streak. I'd done my best to keep on his friendly side. He grunted and went to tugging on one of his bushy side whiskers, said, "I'm not at liberty to give that information, Corporal." His eyes turned this way and that, giving us a going over. "There could be spies about camp."

Well sonny, that riled me a mite. I weren't sure if I should've took them words as a personal insult or not. Figured I'd best let it be, so I held my tongue.

The good sergeant folded his map in two and slipped it in his coat pocket. "You'll be briefed in more detail once we're aboard ship and underway. Until then, see to your mounts and gear. Be prepared to move out by morning."

———————

Heavy clouds was building and a stiff wind howling out of the north when we boarded the steamers three days later. I was dreading the ride, figuring with that wind it would be rough as a dried cob. I weren't wrong either, sonny, that's a fact. We bounced around the gulf for the best part of a day. I went to feeling a mite ill, but managed not to heave. Towards dark we anchored with the rest of the fleet somewheres offshore of the St. Marks River. The wind died, but fog rolled in thicker than my mama's split pea soup.

We stayed anchored there for the next two days. While we sat stuck in that fog, the major called his staff together for another jawing. We learnt we'd be going ashore somewheres near the St. Marks lighthouse, then marching north to capture Tallahassee. That was right troublesome news. Weren't likely the Confederates would let us come moseying into their state capital without putting up one bodacious fight.

On the morning of the third day the fog lifted. All the boys figured we'd be landing then, but we stayed put all day. It was pitch black when the order was give by Major Weeks for a scouting party of some sixty troops to assemble on deck. We was traveling light: pistols, ammunition and canteens only. The rest of the troops and supplies was to land a short spell later. I stood there with the others, shivering in the cold wind while the ship's crew lowered four or five launches over the side. Then the major give the order to board. Over the side we went, climbing down them stiff rope ladders to the launches below.

The navy officer of our boat give the order and his crew went to rowing towards shore. The wind was howling and that boat went to pitching up and down in them waves, till I was sure we was going to capsize and drown in that cold black sea. But them sailors knowed their business, and before long we made it into the mouth of the river. Once we was inside the shelter of the marsh, the wind died down, but the fog closed in till you couldn't hardly see your own hand. A patch of yellow lit up the thick fog somewheres in the distance. I took that to be the lighthouse.

Then come a scraping sound and everbody lurched forward. We had run aground. I heard Major Weeks jawing with the navy officer somewheres near the stern. In a minute or so word was passed down for me to report to the major. I climbed over a passel of legs and feet till I reached the major.

"Malburn, you and Private Wood will go ashore with Mister Buck," he said, pointing to a young navy officer sitting across from him. "Once ashore, you are to test the ground to see if it's passable. If it is, do your best to find a suitable path to the lighthouse, then report back. The Confederates are likely to have sentries about, so avoid contact at all cost."

"We supposed to swim, sir?" I didn't much cotton getting wet with that cold wind blowing so.

"Nonsense, Corporal. Mister Buck will row you and Wood ashore."

That's when I seen two sailors rowing a small skiff alongside. In the dark I hadn't seen that they'd been towing a skiff behind the launch. Me and Private Henry Wood followed Mister Buck as he climbed onto the skiff. Them navy fellers pulled on the oars and we headed upriver. Weren't no time at all till the dark and fog swallowed up Major Weeks and the others in the launch. We sat there listening to the wind and the water slapping agin our skiff. The fog thinned a mite the farther upriver we made. Ten or fifteen minutes passed, then the skiff skidded to a stop.

Mister Buck told me to ease over the side and test the bottom. I held onto the gunnel and put one leg down till I felt mud sucking at my boot. I lifted my foot up and stretched my leg out a mite farther, eased it down and felt grass. Put more weight on it. It held, so I pushed away from the skiff till I was standing at the edge of the bank on both feet.

I reached out a hand, whispered, "Come on Henry, it'll hold."

Henry grabbed my hand and hopped ashore. Henry Wood was from the village of Monticello, a few miles east of Tallahassee. He had signed on as a scout at Cedar Keys after the Econfina raid. He was near my age, but looked so boyish he could've passed for twelve or thirteen. A short and skinny sort, he seemed a mite too jittery to be soldiering. He'd near turned tail and run a time or two when we was scrapping with Captain Dickison's boys along the railroad last fall. More'n once I'd wondered why Major Weeks took him on as a scout.

I checked my pistols and told Henry to stay tight on my tail, then we set out single-file through the marsh grass slower'n a pair of gophers crawling through a palmetto thicket. At first, I tested ever step I took. A few times my boot squished into mud when the grass give way. After a ways, I found that the ground got firmer when I gradually eased to the right as we kept inland towards the glow of the lighthouse. Weren't long till we was on firm ground. A ways later the marsh grass petered out and we come to the edge of a clearing that surrounded the lighthouse itself. We squatted there in the grass, straining the dark with our eyes and listening for sentries. We stayed put for fifteen minutes, hearing nothing but crickets chirping and bullfrogs croaking. Then we turned back.

Mister Buck ordered Henry to stay put where we'd found the firm ground, then rowed me back to our launch. I reported what we'd found to Major Weeks.

"It's maybe a quarter mile from where we come ashore to the lighthouse, Major. Weren't no sign of sentries about, best we could tell. It was awful dark, but there looks to be a road leading north."

A spell later them sailors went to ferrying our troops ashore. In a hour the scouting party was all on dry ground and assembled near the lighthouse, some sixty strong. I'd been right about the road. A little after midnight we set out hoofing it on that overgrown road, heading towards the crossing at East River Bridge, some five miles distant.

TEN

THE ROAD WAS A SANDY rut with a stand of waist-high grass growing thick in the center. Me and Henry Wood set out some thirty yards ahead of the column, one on either side of the grassy road. The fog was still heavy in patches, but the wind was rising and here and there the fog would thin out some. Our eyes had adjusted enough to where we could see where we was stepping, so following the road weren't too hard.

Of a sudden Henry come busting through the grass and run slap into me, near knocking me to the ground. He grabbed a-hold of my arm, said, "Snake!"

Being the excitable sort, Henry had near shouted it aloud. I shook off his hand, said, "Henry, there ain't no snake going to bite, cold as it is tonight. Now get back over there!" and shoved him back through the grass to his side of the road.

I had no sooner felt for my Remingtons to make sure I hadn't dropped one when Henry called out, "Why, it ain't no snake a'tall, just a stick."

I stepped through the grass, said, "If you don't shut your

trap, I'm going to shoot you myself and save the Rebs the trouble. Now get on up this road!"

We pushed on through the night without running across any more wooden snakes or Confederates, but even cold as it was the dern sand gnats like to've chewed my hide off. After two miles or so the grass in the road petered out, making the road one wide rut. Towards dawn, the fog thinned. Scraggly oaks was growing along both sides of the road. Their mossy limbs reached towards us like bony arms. A passel of birds went to singing their morning songs, joining the frogs and crickets greeting the new day. Then a flurry of gunfire broke the spell. I knowed right off it was too far north to be meant for us.

I took a knee and grabbed one of my pistols. "Run get the major," I told Henry. He was gone before I'd near got the words out. That boy didn't need much coaxing to hightail it away from the sound of a fight. I kept my eyes peeled on the road ahead, heart thumping, expecting any second to see Confederates come charging. I swallowed hard, wondered if I'd be able to pull the trigger if it come down to it. So far I'd only fired my pistols to make a show of things. I weren't sure I'd be able to shoot to kill even if my very life depended on it. Hoped I would, but I weren't sure by no means.

Up ahead, muskets kept cracking here and there, then come a shout and the loud *boom!* of a controlled volley. Whoever it was scrapping up yonder, things was starting to get right hot for 'em. I checked my loads again and waited.

A minute or two later, the clomping of footsteps come up behind me. I turned and seen Major Weeks walking towards me, jawing with some of his staff, Henry Woods trailing behind. Troops had spread out on both sides of the road and was wading through the tall marsh grass in a line of battle towards the sound of the fight. I stood up to report to the major, but he strode right on by like I weren't there. "Fall in beside Private Wood, Malburn," was all he said, so I done what I was told.

By then the sun was peeking over the treetops, burning mist off the marsh. Weren't long before a passel of shadows come running out of the low fog up the road a piece. "Hold your fire," a voice called out, "they are Union men!"

Turns out a squad of navy raiders had landed just south of the East River Bridge during the night. They had meant to capture any Confederate sentries that might be guarding the bridge and hold it till we arrived to reinforce 'em. At dawn, they'd opened fire on a small band of Confederates approaching the bridge, but was soon drove back by a full company of Rebs who was hiding on the north bank. Seems our little surprise party had been found out.

We halted while Major Weeks palavered with the navy raiders' officer. Then the sailors took their place in line and we moved forward.

Soon, balls was whizzing and snapping overhead, but they was aimed too high to be worrisome. A ways farther on, the ground rose a mite. The marsh grass give out and soon we was making our way through a thin forest of scattered oaks and tall pines. Up ahead I spied a few buildings, their whitewashed boards shining amongst the shade of the trees. A minute or so later we come to a road that ran east and west. There the major called a halt.

Our officers sent a few squads forward as skirmishers while Major Weeks went to jawing with his staff and the navy officers. Me and Henry hid behind two stout oaks and listened to our boys swap fire with the Confederates. Ever now and again come the *thunk!* of balls hitting trees nearby or the zinging of a ricocheting bullet. This fight was getting a mite too close for comfort, sonny, that's a fact.

A hour passed with no letup. Then I heard Major Weeks calling for me from the back of a house where he'd set up his command post. I told Henry to stay put and lit out towards the major. I ducked and run from tree to tree, balls buzzing by my ears and kicking up dirt. By the time I reached the major I was sucking air like a winded horse.

Major Weeks had his map spread out on the floor of a small porch and was jabbering with the navy officer in charge of the sailors with us. I reported in best I could, being near out of breath. The good major pointed behind me, said, "Malburn, take that horse and get back to the lighthouse quick as you can. Find out if our main force has landed. If so, give this message to General Newton." He handed me the note. "Wait for a reply, then report back to me immediately."

I eyeballed the horse the major had scrounged up somewheres. It was a old gelding, a mite swayback with a grizzled muzzle. The tack and saddle weren't army issue. I put the message in my breeches pocket, mounted up and hightailed it south.

ELEVEN

RECKON THEM CONFEDERATES SEEN ME riding off, because balls went to buzzing around me like I'd kicked up a nest of yellerjackets. I flattened out best I could on that horse's back, dug my heels into his bony flanks and hung on for dear life. All that lead put grit in the old crowbait. I give him free rein and we went flying through the trees, bullets snapping everwhere.

Weren't but a couple of minutes, but it felt like a hour drug by, till we finally cleared them trees and made the marsh. I found the road and lit out south at full gallop. Didn't slow down till them bullets quit whizzing. Then I eased the old boy to a trot. That sandy road weren't the surest footing, and I didn't want to risk him coming up lame or dropping dead.

The major had left a squad back at the lighthouse as guards, so when the lighthouse come into sight I slowed to a walk. I eased ahead the last quarter mile or so, keeping my eyes peeled for pickets. Finally spied a few of our boys sitting around where the road petered out at the clearing. Took off my hat, waved it high and hollered, "Halloo, boys!"

Two big steamers was up in the bay shallows, huffing black smoke and churning the water to mud. Looked to be stuck fast. Three or four other ships was still anchored in the gulf. Weren't no sign that the main body had come ashore. I rode up to the sentries, said, "I got a message from Major Weeks. Where's your officer?"

A skinny, freckle-faced corporal leaning on his rifle pointed towards the lighthouse. "Over yonder. Sounds like a fight is on."

"It sure ain't no turkey shoot," I said, then trotted the horse across the clearing to a cluster of troops sitting around a fire. One feller drinking coffee was wearing lieutenant bars, so I dismounted and walked over to him.

I saluted. "We run into some Rebels at East River. Major Weeks wants to know if the main party is landed yet."

The lieutenant give me a queer look, turned and pointed towards the bay. "You can see they've run aground. An ensign come ashore about a hour ago, said this north wind's caused a lower tide than they were expecting."

"Did he say when they might get to landing 'em?"

The lieutenant was busy pouring hisself another cup of coffee. He looked up. "They're waiting for the tide to turn later this afternoon. You want some of this coffee?"

I shook my head. "Much obliged, but I best be getting back." I give him a quick salute, then mounted up and rode north.

———•—•———

The ruckus was still on when I got back. Major Weeks weren't tickled at all with the news I brung him, that's a fact. This campaign was already a whole day behind schedule thanks to the bad weather. He turned three shades of red and went to bellowing up a storm at his staff and the navy officers. The major hadn't dismissed me, so I tied the horse to the porch rail and sat down agin a nearby tree to wait.

After they was done palavering the major called me over.

He looked all grim-faced, said, "Go find Private Wood. Pass the word to the squad commanders that we will begin a fighting withdrawal at two o'clock. Have each commander send a runner for further instructions."

I took off running tree to tree looking for Henry. The fight weren't as hot as it had been, but there was still balls aplenty whizzing by. I hoped to find Henry where I'd left him. From the looks of the high sun there weren't no time to waste.

Henry was still sitting agin the same tree. Don't reckon he'd moved a inch the whole morning long. "Where you been?" he said, all wide-eyed when I ducked behind the tree beside him. "I figured you was shot."

"Well, I ain't been shot and we got a job to do."

There was four squads spread out on either side of the house the major was using for his command post. I left Henry to get the word to the squads out front of us, then I lit out back towards the house to tell the others. Took the best part of a hour dodging bullets to pass the word, but me and Henry got it done.

A little after two Major Weeks mounted the old swayback I'd rode earlier and give the word to move out. We set off through the trees heading for the marsh and the lighthouse, leaving some skirmishers following behind to slow the Rebs. The Confederates kept hot on our tail for a spell, but once we hoofed it a ways down the marsh road they give it up. Reckon the sight of them navy vessels steaming into the bay took the fight out of 'em.

It was near dusk that evening when we finally reached the lighthouse. I was dern near played out, footsore and hungry enough to eat boot leather. Felt a heap better when I seen the clearing was slap full of troops, mostly colored. The tide had finally rose enough for the sailors to get our boys ashore. I looked around quick but didn't see any Company A boys. Figured I'd look for Jeff come morning if I found the time.

That night I dern near froze. Cold air rolled in from the north, wind just a-howling. Only good thing about the weather was it kept the skeeters down. Weren't no fires allowed after dark, so me and Henry Wood gnawed on hardtack I had carried in my breeches pocket and drank cold water for supper. Our mounts and trappings was still on one of them steamers. We didn't have so much as a horse blanket to cover up with. We took shelter behind some outbuilding near the lighthouse, curled up agin the south side out of that wind and finally fell asleep.

At first light, I got up and scrounged enough wood off a dead pine laying at the edge of the clearing to build a fire. The wind had died during the night, but it was still cold. I woke Henry up and sent him over to the Colored Troops to see if he could fetch us some coffee and bacon or such. The fire was going good when he come back a short spell later with a can of boiled coffee and some fatback. We huddled by the fire to keep warm, drinking hot coffee and eating hunks of fatback we roasted on a stick.

Major Weeks and General Newton was palavering with their staffs inside the command tent pitched near the lighthouse. I looked out in the bay and seen sailors in launches rowing hard, towing a barge covered by canvas towards shore.

Henry pointed towards the barge. "What you reckon that is?"

"Wish it was the horses, but that ain't likely, flat as that barge is."

Turns out it was a pair of twelve-pounder cannons the sailors took off one of the navy vessels and hauled ashore. They weighed dern near eight-hundred pounds apiece, and was mounted on iron carriages. Weren't no horse teams to pull 'em with, so General Newton give the order for a company of the Ninety-ninth Colored Infantry to haul them guns by hand the whole way to Natural Bridge. Them poor fellers had one rough time of it dragging them cannons through all that sand and mud we went through, that's a fact.

A couple of hours after sunrise, we took up the march for East River. The Second Colored Infantry was up front. I seen Jeff and Nebo as they marched off with Company A, but Major Weeks kept me close to hand, so there weren't no chance to jaw with 'em.

The Second Cavalry was next in line, hoofing it as infantry. None of the staff's or scouts' horses had come ashore yet, so we was all afoot, even the major. I figured he'd given that crowbait to General Newton as a courtesy. The Ninety-ninth Colored Infantry come next, including the company dragging the cannons. Supply wagons, ambulances and our horses was to follow soon as they come ashore. One company of the Second Cavalry stayed behind to guard the lighthouse and landing party.

There was near a thousand of us in all. By the time the last of the troops took up the march, there was a line of blue snaking through the marsh from the lighthouse to dern near the East River Bridge. We'd been on the road a hour or so when gunfire broke out, hot and heavy. We was still a good half mile from the bridge, so Major Weeks ordered us forward at the double-quick. I made sure my pistols was fast and trotted after the major.

The sound of musketry growed to a steady roar by the time we struck the forest. Major Weeks called a halt and formed the companies into a line of battle, two columns deep. Orders was hollered out up and down the line and we moved forward, getting ever closer to the sound of the fight ahead. Me and Henry Wood hung near the major as he strutted back of the line barking orders to his staff.

We crossed the road and come to the house that had been the major's command post yesterday. Up ahead, I seen a passel of Colored troops stretched out in a line of battle running east to west facing the bridge. They stood up and fired off a volley, then charged towards the bridge yelling *"Huzzah!"* for all they was worth!

They was maybe twenty-thirty yards from the bridge when a

loud *Boom!* tore the air. Smoke and flame spewed from a cannon on the far bank of the river. Lead went to buzzing and my ears went to ringing and I seen a handful of boys pitch backwards. I swallowed hard, hoping Jeff weren't amongst 'em.

Took a minute for the Colored Troops to regroup. They stood their ground brave as any men I ever seen, reloaded, then give the Rebs another volley and charged again. They no sooner done that than Major Weeks ordered us forward. We moved through the scattered trees and buildings, then halted along both sides of the road that run through the center of the little village and on to the bridge.

The Colored Troops made it to the bridge only to find that the Confederates had pulled up the planks sometime during the night. But them fellers weren't to be stopped, that's a fact. They reloaded again and got off another volley, then went to crossing that bridge, stepping from girder to girder till they was all across. Then they give chase to the Rebels who was hightailing it north towards Newport fast as hounded rabbits.

Well, sonny, the fight was over near fast as it started. Weren't without cost though. Jeff and Nebo was unharmed, but they'd been in the thick of it. Two poor souls from Company A was kilt, a few more wounded. One unfortunate had been blowed in half by the load of canister the Rebs fired. I near puked when I walked past his body in the road, both legs gone. Worst thing I seen since poor Preacher Jubal back at the salt camp.

Weren't no dead or wounded Confederates to be found, but our boys did capture two Rebs along with their cannon. Reckon it was a victory of sorts for the Union, seeing as how the Confederates had cut and run, but it was Union men laying dead in the road at East River. Way I seen it, that weren't much to be crowing about.

TWELVE

BY THE TIME THE SECOND Colored Infantry returned to the bridge with their prisoners and the captured cannon, General Newton had arrived with the Ninety-ninth Colored Infantry. Right off, he ordered Major Weeks to hightail it with the Second Cavalry to Newport before the Rebs could destroy the bridge that crossed the St. Marks River there. So off we went at the double-quick. The general would be along directly, soon as the Colored Troops had the bridge repaired and our supplies caught up.

Well, sonny, it was a ways to Newport as I recollect, some eight miles or so, but we pushed hard and got there in a mite over two hours. Confederate cavalry pestered us a time or two on the march, but weren't much to it. Maybe halfway there we seen big clouds of smoke rising high above the pine forest. When Major Weeks seen that smoke, he dern near made us run the rest of the way. I was ready to drop by the time Newport come into view, that's a fact.

The good major called a halt just outside of town, and we

formed a line of battle amongst the trees and few houses and outbuildings. The Rebs had set fire to a goodly number of buildings on the east side of the river, and the fire had spread to the brush and grass along the bank. My eyes went to tearing up and I dern near choked on the thick smoke till the wind shifted. When it did, we seen the bridge had been lit up too.

Weren't long till Major Weeks ordered us forward. When we got to maybe fifty yards of the bridge, the Confederates popped up in their works on the west bank and cut loose a volley such as as I ain't never heard before. A passel of our boys cried out and dropped, and the rest went to scattering for whatever cover was handy.

I ran and hid behind what looked to be a smokehouse, but it weren't long before the front of it was afire. Well, sonny, I had froze my tail off the night before, and here I was about to roast like a pig on a spit. Bullets was snapping and cracking everwhere, so I stayed put till the heat got too bad. Then I made a run for it towards a big pine maybe fifteen-twenty yards back. I hunkered down behind that pine, making myself thin as I could while our boys swapped lead with the Confederates for the next hour.

Long about midafternoon General Newton showed up with most of the two Colored regiments, the navy cannons in tow. The Colored troops took up positions and opened fire while the navy gun crew got their cannons in position. Them twelve-pounders went to booming and shells went to crashing amongst the Confederate lines and the village beyond. Them sailors weren't the best of shots on dry land, that's a fact.

I was maybe a hundred and fifty yards from the village behind the Reb lines, but I seen a passel of civilians, mostly women and children, leaving their houses and making tracks for the woods to escape the shelling. Later on I learnt that at least five poor wretches had been kilt, and a number more wounded. Seems the good general weren't any more troubled with making war on civilians as Major Weeks was, the scoundrels. Know what

I think, sonny? I'll tell you. Murder is what I call it. Plain and simple.

After a hour of shelling General Newton give it up and called for the cannons to cease fire. We left enough skirmishers to keep the Rebs entertained and fell back out of range of the Confederate fire. The good general ordered the rest of the buildings set afire so the Rebs couldn't use 'em for cover if they took a mind to cross the river and attack us.

Late that afternoon a cheer rose up amongst the Confederate lines. Seems a passel of reinforcements had arrived and took up positions. General Newton weren't a bit tickled to hear that news. He called a big powwow with Major Weeks and the other officers and their staff.

Towards evening, Major Weeks come out of the house the general was using for his headquarters and called for me and Henry Wood. He sat on the steps, pulled out his map and unfolded it. "The Confederates have reinforced their works here, making it unlikely that we will be able to carry them. General Newton has decided to march north along this road and cross the river here, at Natural Bridge," he said, pointing to his map. The St. Marks River disappeared and run underground for maybe twenty-thirty yards till it rose up again. That span of ground over the river was the Natural Bridge we was aiming to cross at.

"I will be staying here with the Second Cavalry to prevent the enemy from crossing the river and moving on the general's rear. Malburn, you will accompany Colonel Townsend and the Second Colored Infantry as courier. Private Wood, you will be with the Ninety-ninth under the command of Lieutenant Colonel Pearsall. Your duty will be to deliver any necessary messages from their commands back to me. Any questions?"

"No, sir," Henry mumbled.

I had a mouthful to say and I aimed for the major to hear it. I put my finger on the map and run it up the road leading north out of Newport. "Well Major, reckon how far it is to this

Natural Bridge?" I was more'n a mite tired of walking. Didn't much cotton to hoofing it up and down that river road between Newport and Natural Bridge.

Major Weeks give his goatee a tug. "One of the scouts familiar with the area assures me that it is no more than four or five miles." Then he cracked a smile, which for the major was near scarce as hair on a baby's behind. "But don't worry, Corporal. We've received word that the supply train is due to arrive shortly. You'll have your mounts."

Me and Henry ate a cold supper of what fatback we had left. A spell after nightfall word come to move out. Me and Henry said our goodbyes, then mounted up and rode off to our new commands. Weren't no way then I could've knowed I'd never lay eyes on Henry Wood again.

We took off north up that pig trail river road heading for the Natural Bridge. It was slow going in the dark. More'n once the column halted while the scouts up ahead figured out what was road and what weren't. Swarms of skeeters and sand gnats pestered us ever foot of the way. It had rained a heap the past week or so, and a goodly piece of the trail was covered in mudholes and quicksand. Them poor fellers hauling the cannons had theirselves a time of it. I was mighty glad to be mounted again, that's a fact.

The Second Colored Infantry was leading the way. Colonel Townsend and his staff, which I was now a part of, rode a piece behind the first two companies. Then come the Ninety-ninth boys that was hauling the cannons, and then General Newton and the rest of the Ninety-ninth. All told, we numbered some six hundred or thereabouts.

Around midnight a halt was called to rest a spell. We hadn't covered but maybe three miles, but we was wore out from two days of near steady marching and fighting. I tied my horse to a nearby bush, then found a dry spot of ground to stretch out on. Rolled up in my blanket and tried to get some sleep. I did manage to sleep a mite despite all the bugs, but it was fitful. Kept dreaming I was running butt naked through a swamp with a passel of gun-toting Rebs fast on my heels. I woke up in a cold sweat, feeling sick in my belly. Took that dream to be a bad sign, but I hoped it might just be the rancid fatback me and Henry Wood had eat for supper that night.

It was still two-three hours before dawn when we set out again. We stumbled along for the next two hours, making the best time we could in the dark. It was near dawn and we still hadn't made Natural Bridge. That scout had told Major Weeks wrong. Turned out to be near eight miles from Newport to Natural Bridge.

The sky was just hinting gray and early birds was singing their predawn songs when a single gunshot rang out up ahead. After a few seconds, the woods swallowed up the sound. A minute or so passed. I had near decided that somebody had went and fired off a shot by accident when a volley thundered out. A passel of balls cut leaves overhead. Then come two more volleys. From the sound of things, our boys had stumbled into a heap of trouble.

Colonel Townsend went to shouting orders to his staff, then spurred his horse and took off up the road towards the fight. I dug my heels in and followed after the colonel. I leaned low over my horse's neck, hoping he could see a heap better than I could.

A cannon boomed and lit up the dawn. Then come another and another. Cannons went to roaring and muskets went to crashing and sheets of flame flared through the trees as our boys swapped fire with theirs. Spent balls and shrapnel was buzzing everwhere like mad hornets. Lead was flying so thick I figured there weren't no way I was making it alive out of this fight.

In a minute or so I caught up to Colonel Townsend at the edge of a cut-over field. He had dismounted and was shouting orders to his captains and lieutenants to form their troops for battle. Other soldiers was busy digging trenches and felling trees for works. Up ahead our lead companies was making another charge at the Rebs across the Natural Bridge. Our boys was screaming *"Huzzah!"* for all they was worth, but their cheer was near drowned out by the sound of the Rebel Yell. It was still more night than day, and I wondered how anybody could tell just who was shooting at who. I hoped Jefferson was keeping his head down.

Weren't long before the heavy Reb gunfire had our boys scurrying back across the Natural Bridge, taking cover amongst the thick forest which covered the crossing between us and the Confederates. They stayed put there, hiding in the trees and trading fire for the next hour-hour and a half till the sun was well up.

Our boys had took a terrible pounding from the Reb cannons, but after a spell the firing eased up a mite. Both sides seemed of a mind to hunker down and swap just enough lead to keep the game honest. I kept close by Colonel Townsend, hoping he'd send me back to Newport with a message for Major Weeks, but it weren't to be.

Meantime, the pioneer company from the Ninety-ninth Infantry worked like beavers, digging trenches and chopping pines. Weren't long till they had a fine line of works at the edge of the field near the east bank of the river. Them two navy cannons and the captured Confederate gun was hauled up and put in place near the center of the works.

Judging from the sun, it was near nine o'clock when the colonel called me over and said, "Corporal, ride south along the river a mile or so. There's supposed to be a ford somewhere in the vicinity. If you can locate it, see if it is suitable for crossing. Report back within the hour."

Well, sonny, a hour was a hour and that was just fine by me. I could cotton to not having to duck spent lead for a spell. Least

I'd be heading in the proper direction, away from the fight.

I mounted up and rode a piece down the road, then cut through the woods towards the river. Weren't long till the brush got so thick that I had to dismount and walk my horse through. After a spell I tied him to a stout bush and set out on foot. The river was high and muddy and running fast. I was tromping through a thick bog of wet leaves and pine needles. It was hard going, but it muffled my footsteps.

I eased on through the brambles and briars, keeping my eyes peeled and my ears open for something other than the sound of the river or the ruckus of battle. Through the trees ahead, I seen the river as it took a bend to the left, then slowed and widened out to what looked like might make a passable ford. I pushed on through the brush till I come out on a overgrowed trace leading down to the bank. Of a sudden, I froze. On the far bank I seen a flash of sunlight glinting off metal. Quick as I could, I ducked back into the bushes and hid. Weren't long till I heard some fellers jawing, then four-five Rebs on horseback come into view. They went to pointing here and yonder, then got off their horses and spread out on both sides of the trace leading up from the river. I waited around long enough to see a passel more ride up and dismount. Looked like they weren't going anywheres for a spell. Figured my scouting job was done, so I snuck back through the woods to my horse.

———•◦•———

I reported what I'd seen to Colonel Townsend. He looked all solemn-like, said, "Very well." Then he walked off towards General Newton's headquarters in a thick pine grove well back of our works.

I found myself a stout tree, sat down agin it to rest and wait while the highfalutin brass was powwowing over what to do. The Confederates kept tossing shells our way, but being as our lines was dug in on low ground near the river they mostly overshot and exploded in the woods behind. Skirmishers kept up a lively fire in the thick woods that surrounded the Natural Bridge, but the cover was so heavy it was more bark than bite.

Weren't long before Colonel Townsend come back and called his staff together. Being a lowly corporal, I stood back a ways, listening to the grand plan the good general had hatched. From the sound of things, it seems General Newton had come up with a surefire attack that would send the Confederates scurrying back towards Tallahassee, and win the day for the glorious Union.

While a hot barrage from our three cannons kept the Rebs hunkered down in their works, the Second Colored Infantry was to lead the charge across the Natural Bridge. Once across, half the regiment, including Captain Tracy's Company A, would charge left between the road and the river to attack the Confederate right. The other half of the regiment would make a beeline straight up the road and strike the Reb middle. The Ninety-ninth Infantry was to follow behind and attack wherever they was needed.

Well, sonny, them officers might've thought it to be a right dandy plan they'd thunk up, but I had a heap of doubts. For one, weren't nobody really knowed for sure just what the Confederates had waiting for us on the other side of them thick woods covering the bridge. What troops of ours that had made it to the other side in the first two charges at dawn was still over there, laying dead or wounded. I weren't any too antsy to follow 'em, that's a fact.

It was near high noon when our guns opened up and we moved up the road towards Natural Bridge in a rough column of fours. I seen Company A's flag flying next to Old Glory up near the front of the column. I weren't much of a praying man in them days, but I ain't ashamed to say I said a quick one for Jeff and Nebo.

I weren't never fond of officers, but I'll give that Colonel Townsend his due for having enough grit to put his command directly behind Company A and in front of the other two companies he'd be leading in the charge agin the Confederate right. Seems he weren't the kind to hunker back in the rear while his troops faced all the lead and done all the fighting.

The column had scarce entered the woods near the Bridge when a storm of cannon fire and musketry blowed in like a howling hurricane. I ain't never seen or heard the likes of it, sonny, that's a fact. Canister and musket balls tore through them woods and our poor troops, busting tree limbs and flesh and bone alike in a horrible shower of carnage. Bodies and pieces of such went flying everwheres. What boys of ours weren't hit fired off a volley and went charging forward across the Natural Bridge. I seen the colonel ride ahead, so I flattened out on my horse best I could and took off after him. Somehow my horse made it through that wall of lead and into the thick woods without us being hit.

It sounded like the gates of Hell itself had opened and ever screeching demon and stinging pestilence from the Bible had been loosed on the earth right then and there. Bodies was laying all over the Natural Bridge, some screaming with pain, others laying still in death. My horse near stumbled over the heaps a time or two, but then we was across the Bridge and out into a overgrowed field.

I lifted my head a mite to chance a quick look around. Through the thick gunsmoke, maybe fifty-sixty yards, ahead I seen the Confederate works. They stretched out in a long half-moon with both sides anchored near the river. A passel of cannons was spaced out along their lines, belching flame and canister like there weren't no end to it. Reb muskets by the hundreds was spitting smoke and lead. Balls was buzzing by so thick it sounded like I had stuck my head slap inside a hornet's nest.

Well, sonny, I figured right then and there I weren't going to live through this. I'd never see my home or my family or my dear Annie again. I called Annie's name out loud a time or two, wanting it to be the last word that ever passed my lips in this cruel life that was fixing to come to such a inglorious end.

Of a sudden my horse stumbled and pitched forward. I went tumbling through the air head over heels, struck the ground so hard for a minute I thought I'd been shot. My head ached and I couldn't breathe. Figured I was a goner for sure. I felt blood running down my face, reached up and felt a gash in my forehead near my hairline. In a minute my breath come back. I rolled over onto my belly and seen I had struck my head agin a tree root. I was relieved that I hadn't been shot, but from all the lead still flying around I figured it weren't long before I would be.

With all the fear of dying I'd plumb forgot about my horse. I looked around and seen him laying on his side with his neck twisted backwards. His muzzle had been blowed half off and blood was puddled around what was left of his face. He weren't moving none that I could see, so I figured he was done for. No need in wasting a bullet to put him out of his misery. I reached down and found I still had one of my Remingtons. Figured I'd pass on trying to find the other.

The Rebs was pouring load after load of canister straight down the road, cutting the other companies of the Second Colored Troops to bits. On the Confederate left, other cannons joined in, catching our poor boys in a murderous crossfire. My horse had went down just off the road, so I made myself flat as I could and wormed my way through the grass and bushes towards the river to my left. Weren't long before I was crawling amongst a passel of bodies. I went to shivering, done my best not to get too close to the poor souls.

I aimed to make it to the river, then swim across if I could manage to stay alive long enough. I soon come upon a pair of fancy boots. A feller was laying on his belly with his arms sprawled out, curly blond hair sticking out beneath his kepi. I crawled up beside him and took a better look. Captain Tracy stared back at me through dead blue eyes. There was a big ragged hole blasted in his back. Clots of blood had oozed out of his mouth and nose and stained his fancy waxed moustache red. The good captain had give me grief a time or two, sonny, that's a fact, but it still troubled me some to see him laying there dead.

I crawled on towards the river, keeping low as I could manage. Musket balls and canister kept zinging by, cutting bushes overhead. It dawned on me then that Jeff was out there somewheres. He might be hurt or dead, so I quit dodging bodies. Instead, I give a quick look at ever one I come across, dreading what I might find.

After a while I found a couple of poor wounded fellers laying near each other. They was both grievous hurt, rolling their heads and moaning something awful. Made me shiver to hear it. One had been shot through the chest and belly. He kept gurgling, coughing up blood. The other poor feller had a leg blowed slam off near the hip. I give 'em both some water and told 'em help was coming soon. Figured that to be a lie, but there weren't nothing else I could do for 'em, them being in such a bad way. Then I crawled on.

The fight was still going hot and heavy. A ways off, I seen two of Colonel Townsend's lieutenants carrying him back towards the Bridge, his arms slung over their shoulders. One side of his coat was all bloody, but he was alive and seemed alert. For a minute I wondered if I ought to turn around and go after them, but Jeff was still out there and I aimed to find him if I could.

Seems our attack on the Confederate right had near petered out, but them boys attacking up the road was giving the Rebs all they could handle. Three times them brave fellers went charging up that rise towards them works, only to be hurled back by the fierce Reb fire. After near a hour they finally give it up. Them that was able made it back across the Natural Bridge, carrying or dragging with 'em what wounded they could manage.

It was near two o'clock, best I could figure by the sun. By

now most of our boys that was able had quit the field and made it back across the river to our works. Skirmishers from both sides moved back into the thick woods and kept the ruckus going. Here and yonder, groups of Confederates was walking across the field looking for Yankee wounded that might need tending to or took prisoner.

A ways back, I had crawled past two flooded sinkholes that lay near the river. Both had three-four bodies floating in 'em. Up ahead I seen another sink. This one was a mite closer to the river and well hid by bushes. Figured it might be a good place to hide out for a spell. I crawled over towards it, then froze.

Voices! I listened hard, straining my ears agin the noise of the battle. Sounded like somebody singing, which struck me as being a mite strange. I pulled the Remington out of my belt, checked the loads. Then, quiet as I could, I eased my way into the brush.

THIRTEEN

WELL, SONNY, IF I HADN'T been laying flat on the ground already, I surely would've fell over at what I seen when I pushed through them bushes.

"Eli? That you?"

Jefferson was sitting at the edge of the sink, cradling a bloody head in his lap. His face was pale as wood ash. I crawled closer, seen it was Nebo stretched out alongside him. "You be shot too?" said Jeff, rocking back and forth like he was holding a newborn baby instead of a bloody head. "Nebo, he hurt. I been takin good care o' him. Been singin to him. Nebo like singin', make him feel better."

I remembered my cut, reached up and touched it. "No, I ain't shot. Fell off my horse is all."

Jeff grinned, said, "That good." Then he went to singing, "Now if you get there afo' I do, God's goan trouble the water. Tell all my friends I's coming too, God's goan trouble the water."

I seen Nebo was a goner before I reached Jeff's side. There was a hole over his left eye, and from all the blood Jeff's uniform had soaked up, it was a sure bet the back of poor Nebo's skull was blowed out.

"God's goan trouble the water."

"Look here Jeff," I said, easy as I could manage, "Nebo is dead."

Jeff looked at me like I'd went and slapped his face. He looked down at Nebo, then at me and shook his head. "Ain't dead. He restin a spell is all. I sing him asleep. Nebo like my singin'."

Now the Rebel Yell rose up over the noise of the guns, then come a thundering of cannons and muskets. I scurried over and peeked out through the bushes. The Rebs was making a charge across the bridge towards our works. I hurried back over to Jeff.

"We got to go now. The Rebs is charging our works. This is our chance to get away."

Jeff just sat there shaking his head. "Cain't. I gots to take care o' Nebo."

Well, sonny, I was flat out of patience. I grabbed Jeff's shoulder and give him a good shaking. "Bring him along then, but we're hightailing it for the river now!"

That seemed to satisfy him. Jeff stood up and slung Nebo's limp body over his shoulder like a sack of grain and we lit out through the bushes towards the river thicket.

———————

Me and Jeff had spent many a summer day swimming in the swift-flowing Econfina when we was growing up, so it weren't no problem getting across the St. Marks. I took off my boots and held them above the water and side-kicked my way across. Jeff laced his brogans around his neck and swam, towing Nebo behind. When we made the other bank we hunkered down a spell, making sure there weren't no troops stirring about. Way I seen it, it was best to duck Rebs and Yanks alike now, things being what they was.

When I was satisfied it was safe, we eased on through the woods away from the river. I figured the woods threabouts would be crawling with troops before long, so we crossed the river road and kept heading east. From the sound of things, the battle was still going strong. Well, let 'em keep fighting if they had a mind to. I'd had more'n enough of that foolishness. The way I seen it, my soldiering days was over. I aimed to find me and Jeff a place to hide out for a day or two to rest up, then head for home.

We skirted a cypress swamp, then followed a game trail that wound through a stand of tall pines and palmettos for near a mile. A time or two we rested. It had warmed up, and strong as Jeff was, toting Nebo all that way had him a mite winded. The trail petered out at a oak hammock that sat on a rise of ground. It would make a fine place to hide a spell. The skeeters weren't too bad. There was good cover, and acorns aplenty to eat from last fall's crop. And we could always pull us some palmetto hearts back down the trail a ways. I'd figure out what to do about Nebo later, when Jeff come to his senses.

It was cold again that night, but we didn't dare chance a fire. The distant battle had petered out before dark. We was far enough away that I figured it was safe for us both to sleep without keeping watch. If our boys come across us, I'd tell 'em we got lost retreating from the Rebs. If the Confederates was to find us, well then I reckoned we'd wind up in a Rebel prison camp somewheres.

Jeff huddled up agin Nebo's stiff body, still not wanting to face up that he was dead. I covered up best I could under a pile of oak leaves and managed to sleep tolerable. Next morning I was up with the sun. Jeff was still asleep, so I left him there laying beside Nebo's body while I went to do my business away from our campsite.

I was standing there listening to the morning birds and shivering agin a light northeast breeze when I caught the scent of wood smoke and bacon. I near panicked for a minute, then remembered the fight was back off towards the west a good two-three miles. Weren't likely that smoke was coming from any troops. Just might be a house yonder somewheres. There was things me and Jeff needed for our trip home, so I aimed to find out.

◆

It was near midmorning by the time I reached the little log cabin that sat in the middle of a acre of cleared ground. Smoke was still rising from the chimney, though the day was warming fast. Behind the cabin was a barn and a lean-to tool shed, and near it stood a small smokehouse. A passel of scrawny chickens was scratching and pecking and chasing bugs and such around the yard. Next to the cabin was a garden with a good stand of winter greens and rows of sprouts from a early spring planting.

I had left Jefferson behind to watch over Nebo till we could get him buried proper. No sense in him coming along, toting Nebo's stiff body. Jeff had finally found his wits and accepted that his good friend was dead. This dern war had took both of our best friends from us. Figured it would be a good idea to let him grieve a spell in private while I went looking for where that smoke was coming from. When I left him he'd looked up at me with tears running down his cheeks, said, "Nebo sleepin in the arms o' Jesus." Near brung me to tears seeing him grieve so.

I stepped out of the woods and eased my way across the clearing towards the cabin. When I got within fifty feet I stopped and hallooed. I'd left my coat and pistol with Jeff. Didn't want to chance getting shot at. The Remington weren't of no use anyhow. All the loads had got ruint when we'd swum the river. I was wearing a shirt my mama had sent me from home, but I still had on them Yankee blue breeches. My boots was my own, and them breeches was dirty enough to where they might pass for civilian clothes.

A minute passed, so I hallooed again. The front door creaked open and I seen a young girl with long stringy hair stick her head out. When she seen me she ducked back inside and the door swung shut. Weren't long till it opened again. This time a thin woman stepped through the door and onto the covered porch. She was toting a old hunting musket with the hammer cocked back.

I held up my hands to show her I meant no harm, said, "Morning, ma'am. My name is Malburn, from over Washington County, west of here. I'd be obliged if you'd spare me a minute to talk."

She stared me down a bit, then waved the rifle barrel for me to come closer. "Close enough," she said when I got near the porch steps. Her hands was gripped so tight on that rifle stock her knuckles was white. "What you want here?"

She was a fine-looking woman, maybe thirty or thereabouts. Reminded me a mite of sister Sara. Her brown hair was pulled tight in a bun, and there was a wrinkle or two creeping along the edges of her dark eyes. The hard work of scraping a living out of these woods had put a few years on her, but she wore 'em well enough.

I lowered my hands and give her a friendly smile. "I could use some help, ma'am. Is your man around?"

She give me a frown and her eyes narrowed up, mean-like. Raised the barrel of that musket. "My man was kilt up north a year ago, fighting with Gen'ral Lee."

I seen the pain behind that hard look she give me. I shook my head, said, "I'm right sorry to hear of your loss. My own brother was kilt fighting with General Johnston up in Georgia."

Her eyes near burned right through me then. "Ain't you got no shame? Your own brother kilt by Yankees, and you one of them?"

Before I could find my tongue she said, "You with them Yankees what's been fighting over to the Natural Bridge?"

I near fell over when I heard that. Derned if I could figure how she knowed about that fight yet, other than the racket. But that was a good three miles from here as the crow flies. Reckoned folks hereabouts had their own way of knowing things. What she said next made things a whole heap clearer.

She pointed across her cleared field, said, "These woods is crawling with nigra soldiers. Done had to run off a couple what tried to steal from me. I don't cotton to no thief."

I stared at the muzzle of that musket, figured I'd best tell the truth. "I ain't going to lie to you, ma'am," I said. "I am with the Second Florida U.S. Cavalry, and I was in the fight at the Natural Bridge. But I ain't with 'em by choice, no ma'am. Me and a family slave was working at the salt works up on St. Andrew Bay near to home. The Yankees come raiding and we was captured. They give us the choice of going to prison or joining up. I ain't got no use for this war. I only want to get back home to my family."

That seemed to ease things a mite. The woman lost her hard look. She kept a-hold of the musket but lowered the barrel till it was pointing at the porch floor. After a spell she leaned it agin a post, give out a long sigh, said, "I fancy myself a Christian woman. Lord knows these be hard times for everybody. It ain't my doing to judge others, so if I can help you, I'm a-willing."

———•———

By noon I was back at camp with the bundle of clothes and food I had bought off the Widow Cordell. Turns out I was near the same size as her late husband, and being he had no further need of them, she was pleased to swap a couple of his shirts and breeches and other such for the nine dollars in U.S. greenbacks I had on me. She also throwed in a old raggedy quilt to guard agin the cold nights.

Me and Jeff got shed of the army issue we wore and put on the new things. My new breeches fit a mite loose, but plenty fine. Jeff's shirt fit well enough, but the breeches was a mite short and tight about the middle. They would have to do, though. I made

Jeff get shed of his brogans too, which meant he'd be walking barefoot. Couldn't chance getting caught wearing army issue on our way home, Union or Confederate.

By rights, I reckon me and Jeff was now officially deserters. But the way I seen it, neither one of us had joined up on our own. And there was bound to be a heap of dead and missing after the big fight at the Natural Bridge. Figured me and Jeff would be counted amongst 'em. It weren't likely the army would ever account for them all, or bother trying to track us down.

The kind widow had give me the loan of a shovel, so me and Jeff set about digging a proper grave to lay poor Nebo to rest. When it was done, I said a little prayer, and Jeff sang one of Nebo's favorite hymns over his grave, which laid beneath the sprawling branches of twin live oaks. I made a cross from a scrub oak sapling and hammered it into the ground at the head of the grave. Promised Jeff we'd come back one day and give Nebo a proper marker, but it weren't to be.

Still couldn't chance a fire, so that evening we ate cold collards with fatback and cornbread till we was near stuffed. Then we huddled under the quilt and drifted off to a peaceful sleep, knowing we'd done our duty for poor Nebo.

Next morning I got up before daybreak and left Jeff sleeping while I returned the shovel to the Widow Cordell. When I got back the sun was shining bright in as purty a blue sky as I'd ever laid eyes on. Birds was flitting about the trees, singing their happy spring songs. It was a fine day for walking, and we was going home!

Jeff was near bubbling over with joy as we set out. A time or two I had to hush him up. There was still soldiers about and we couldn't chance running into them. Thing is, I was ever bit as excited as Jeff was. We was going home. Another week or two and I'd see my Annie again.

For us, the war was over at last! Leastways, I thought it was.

Daniel Malburn
Rock Island Prison
June 1864

FOURTEEN

WELL, SIR, MY PRISON DAYS is a mite muddled, even to this day. I can recollect much of what went on, but it's like things was throwed in a bowl and mixed all together rather than being set out in a orderly fashion. Truth be told, if it weren't for a feller name of Jacob Newsom, them days would've been lost to me forever. The Yankee ball that plowed a furrow in my scalp give me a bad case of the fugues. For a goodly spell after I come to, I couldn't recollect a goldamn thing about my life, not even my own name. But I'll tell it best I can.

Poor Jacob had the misfortune of catching a piece of canister in the leg whilst we was making our charge that day. He weren't bad hurt, no bones broke or such, but it crippled him enough that he was captured. He was sitting in the Yankee works the next morning when I come crawling towards their trenches on all fours.

"You was a sight to behold," Jacob told me later at Rock Island, after my memory come back some. "Them Yanks thought you was some kind of critter when they first seen you. You was covered in dried blood. Big clots of it was hanging off your face. Looked like a ugly cur dog or a wild boar or the like. They come mighty close to shooting you before they seen you was human."

Jacob's bad luck proved a godsend for me. We hadn't knowed each other before the war, him being from over Jackson County way, and me and him was in different squads. But all the while I was touched in the head like a dullard, Jacob Newsom watched over me like a mother hen. After the Yankee doctors patched us up best they could and sent us to the prison train, Jacob took me under his wing. He kept me from harm and seen I got a fair share of what little rations we had on the journey to Rock Island. Reckon I owe my very life to him, gospel truth.

I don't recollect much about our train ride north, but from Jacob I learnt we traveled through Chattanooga, Nashville, Louisville, and on to the northern cities of Indianapolis and Michigan City. From there, the railroad turned west along the shore of Lake Michigan for a ways, which Jacob told me looked ever bit as big as the Gulf of Mexico.

After a week, we finally arrived at the new Yankee prison camp at Rock Island. The prison was built on a island that sits in the Mississippi River betwixt the cities of Rock Island on the Illinois side, and Davenport, Iowa to the west. The island itself was some three miles long, and maybe half a mile wide. The prison stockade was roughly a quarter-mile square. It was surrounded by a planked fence twelve foot high, with a catwalk around the outside for the guards to patrol along and keep a eye on us. Ever hundred foot or so along the wall was a covered shack to shelter the guards from the sun or rain. A row of posts was sunk in the ground twenty foot from the fence all the way around the stockade. This was called the deadline, and it weren't to be crossed by the prisoners. Guards had orders to shoot any fool that did.

Inside the stockade was eighty-some barracks to house prisoners. They was crudely built affairs, hardly better than shacks. Each was a hundred foot long and twenty foot wide. There was a door at each end, and five or six windows along each long wall. Inside was bunks enough for a hundred or so prisoners.

Well, sir, cain't say as I rightly recall much of my first two or three months there, not even our arrival. Later, I learnt from Jacob that I had been put into one of the hospital barracks at the south end of the compound for the first month or so.

One hot morning in July I woke up in that hospital bunk and remembered who I was and where I was at. It was like I had awoke out of a trance, which I reckon I had. I looked around the room and called out to the orderly tending another feller in a bunk two or three down from mine. Asked him could I have some water as I was powerful thirsty. That orderly stiffened up and stared at me like he'd seen a ghost. Come to find out, them was the first words I'd uttered the whole time I'd been there. The orderly went and fetched a doctor and they made a fuss over me for nearbout a hour. Kept jawing at me, asking me all sorts of questions. Most, I had no answer for.

I still didn't know much more than my name and that I had been took prisoner sometime back. Couldn't recollect where or when. My memory didn't come back all at once. It snuck back inside my head a piece at a time. After a few days, I recollected Jacob Newsom, told the doctor how he had watched out for me since we had been captured somewheres in Georgia. Even recalled that I'd been with the Sixth Florida Infantry, though I weren't sure which company.

A week or so later they released me from the hospital. Seems they'd done what they could for me. Seeing as I'd mentioned being captured with Jacob Newsom, they assigned me to his barrack, Number Forty-eight. Reckon the doctor figured rubbing elbows and jawing with fellers I knowed might do me some good and help me to remember things.

It was a pitiful lot of scarecrows I seen that morning when

I followed a guard down the long prison street betwixt rows of barracks towards Number Forty-eight. The bright sun nearbout blinded me. I had long ago lost my hat, so I held a hand above my eyes agin the glare. Weren't much stirring in the heat that didn't have to be. Down a side street I seen a passel of prisoners armed with shovels and picks digging a long trench in the middle of the road. I didn't much envy them boys, working so in the hot sun. Others sat agin the side of barracks in what shade there was to be had. Some was playing checkers or cards, others was reading, and a few appeared to be whittling on sticks or what looked to be shells. I thought that a mite peculiar, wondered where they could've picked up shells in a place so far from the ocean. None of 'em paid me much mind, other than a quick look.

After a spell we come to Barrack forty-eight. The guard told me to go on in, so I walked up the steps and through the open doorway. The sun was already high and there weren't much light coming through the windows. Took a minute for my eyes to adjust. Here and yonder, I seen prisoners laying or sitting on bunks about the long barrack. Near one of the windows a few fellers was sitting in a circle on the floor betwixt the long rows of bunks. Looked to be playing cards.

"Beg pardon," I says, "any of you boys know where... where there is a empty bunk I can use?"

One feller looked up from the card game. He had a long beard and was so skinny he'd have a time getting wet in the rain. "Down yonder's a few," he says, pointing towards the far end of the barrack.

"Much obliged," I says. I walked on past them, then stopped. "Say, any of you know a feller... name of... name of Jacob Newsom?"

Nearbout ever one of 'em looked my way when I said that. "We do," says a redheaded bean pole that looked young enough to where his face ain't touched a razor yet. "Who is asking?" he says, staring at me hawk-like, like I was a no-good thief or worse.

Well, sir, I was starting to feel a mite unwelcome, something I ain't expected to find amongst them in the same unfortunate straits as me. I was still woozy in the head some, and found it a struggle at times to keep my wits in order. I rubbed the raw scar on the side of my head and took a minute to think. "I'm Dan... Malburn. Sixth Florida," I says, fighting to get the words out straight. "Me and Jacob, we was took... took prisoner together. Somewheres in Georgia."

Another of the boys put down his cards and stood up, all six foot-some of him. He brushed a shock of dirty blond hair out of his eyes and stepped towards me. "You the one been in the hospital all this time?"

"I am," I says, wondering what it was I had said to irk him so.

"Well hell, why didn't you say who you was when you come in here." He grinned. "We thought you might be a spotter."

Reckon he seen I was a mite confused. Before I could ask him what a spotter was, he says, "Some calls 'em doves. Spies. The damn Yankees is always bribing prisoners from other barracks to spy on us."

I rubbed my head again, felt one of them powerful headaches coming on. "I ain't no spy... dove, what you said."

"Well hell," he says, and shook my hand, "we know that. Jacob told us about you. He's out on work detail. This sorry bunch here is all Florida boys. I'm J.C. Kemp, pleased to make your acquaintance. Reckon you'll be bunking with us."

———◆———

Whilst I had been laid up in the hospital getting my senses back, orders had come down from the prison commandant, one Colonel Adolphus Johnson, to severely cut rations for the prisoners. Seems the bluebellies was determined to punish us for the wants and suffering of Union prisoners sitting inside Confederate stockades, namely Camp Sumpter near Andersonville, Georgia.

Well, sir, what the Yankees failed to consider was, the United States government had stopped prisoner exchanges so that paroled Southerners couldn't take up arms again after their release. The long years of war had already made food and other goods scarce as hens' teeth in the South. Our own armies was close to starving, and most civilians weren't a heap better off. Stood to reason the Confederacy would be hard put to feed and care for Yankee prisoners proper-like. The South's cupboards was bare, but the North had aplenty. But they weren't about to share with them that took up arms only to protect home and family from invasion. Reckon the Yankees was more a "eye for a eye" than a "do unto others" sort. They done a right fine job of it, too.

Not only was our rations cut in half, but instead of each man receiving his daily share, all rations was issued in bulk to ever barrack. There was a hundred-some prisoners in each, with one kitchen to share the cooking duties in. We split up into messes of ten or twelve fellers and made do best we could. It was a tussle divvying up them meager rations even-like, and it weren't no rare sight for fights to break out amongst messes that thought they'd been cheated. You might think it strange for fellers to go to blows over spoilt meat and cornmeal so full of lye it could barely be eat, but hunger can be a mighty powerful master.

It weren't long till we was all little more'n walking skeletons. Them that still had strength and health enough to walk, that is. We was down to one meal a day, and that a meager one. Weren't a fresh vegetable to be had, and divers ailments soon broke out in camp, scurvy amongst 'em. Some poor souls commenced losing their teeth, and their gums was so swole up and sore they couldn't eat. I lost one or two my own self, but managed to eat my share, though it was a struggle at times.

We soon took to hunting rats to sweeten our stew pot. We would block off any holes in the walls or floor except our "hunting hole." The hunters would take turns kneeling on a bunk next to the hole where we had sprinkled a bit of cornmeal on the floor. Armed with a gig made from a nail hammered into a scrap of board, we would wait till a unsuspecting rat come looking where he thunk he could find hisself a easy meal. Then we'd strike! Them rats was right tasty too, nearbout tasty as squirrel. Course, there weren't much to 'em.

We was always on the lookout for some morsel or other to add to our measly rations. When Colonel Johnson had give the order for our rations to be cut, he also forbid the local sutlers from selling their wares to us prisoners. Reckon he figured that would help to keep us near starved. The colonel did, however, let the sutlers hawk their goods to the boys in the "calf pen," which was where the traitors amongst us that took the Union oath was held.

The calf pen barracks was separated from the rest of the stockade by a fence. To get to the calf pen the sutlers had to pass through the main stockade. For some reason or other, it weren't long till the colonel give one sutler in particular, feller name of Dart as I recollect, sole permission to peddle his wares to the calf pen.

Now, sutler Dart just happened to have hisself a fine pet bulldog that stuck to him like a shadow. One day me and Jacob and J.C. Kemp got wind that some fellers from Barrack Forty-seven was planning to steal that dog. Well, sir, we aimed to beat 'em at their own game.

Mister Dart's bulldog had the habit of running along underneath the wagon when folks got too close. On this particular day, he stood outside the calf pen under the center of that wagon whilst his master was busy doing business inside with them "galvanized Yankees," which is what we called them that took the oath and went over to the enemy.

That was one smart dog. It was like he knowed what we was planning. He kept looking this way and that, growling and snapping at anything that come near the edge of that wagon.

Whilst Jacob kept a eye out for Dart, I took to my knees and made a lunge for that dog, intending to grab him by the scruff of his neck. Then quick-like I'd pass him to J.C. who would hide the dog under his coat and skedaddle for our barrack.

Well, sir, that bulldog was a mite quicker on the draw than me. I no sooner laid a finger on him than he turned quick as a cornered rattler and sunk them chompers of his into the back of my hand. I let out a holler and that dog bolted to the other side of the wagon where one of the boys from Forty-seven grabbed him up in a flash. I nearbout cried when I seen that dog disappear under some other feller's coat. It weren't the bite on the hand that caused me to tear up, it was the sight of that tasty feast being toted off towards Barrack Forty-seven.

FIFTEEN

A WEEK OR TWO WENT by, then one morning Jacob took ill. We was due to be out on the street in front or our barrack for morning roll call, but he was so sick he could barely sit up.

"You best lay here and rest," I says. "When they call your name I'll tell 'em you're ill."

When my name was called, I give out the usual "Here!" and waited the few names till they come to Newsom. When the guard captain called Jacob's name, I raised my hand. "He's inside feeling poorly, cain't hardly stand."

The captain, whose name was Graham as I recollect, looked at me like I'd committed a mortal sin. Then he says again, "Newsom, Jacob!"

I stuck up my hand again. "Jacob Newsom is ill, Captain. He's ain't fit to be out here."

The captain turned to the sergeant standing to his left and said something I couldn't make out. Next thing I knowed, the sergeant stomped into our barrack and commenced to hollering and cussing at poor Jacob to beat all hell. Then Jacob come

flying out the doorway and landed in a heap at the bottom of
the steps. The sergeant come tromping down them stairs and
commenced kicking Jacob in the ribs and head, all the while
cussing and hollering at him to get up on his feet and stand in
formation with the others.

That was all I could stand. "Leave him be!" I says. "He ain't
no cur dog for you to be kicking so!" I was madder than a nest
of stirred-up hornets.

I commenced walking towards Jacob, intending to keep
the sergeant from doing him further harm, when the click of
a hammer stopped me in my tracks. "One more step and I'll
relieve you of your brains," Captain Graham says.

I turned around and seen that pistol staring me in the face.
"Captain," I says, "you can go ahead and shoot me where I stand,
or you can call him off Jacob, because if you don't stop him I'm
going to, or else die trying."

The captain decided I weren't bluffing. Reckon he didn't
care explaining to Colonel Johnson how he'd shot a unarmed
prisoner who was just trying to stop one of his own from getting
beat to death. So he ordered the sergeant to stop. A few of the
boys pulled poor Jacob to his feet and helped him stand in line.
When the captain called out his name again, Jacob spit out a
mouthful of blood. "Here," he says, barely more'n a whisper.

When he was done calling roll and assigning work details
and such, Captain Graham dismissed our company. But he
weren't done with me yet, no, sir. He ordered me to stay put,
then called over another guard and commenced jawing with him
and the sergeant.

When they was done talking amongst theirselves, Captain
Graham walked over to me. "Private Malburn, you are guilty
of insubordination and threatening a non-commissioned officer
with bodily harm. Punishment will be carried out immediately."
The he turned on his heels and strutted off.

Them other two marched me down to the end of our street

where one of the stretching poles stood. They tied my hands over my head and pulled that rope tight till my toes was barely touching the ground, cussing and threatening me all the while. I won't repeat what they said, but it weren't nothing you'd ever hear inside a church, gospel.

They left me dangling there in the hot sun for the next three, maybe four hours. It was a struggle to keep on my toes. Ever now and again I'd give 'em a rest and try to stand flat on my feet, but the ropes would burn and nearbout pull my shoulders out of their sockets. Weren't long till my hands and fingers was dead numb.

Ever now and then a prisoner would come walking by and give me a sorrowful look, but they knowed better than to try and help in any way. Them poles was set not far from the deadline, and the guards had orders to shoot anybody that might try to aid a prisoner being punished.

Around noon the sergeant and the other guard come and took me down. My arms was so stiff I couldn't lower 'em below my shoulders. I must've been a sight walking back to our barrack, my arms sticking out like I was trying to fly. When I got there, J.C. Kemp and another feller from our mess, Pete McDonald if I remember correctly, each took one of my arms and rubbed the life back into 'em. It took a spell, but after a while they got my blood to flowing again.

I looked around, didn't see Jacob anywheres about, so I asked J.C. where he was. He pointed towards the door. "He passed out on the floor yonder after we come back in from roll call. Couldn't wake him up, so we called the guards. They fetched a stretcher and took him to the hospital. He's in a bad way, I'm afeared. He had shat his breeches and was bleeding out his ass."

Two days later they struck Jacob Newsom from the rolls of Barrack Forty-eight. Dead from brain fever, they told us. But we knowed better. Them goldamn Yankees had beat the poor soul to death.

SIXTEEN

ONE NIGHT A FEW WEEKS after Jacob Newsom died, I was laying awake thinking about my Annie and home and generally feeling sorry for myself, when of a sudden a gunshot rang out. Before I could think about it, I rolled off my bunk and hunkered down on the floor. Weren't a minute later another shot was fired, then two more.

"Them fuzz-chins is at it again," says somebody a ways down the barrack. Another musket fired and the building went to shaking as more and more of the boys took to the floor.

This had been going on for nearbout two weeks now, ever since them Illinois boys had took over the guard duty. When I say boys, I mean it literal-like. Them new bluebellies was young fellers, most not over sixteen or so. Now, it's a fact that our own army was full of such, but they was real soldiers fighting for a cause. This here group was nothing of the sort. Word was the Yanks had raised many a like regiment to free up other units so they could be sent south to fight the war. These boys had signed on for one hundred days of duty, and they had about as much military training as the average flea-bit hound. A few had blowed off their own fingers or toes, and it was said one or two had shot theirselves to death whilst fooling around.

They was a trigger-happy bunch, gospel truth. A week or two earlier one of the guards had fired into a group of prisoners on work detail whilst they was gathered around the water bucket. That single ball struck down three men, one that died. It was a rare day or night when there weren't at least a dozen or so muskets fired. Betwixt starving us and shooting us it seemed them goldamn bluebellies was hankering to get shed of us once and for all.

"Some feller told me on work detail today them bastards shot Barrack seventy-eight full of holes last night," Pete McDonald says, hugging the floor not far from me. "Said near twenty prisoners was sent to the hospital wounded."

"Don't doubt it a bit," says Charlie Harris, another of the Florida boys in our mess. "Why, t'other night a Alabamian from fifty-seven got shot dead whilst walking to the sinks. Pard of his told me he seen it with his own eyes."

"Them boys got a heavy finger all right," says J.C. Kemp. "Damn if I won't piss my breeches before I use the sinks after dark."

"Well boys," I says, "I'm getting a mite tired of sleeping on this hard floor dodging balls ever night. Figure it's about time we done something about it."

Next morning after roll call I told the boys my plan. The island was full of rocks of all sizes, inside the stockade and out. If everbody was to gather up a pocketful of good throwing rocks whilst going about our daily business, in a couple of days we could have ourselves a fine arsenal to teach them fuzz-chins a lesson or two. And if we was to share our plan with some fellers we trusted in other barracks, we could cause them young Yanks a heap of grief. So that's what we set out to do.

Two nights later me and my messmates slipped out the door at eleven o'clock, the time agreed on with the fellers from the other three barracks we recruited. It had clouded up that evening, so the moon was swallowed up. We snuck along the back side of our barrack, then split up into two groups, each assigned to a particular guard on the wall. That would give us eight groups of five or so for ever guard we aimed to attack. With that many rocks flying we was bound to score some hits.

We was in place before quarter-after, the time the attack was set to begin. We hugged the side of the barrack single file. I eased my head around the corner and chanced a look. In the light of the reflecting lanterns that hung from the stockade fence I seen our guard leaning with both arms resting atop the wall, his musket beside him. Looked to be half asleep.

I give J.C. a nod, which meant our target was in range. J.C. pulled out his watch and snuck a close look, then give us the signal. We jumped out into the road with our hands full of rocks and commenced slinging them at the guard. A heap of rocks clattered off the wall, then come the dull *thunk!* of stone striking flesh and bone. The guard cried out and went down in a heap.

Our duty done, we scurried back down the road and slipped inside our barrack to our bunks. Up and down the stockade wall guards went to wailing and shouting, wondering what had hit 'em. Here and yonder, a few muskets blasted into the dark. Then things fell quiet.

Next morning at roll call, our new guard captain was madder than a wet cat. Don't recollect his name, but he was a young feller, not much older than them boys on the wall. He had took over for Captain Graham when that bastard's regiment was relieved from guard duty. The new captain commenced strutting up and down our formation, spouting all sorts of threats and dire consequences to come if we didn't turn in the cowardly rogues that had attacked the guards last night. Seems one unfortunate soul had caught a rock in the mouth and lost some teeth. Two others had their skulls cracked and one broke a leg when he tumbled off the wall.

Well, sir, that shavetail spoke so eloquent he nearbout brung me to tears, hey-hey. I was sorely tempted to confess my sins and beg his forgiveness, but I managed to hold back like the rest of the boys.

As I recollect, the Yanks never did find out who any of the rock-throwers was, but most of them guards got our message. Weren't near as much shooting from the fuzz-chins afterwards.

———————

Around the same time Colonel Johnson cut our rations, the boys began to notice that mail from home had dropped off considerable. Weren't long till donations for the prisoners from the kind citizens of Davenport and Rock Island all but disappeared. Being as our rations was so meager, packages the boys received from home and charity from the good neighbors of the nearby towns had kept us from starving. Now, that well had dried up too.

It had been a month or so since I had wrote the first letters home to my mama and Annie, letting them know I had been wounded and took prisoner, but that I was alive and doing tolerable. Ever day I looked forward to a answer from home, but as yet no letter had come. Now and again some lucky fellers in our barrack would get word from their wife or sweetheart or family, but packages with food and money and such weren't to be had. That evil tyrant Johnson was to blame, weren't two ways about it.

Our circumstances was growing worse by the day. Spirits was low, even amongst the heartiest of us. Fighting commenced over rations or work details or who had turned spotter for the Yankees or other such. Then word come down from the prison commandant that any prisoner willing to take the oath would be paid a bounty of a hundred dollars a year. They would not be sent south to fight agin their former countrymen, but would be sent west to fight the Indians. Reckon everbody has their breaking point, and it weren't long till prisoners was taking the oath in droves. Them that swore allegiance to the Union was transferred to the aforementioned calf pen where they was given full rations and new clothes and other such niceties. It ain't wrong to say that hunger and want drove many from our ranks to the enemy camp, but greed took its share too.

Well, sir, I was ever bit as hungry as the next man, but there weren't no way I would take that oath and go over to the bluebellies. They had invaded our land and plundered our homes and visited all sort of misery on our people. I'd seen too many of my pards die from Yankee shot and steel. I'd sooner starve to death and be cursed to Hell before I'd be counted amongst their number.

Truth be told, some good-hearted fellers took the oath so they could help them that was left behind in the main stockade. Them new "Union men" commenced tossing beef and bread and other such over the calf pen fence to their hungry pards. Weren't long before Colonel Johnson got wind of things and put a swift end to it. He ordered that a new deadline be built in front of the calf pen fence and posted guards to keep the prisoners a proper distance away from their galvanized pards.

Though Colonel Johnson had halted the delivery of charitable goods from civilians, some mornings we would find potatoes or turnip roots or cabbages and such vegetables that some kindly souls from the nearby towns had throwed over the fence during the night. They done this at considerable risk, though I never heard of any civilians being shot. Most likely they resorted to bribing the guards to let 'em toss them goods into the stockade. Whatever the circumstances, it was "manna from heaven" to us suffering prisoners, and kept many of us alive and in tolerable health.

It weren't unusual to find a cabbage or such had landed betwixt the stockade fence and the deadline. The guards had a heap of fun goading us to step inside the deadline and fetch it:

"Say Reb, that cabbage would be right tasty with them rats you been eating. Believe I'll just mosey on down the wall a piece, see if it's gone when I get back."

Them guards could be a cruel sort, gospel truth.

———•———

Well, sir, by late summer hundreds of the boys had gone over to the enemy. Incoming mail had all but ceased, and there weren't no way of knowing if the letters we wrote home was getting there or being waylaid. What clothes we had was little better'n rags. Winter weren't that far off and there weren't blankets enough to go around. Our rations got shorted again when the number of "volunteers" taking the Union oath dropped off considerable. Then to add to our troubles, one morning in early fall at roll call we looked up to find we was now being guarded by colored troops.

Them coloreds proved to be less disciplined and even more trigger-happy than the fuzz-chins was, and it weren't long before another rash of shootings broke out through camp. One morning me and John Boykin, one of the Florida boys from up Quincy way, was out gathering limbs and such for the stove. It had turned chilly at night, and our barrack had done used up our meager coal ration for the week.

John was picking up dead limbs from a tree near the deadline when this colored guard hollers out, "Hey you, you drop dem limbs and get back fum de dead line!"

Well, sir, John knowed he weren't doing nothing wrong, so he just ignored that colored sentry and went on about his business.

"Drop dem limbs, you damn Rebel!" the guard hollers again.

John was bent over reaching for another limb when I seen

the guard raise his musket and take aim. "You best do what he says, John," I says. "That guard means—"

The musket boomed and spit smoke and flame and poor John Boykin went face down, shot through the right hip. I dropped my load of wood and drug him behind that tree before the guard could reload for another shot. John was hurting bad. The ball had burrowed deep. I couldn't tell if bone was broke or not, but he was bleeding a heap. We stayed hid agin that tree trunk till the sergeant of the guard come running to see what all the ruckus was about.

"That goddamn nigger back-shot me for nothing," says John.

"It's true, Sergeant," I says. "We was just fetching stove wood."

I kept a handful of leaves pressed tight agin the wound whilst the sergeant walked over and jawed a spell with the colored sentry. When he come back, he says, "The sentry says you crossed the deadline to get wood. He has witnesses who will swear to it."

"They are goldamn liars!" I says. "He weren't nowhere near it."

The sergeant sneered and wagged a finger in my face. "One more word out of you and I'll have you in irons."

That was that. They fetched stretcher bearers and toted poor John Boykin to the camp hospital. That was the last we seen of him. Some feller from Forty-seven said John took sick and died of lung fever. Another heard he took the oath and, being found unfit for duty on account of his wound, got sent home a free man.

Never did find out for certain the fate of John Boykin, but a week after he was shot, that same guard shot another prisoner headed for the sinks after dark. That unfortunate soul was kilt outright.

SEVENTEEN

FALL SET IN. DAYS GROWED shorter and the weather turned cold. It was a struggle at times to keep warm, and we commenced sleeping in heaps around the stoves during bitter nights.

Mail from home continued to trickle in for the more fortunate prisoners. I had wrote to home and Annie a passel of times, but still hadn't received even one letter in return. I was homesick and heartsick.

Some of the fellers, like J.C. Kemp and Charlie Harris who'd been captured at Missionary Ridge, had already faced one bitter winter on Rock Island. They weren't none too happy about the prospects of bearing another. More and more, talk about escaping swept through camp.

There had been a heap of attempts to escape the island, but only a handful had made it. One young feller had "hitched" a ride underneath a camp doctor's buggy and rode through the stockade gate to freedom. Another clever soul somehow fashioned hisself a Yankee uniform of sorts, complete with a pistol carved of wood and holster made from the top of a cavalry boot. One morning this bold feller took command of a prison work detail, marched his "charges" out the stockade gate and set them to work clearing a field. Whilst the prisoners was busy with picks and shovels, this "guard" made good his escape.

Just a month or so back a handful of prisoners had slipped into the camp sewer trench and crawled their way outside the stockade fence. Three of them fellers was captured before they made it to the river, two poor souls drowned whilst trying to swim the Mississippi, but another two made their way to freedom.

One evening J.C. come back from a work detail and was warming hisself near the back stove, looking grim. "Them nigger guards is up to no good again," he says, blowing on his hands and rubbing them together.

Pete McDonald picked another grayback out of his shock of red hair and flicked it onto the hot stove. "They shooting up the sinks again?"

"Worser than that," says J.C. "They murdered one of the Tennesseans over in Number sixty-two. He give a guard twenty dollars to let him cross the deadline and dig under the fence. He no sooner got to the other side when the bastard shot him dead."

"Sorry sumbitch!" Charlie Harris says. "What we going to do, J.C.? Them black devils is tetched, just soon shoot you as look at you. And ain't nobody tells 'em no better."

"I don't cotton to being at the mercy of no Yankee," says Pete. "Specially no Yankee nigger."

J.C. looked around the barrack to see who might be listening, then motioned for us to lean in a mite closer. He pulled back one side of his jacket. There was a posthole spade with a broke-off handle hid down one leg of his breeches. "We going to dig us a tunnel boys," he says, grinning.

———◆———

For the next few weeks we dug like gophers towards the

stockade fence, some hundred-fifty foot from our barrack. Most ever night after taps, we would lift up the floor boards we'd pried loose under a bunk, drop down into our tunnel and dig till just before first light. We took turns at it, usually a hour or so at a time. That was nearbout all a body could handle, what with our poor rations and the foul air inside the tunnel. We shoveled the dirt and rocks onto a blanket, then drug it back to the entrance where another feller would lift it out and spread it over the crawl space underneath the barrack floor. A time or two we had to detour around a rock that proved too big to move.

Three or four other messes joined our little adventure. There was always the danger of a spotter being amongst us, but that was a risk we had to take.

I still hadn't heard from home. Word had come through the local newspaper that Sherman's army had captured Atlanta and was on the march through lower Georgia. I was more'n a mite fearful a wing of his army might've turned south into West Florida. Couldn't shake the feeling that bad times had befallen my loved ones. That made me more determined than ever to make good my escape and head home.

After a month we figured the tunnel had passed under the street and was now somewheres betwixt the road and the dead line. Another week and our tunnel would be outside the stockade wall! Or so we hoped.

It was my misfortune to come down with a case of the trots that ailed me enough to where I was spending nearbout as much time at the sinks as the barrack. One night I was heading for the sinks again, being quiet as I could manage. I crossed the road and turned down the path towards the sinks when I noticed two fellers standing by a tree down the road a piece.

I stopped in my tracks, making sure it weren't guards fixing to waylay me. They was too far away for me to hear what they was saying, but I had a hunch. After a spell, they went their separate ways. I stood fast in the shadows whilst one feller walked down the road past me and turned towards our barrack. In the faint glow of the reflecting lamps I recognized him as a young feller that had been assigned to our barrack two or three weeks earlier. Don't recollect his name, but he was a standoffish sort. Couldn't make out the other, but he was decked out in a fine Yankee uniform, most likely a officer.

When I got back I woke up J.C. Kemp, told him what I'd seen. Next morning we passed the word for everbody to lay low a spell. That night we set about cleaning up any signs of our work, then stretched a blanket over the hole, weighted the edges with rocks and covered it with a thin layer of dirt. Even tapped the nails back into the floor boards.

Two days later at morning roll call the captain and sergeant of the guard showed up with a squad of coloreds armed with muskets. The captain commenced calling out a list of names, which included our whole mess plus most of the other boys that was in on our little scheme. They separated us from the others and we stood there under guard whilst the captain and sergeant searched our barrack.

Whilst they was about their business I looked hard at the other row of prisoners, trying to find the feller I'd seen palavering with the Yankee officer a few nights before. He weren't nowheres to be seen. Most likely that Judas was over in the calf pen, eating high on the hog whilst counting his bounty money.

Didn't take the captain long to find what he was looking for, since he knowed right where to look. The game was up. We'd been sold out.

———•———

They moved us miscreants to a guardhouse barrack for the next few weeks. We spent our days on the dirtiest work details the Yanks could conjure up, toting slop buckets and cleaning out the sinks and sewer trenches and such. At night they chained each of us to a iron ball that weighed thirty pounds. That made any trip to the sinks a struggle.

Our rations was thinned even more. We was getting by on moldy lye cornbread and water. Seemed ever day I cinched the rope holding up my breeches a mite tighter. It turned bitter cold, and we was suffering mightily. Our clothes weren't nothing but rags, and though they give each prisoner a blanket, there never seemed to be enough coal for the stove. The river had froze over, and our water supply run low. At times we took to melting snow to get enough to drink.

As the days drug by our numbers thinned out. Some fellers took sick and was toted off to the hospital. Others, sad to say, slunk off in the dark of night and took the oath. Weren't nobody amongst us getting mail from home. I had nearbout give up on ever hearing from my family or Annie again. Them bad headaches had come back to plague me, and there was spells when I would disremember things.

One cold morning the guards ordered us to gather up our belongings, such as they was, and marched us back to Barrack Forty-eight. Reckon Colonel Johnson figured we'd suffered enough for trying to escape. Things was a mite better then. Weren't no ball and chain to tote around, and most days our rations included a bit of blue beef or wormy pork.

Ever now and again one of the boys would somehow get hold of a recent newspaper from one of the local towns. That's how we come to find out that Christmas had come and gone. It was now January eighteen sixty-five, and things was going poorly for the Confederacy. General Hood, who had replaced Ol' Joe Johnston at Atlanta, had bled the Army of Tennessee dry at Franklin and Nashville. General Lee's boys was barely hanging on agin Grant in the trenches around Richmond. That devil Sherman had burned a path fifty miles wide through Georgia and was aiming to do the same through the Carolinas. Things was looking so bleak for the Southern cause ever day more and more prisoners took the oath. Even some amongst our own mess seemed sorely tempted.

"What's the use in us holding out any longer?" says Pete McDonald one evening whilst we was huddled around the stove. "They've whipped us."

Charlie Harris raked his fingers through his long beard, scratching at graybacks or such. "The Yanks kilt your brother at Stone River," he says. "Now you a-wanting to join up with 'em?"

Pete looked like Charlie had slapped him. "I didn't say nothing of the sort. I'm just wondering why we stay here cold and starved when we could be fat and warm. Besides, we'd be off fighting Injuns, not our own people."

I pulled my blanket tighter around my neck. "You'd still be doing the Yankees' dirty work for 'em. I'd just as soon starve."

"Well, Danny, you are doing a right fine job of it," says Pete.

J.C. Kemp had been studying the newspaper. Now he set it down. Took off his hat and scratched at his scalp. "Boys, there's talk of exchange starting up again. If we can hang on a mite longer—"

"Hell, J.C., they been talking that shit since we got here," says Charlie Harris. "Yanks is filling up their army with foreigners from across the ocean. Why would they turn us a-loose to fight again?"

"I tell you, there's a chance for it," says J.C., holding up the newspaper. "This here Davenport paper is calling for exchange. Says here that editors all over the North is pushing for it. There is hope, boys."

Come morning, Pete McDonald was gone.

EIGHTEEN

THE COLD NORTHERN WINTER CRAWLED by slower than a three-legged gopher through molasses. I took ill and spent a spell in the hospital again, but I cain't recall how long I might've been there. Seems ever time I recollected something from my past life, I would disremember two other things. Rumors of prisoner exchange kept floating through camp, but there weren't many amongst us put much store in it ever happening.

One night in February, I was laying on my bunk staring out the window up at the cold black sky. Stars was shining like diamonds, the crescent moon climbing above the stockade fence. It was a beautiful sight, and if I'd not been behind prison walls. I might've took some comfort in it.

There still weren't no word from home, but truth be told, I'd done give up hope. I was feeling right sorry for myself, thinking that only a year before I'd spent such a beautiful night as this with my Annie. It had been a warm day for early February. I had arrived at the Gainer plantation late afternoon for a supper invite to find that Annie had packed us a picnic basket full of baked ham, roasted corn and real flour biscuits. She'd even snuck a bottle of Muscadine wine from her father's cellar, risking her ma's wrath but knowing how much it would please me.

We walked hand-in-hand down the path to the big springs. The breeze was whispering through the green pine boughs, and the late evening sun shined like gold on the moss draping the branches of live oaks. We spread a blanket on the limestone outcropping, and sat there listening to the bubbling spring whilst feasting on fine food and drinking sweet wine.

The sun set and the crescent moon rose above the dark wall of trees. I took Annie in my arms. We hugged and kissed till I thought I'd bust wide open from the love and joy I felt.

It was our last night together before my return to Dalton and the war. It's been sixty-some long years, but I still ain't forgot how beautiful Annie looked, standing on the porch steps under that diamond sky, waving and calling goodbye till the dark swallowed her up.

———◆———

One morning in the middle of March we rolled out of our bunks, trudged outside to line up for roll call. It had turned bitter again after a few days of false spring. My head hurt something fierce, and I could barely feel my toes agin the frozen ground. The soles of my brogans was more hole than leather. I'd wrapped them in rags best I could to keep the cold out. I hunched under my blanket trying to shed the chill, fighting off the cough that plagued me for the past two weeks. Felt a mite more tuckered than I had of late.

"You ain't fit for work detail, Danny," says J.C. Kemp, standing beside me. "I'll see to it the captain lets you rest today."

I finished up a coughing fit, wiped my mouth agin my sleeve. "I'm obliged, but I can hold my own. Besides, there ain't no coal to spare. It'll be a heap warmer out in the sun than inside the barrack once I get to moving."

Just then, the sergeant called us to attention. The captain strutted up and down the ranks, eyeballing us. He had his hands behind his back, holding what I took to be the roll. After a minute he held up the paper like he wanted us all to get a good look at it.

"When you hear your name called, step forward and line up beside the sergeant," he says. He commenced to call out two dozen or so names, J.C. Kemp and Charlie Harris amongst 'em. When he was done, the captain turned to face the rank of scraggly scarecrows. "Upon order of Colonel Adolphus Johnson, Commanding Officer, Rock Island Barracks, and the United States War Department, you men are being exchanged. You will return to your barrack to gather your personal belongings and report back here in five minutes. Dismissed."

Well, sir, them words come as a surprise. I was downright stunned as I stood there watching my pards walk back towards the barrack, knowing they'd soon be free men whilst me and the others would be left behind to rot on this island. Them fellers looked dumbfounded, like they didn't dare believe their ears, which I reckon most didn't. I was glad for 'em, knowing they'd soon return to hearth and home, but truth be told, I was mighty envious.

Feeling a mite shamed, I hollers out, "Whoowee!" loud as I could, waving my hand in a high circle. "You boys is going home!"

"Quiet in the ranks!" the captain shouts back whilst I bent over coughing my lungs up. Others amongst us ignored the captain and took up the cheer and soon it rose up and echoed around the stockade walls till it growed into the Rebel Yell. Only after the captain threatened to call out the guard did we finally give it up.

Well, sir, imagine my surprise when I come back from work detail that evening and seen J.C. Kemp sitting on his bunk reading the latest newspaper he'd managed to scrounge up.

Before I could ask, he says, "They told us we had to swear the oath before we left the island. I couldn't bring myself to do it, Danny. The others did, even Charlie, but I just couldn't."

I knowed right then that I wouldn't either, and I said as much to J.C. They could bury my scarecrow carcass in the prison graveyard where so many other poor souls that had perished on that godforsaken island would spend eternity, but I would never take their goldamn oath.

NINETEEN

THE WEEKS WORE ON TILL the cold finally loosed its grip on Rock Island. Trees and bushes commenced leafing out and grasses sprouted in the places that weren't kept tromped down. Songbirds returned from points south, singing their happy songs and building nests.

Ever week, more and more prisoners got exchanged. I lost track of the number of times we switched barracks as our numbers thinned. Rations was increased and the sutlers was allowed back inside the stockade to sell goods to them that had the money for such. Things overall turned a mite better then they'd been for many a month. Reckon the Yankees didn't want a passel of starved skeletons showing up when it come time for prisoner swaps. Then one day in early May a heap of disturbing news swept through camp like a wildfire.

Seems General Grant finally forced General Lee's army out of their works around Richmond. Our boys had made a gallant fight of it on the run for the mountains, but Lee finally give it up at Appomattox Courthouse. Then, a couple of weeks later,

General Joe Johnston, who was again in command of the Army of Tennessee, surrendered to General Sherman somewheres in North Carolina. If all that weren't bad enough, some fool had went and shot President Abraham Lincoln dead. I weren't no admirer of Lincoln, truth be told, but his murder didn't bode well for the South.

Rumors commenced flying about camp that the Yankee government was planning on revenging Lincoln's death, and us prisoners was to be the object of their vengence.

"I heard tell they's going to hang us all," says one of the boys after roll call one morning. "And a feller over in Sixty-two says he heard them nigger guards is going to line us all up in the sewer trench and shoot us."

Things was mighty antsy for a spell, but fortunately the rumors proved false. Weren't long till the whole kettle of fish was spoilt. Word come that the rest of the scattered Southern forces had surrendered. The Confederacy was done in for good. The war was over. Weren't no more exchange of prisoners to be made now. We was all free to go home, just as soon as the prison officials could arrange for our transportation to points south… *and* we took that goldamn loyalty oath.

"I ain't going to do it," I says to J.C. Kemp one night after we eat our supper rations. "I'd sooner rot right here on this island."

"Well Danny," says J.C., "we got no country to defend now. I don't see the sense in being mule-headed about it. We done all we could. It ain't like we're going over to the Union army. We're being paroled. Besides, I'm hankering to get home."

"Least you got one to go to," I says, feeling right sorry for myself. "Reckon if I had a wife waiting for me, I'd do the same." Not hearing from home all these long months was the cause of my stubbornness, I knowed that, but I was bent on playing out the hand I'd been dealt.

"A lot of the boys ain't heard from home," he says, trying to cheer me. "That don't mean your people have forgot you. The war just has things messed up is all."

Next morning J.C. Kemp was amongst them called for parole, and this time he went.

—————•————

A couple of weeks later I was laying awake staring at the stars when a thought struck me. I'd take their goldamn oath without really taking it! It was a right smart idea, but so simple I wondered why I hadn't thought of it long before. I laid awake the rest of the night, too excited to sleep.

The days crawled by. There was only a hundred or so of us left inside the stockade. Only three or four names was called the past two mornings. I feared the Yanks meant to keep some of us prisoner as a example for them that might dare take up arms agin the Union again.

Of a sudden I heard it—"Malburn, Daniel!"

This time instead of turning around and walking back to the barrack, I took my place in line with the other few that was called out. This time I would take their oath. Only I wouldn't. I aimed to beat the Yanks at their own game. I stood there with the other dozen or so fellers whilst them not called was dismissed to go about their daily business. After a spell the guard captain says all solemn like, "Raise your right hand and repeat after me.

Well, sir, I don't rightly recollect the exact words of that oath, but the captain had us spout such like, "*I do hereby swear this, that and the other, to uphold and obey and defend the Constitution of the United States of America,*" and on and on.

I nearbout laughed out loud when he come to the part about the Constitution, knowing as I did how Mister Lincoln had trampled all over that most precious document to preserve his so-called Union. Anyhow, thing was, ever time they had us say "*I swear,*" I'd mumble, "*I swear not.*" So, after we was done, I had swore *not* to do all they had made us swear to!

Then all us new law-abiding citizens was marched off to

another barrack where we was given a new blanket and set of clothes if the ones we had on was considered too ragged. Then we was marched to another barrack where we was instructed to sign a written copy of the oath we had just swore aloud to.

Well, sir, I hadn't counted on that. Had to do some quick thinking on my feet. When it come my turn, I had it figured out.

"I cain't read nor write," I says to the officer sitting behind the desk to witness our signing.

He looked at me like I was lower than pond scum. "Well then, make your mark on this line," he says, pointing to the blank line where we was supposed to write our name. He dipped the pen in the inkwell and handed it to me.

I took the pen and scratched a big "X" right through the center of the oath.

"You ignorant bas—" he says. "On the line, prisoner, right here." He tapped a finger on the paper.

"Sorry," I says. I made another mark on the proper line.

A hour later they loaded us onto wagons. When we passed through the stockade gates I teared up as I looked east towards a grove of trees. Beyond them trees was the graves of Jacob Newsom and thousands of other poor souls that perished on that damnable island.

Soon the road curved south and the wagons headed for the causeway that would take us to the town of Rock Island and freedom. It was the twenty-eighth day of May in the Year of Our Lord eighteen sixty-five, one year to the day that a Yankee ball had struck me down outside Dallas, Georgia. In just a few weeks at most, I would be home and marry up with my beloved Annie.

Leastways, that's what I thought. Couldn't know my troubles was just beginning.

Elijah Malburn
March–April 1865
Journey Home

TWENTY

THE NIGHT BEFORE WE SET out I done some thinking about the best way for me and Jefferson to get home. I remembered from my schooling that a huge forest full of swamps and such covered most of the land to our west. Weren't no way we'd ever find our way through that, so I figured we would swim back across the St. Marks River and follow the road south to Newport. From there we'd take the crossroad that led west across the Wakulla River, then turn south to the coast. The coastal road would get us to St. Andrew. There would be food aplenty to be had from all the bays and bayous along the way. Once we made St. Andrew, all we'd have to do was head north on the Marianna Road to home.

Well, sonny, it didn't take long for me and Jeff to learn we'd have to do most of our traveling by night and hole up days. We'd just swam the river and set out down the Newport road when hoofbeats clattered behind us. Weren't no time to hightail it for the woods. I turned and seen it was Confederate cavalry, maybe five-six strong.

Jeff seen 'em too. His chin went to quivering. "Oh Lawd Eli, what we goan do?"

I shifted the quilt bundle to my other shoulder. "You keep quiet and let me do all the talking."

Jeff give a nod.

A minute later the first rider overtook us. He was mounted on a scrawny sorrel nag that had seen its better days long ago.

I looked up, said, "Howdy." He was a rough-looking sort with a scraggly beard and a ugly red scar across one cheek. Looked to be near thirty. Couldn't see no sign of rank, but the brace of pistols tucked under his wide belt give him all the authority he needed. He ignored my greeting, rode on ahead a few feet then wheeled his horse around, blocking our way. I heard the others pull up behind us.

Scarface spit out a brown stream and pushed his chaw to the other cheek. Swung a leg over the pommel. Stared me down with rattler eyes, said, "Who are you, and where you headed?"

"Name's Elijah Wachob," I said, borrowing my mama's maiden name for the occasion. "This here is Jefferson, of the family. We heard tell there's work to be had on the coast, making salt."

Out the corner of my eyes I seen two other riders move up on either side of the road, blocking our way if we was foolish enough to bolt for the woods. Scarface darted them snaky eyes all over me, then locked them onto my own. "What's in the bundle?"

I slid the quilt off my shoulder and held it out to him. "Just a change of clothes. Ain't got no weapon if that's what you're asking, other than my jackknife. Left my pa's shotgun back home with my ma."

Scarface paid the quilt no mind. "And just where is your home... Wachob, is it?"

"Yes, sir, Elijah Wachob." I wondered if these boys might've been amongst them I'd seen guarding the ford below Natural Bridge. "We're from Statesboro, up in Georgia. That damn

Yankee devil Sherman burnt us out a spell back. Figured I'd come down here, hope to make some money to help out my poor widowed ma and family."

Some of the meanness left his eyes when he heard that. He brushed away a fly that lit on his horse's ear. "We heard of your trouble. Wisht I could lay a-hold of that devil."

"Do tell?" I said, cracking a grin. "Reckon you and your boys might teach his sort some proper manners at that. Say, how far you reckon it is to the salt makers?"

He turned to the rider on my right, a tall skinny feller with pale skin and cotton white hair. "Martin, how far to Shell Point?"

Martin turned in the saddle and stared out from under his slouch hat towards the southwest, like doing so would help him better judge the distance. "Afoot? Two, maybe three days, Cap'n."

"Much obliged, sir," I said, nodding to Martin, though he weren't much older than me that I could tell.

There come the distant rumbling of musketry to the south. "Sounds like rain's a-coming," I said, hoping to impress Captain Scarface and his boys with my ignorance.

The captain laughed and slid his leg off the pommel and back to the stirrup. "Hell boy, them's muskets. You and your nigger best keep a sharp eye out for Yankees. They still running around these woods from the whupping we give 'em t'other day."

"That so?" I said, trying to look surprised. "I thank you kindly for the warning."

Captain Scarface tipped his hat, then wheeled his horse and lit out towards Newport with the others close on his heels. I looked over at Jeff who was a mite pale and shaking but still had his mouth shut tight. "You done fine. Now, we best get off this road while the getting's good."

———◆———

We holed up in the woods till dark, then hit the road and

walked the few miles to Newport. It was a mite cold, but clear, with a waxing moon that give what light we needed. I figured the Confederates would have the town heavily guarded, being they fought the Yankees there a few days back, so we kept a sharp eye and ear peeled for pickets. Sure enough, we seen their fires burning a ways outside town. Me and Jeff left the road and cut through the woods, keeping in sight of what lamps we could see burning in the village as we skirted it. Here and yonder, a dog went to barking, but we was soon west of town. When I was satisfied we had gone far enough, we turned south and struck the road that would lead us to the coast.

We made good time that night. The road was hard-packed sand with crushed oyster shells in places that might prove troublesome come a hard rain. A hour or so outside Newport come the clinking and clanking of a wagon. We slipped into the bushes and watched it pass by. It was hauling fish or such from the smell of it. My stomach went to growling. Me and Jeff had eat the last of the food the Widow Cordell had give us for breakfast that morning. Tomorrow we'd have to scrounge up something for our bellies to work on.

Over my left shoulder the sun was just peeking above the marsh, so we searched for somewheres to hide out for the day. After a spell I spied a oak hammock a short piece out in the marsh. We left the road and lit out for it. That saw grass was near shoulder high in places and would slice like a razor if a body weren't careful. Fact is, I was a heap more worried about kicking up a water mocassin than I was getting a cut or two. I hoped the cold still had 'em feeling sluggish. There ain't nothing ornerier than a stirred-up cottonmouth, that's a fact.

For the next week or so we followed the coastal road best we could, traveling nights and resting days. When we was able to stick near the coast we feasted on raw oysters and scallops.

There was times we had to skirt around villages, keeping to the woods and swamps. The skeeters and sand gnats made us pay dearly for it too, that's a fact. But we couldn't chance running into no army patrols or such.

When me and Jeff made Eastpoint we had ourself a problem. Somehow we had to find a way to get across Apalachicola Bay. Weren't no walking around it. It would take a month or more even if we managed not to get eat by gators or struck dead by snakes. If that weren't trouble enough, there was Union outposts thereabouts, mostly on the coastal islands. So we laid low in the piney woods a couple of days and kept our eyes peeled.

We soon noticed a oysterman who had a cabin near the edge of the woods where we was hiding out. Ever morning at daybreak this feller set out in his boat to work the oyster beds. He'd get back midafternoon and spend the rest of the day breaking up clusters and washing the mud off the oysters and loading 'em into gunny sacks. Then he'd cross the bay to the town of Apalachicola to sell his goods.

Well, sonny, two-three days passed and we was getting antsy to move on. Figured this feller was about as good a chance as we was going to find to get across the bay. So, when he come back in with his day's catch the next afternoon, me and Jeff left our hideout and headed for his shack. He was sitting on a rough bench in the shade of some pines, busting up clusters of oysters with a queer looking hammer.

"Howdy," I said when we got within earshot. I didn't want to chance spooking him. He turned, give me and Jeff a quick look and went back to his work. Caught the smell of salt and pipe smoke drifting on the breeze as we come up behind him. "Wondered when you boys was goan come see me," he said. "What y'all doing hiding out in my woods?"

He didn't sound like a unfriendly sort, so I walked on around to face him. Had to give Jeff a tug to get him to follow me. The man stopped his work and looked up at me and Jeff from beneath a ragged hat wove out of palmetto fronds. The sandals he wore appeared to be made of the same, and his short breeches and shirt was cut from gunny sacks. He was black as any nigra I'd ever seen, but sharp of jaw and cheekbones. His silver-streaked black hair hung over his shoulders, his skin was wrinkled like weathered leather. I took him to be sixty, maybe older.

"My name is Eli, this here is Jeff," I said, a mite uneasy under his stare and that hammer he was holding. Them dark eyes seemed to look right through into my soul, so I figured I'd best be honest with him. "We was hoping you could carry us across the bay."

He set down the hammer, took a puff on his cob pipe. Pointed south, said, "Ferry be right down yonder."

Well, sonny, me and Jeff was neck deep in the brine barrel, and I needed to come up with something quick to get us out of it. We was flat broke, but even if we had money for the ferry we couldn't dare risk it. Before I could find my tongue he set them dark eyes on me. "You boys be in trouble?"

"Yes, sir, of a sort." Then I went to telling him our sad story from the beginning, how me and Jeff become salt makers, how we was captured and drafted into the Yankee army, the whole can of worms. When I was done I looked him right in the eye. "Me and Jeff don't want no part of this war, Mister. All we want is to get home to our family."

Know what he done then, sonny? I'll tell you. After a spell he give a grunt. Took off his frond hat and fanned hisself, said, "You boys know oystering?"

"Know how to shuck and eat 'em," I said, and chanced a grin.

The old man laughed at that. "Ol' Black Buck will see you boys across, but fust you gots to earn you keep."

That night, after our work was done, we feasted on smoked mullet and oysters roasted in the shell and fried cornbread and turnips. It was the best me and Jeff had eat since we left home. After we had our fill, Black Buck give us some sort of ointment to rub into our hands. "Cure them cuts right up," he said.

Later, he fetched a jug and poured us a snort or two of good corn whiskey. When his tongue was loosed up good, we learnt a mite about his life. Black Buck had been born near seventy years ago of a runaway slave father and a Creek Injun mother somewheres up in Alabama or Georgia, he weren't quite sure which. As a young man, he had fought the white soldiers, and after both his ma and pa died he drifted south with his Creek wife. He tried to make a go of it farming along the Flint River near what today is Brainbridge, Georgia. Then the fever come one winter and took his wife and both their young'uns, so the next spring he followed the river south till he reached the coast at Apalachicola. He lived and worked there for many a year, oystering and netting mullet for a big fishery. After a spell he tired of town life and working for others on their terms, so he bought hisself a boat and moved across the bay to strike out on his own.

"Done right fine for myself, I has," Black Buck said of his life. "Folks knows my oysters be fresh and clean, and I makes the best whiskey and smoked mullet they is in these parts."

Well, sonny, he weren't about to get a contrary word from me or Jeff. We had tasted Black Buck's wares and they weren't wanting for nothing, that's a fact. Later, when I was near to falling asleep, I got to thinking that if the war weren't on I might've been tempted to stay right there and partner up with Black Buck, if he'd had a mind to take me on.

But the war *was* on, and me and Jeff was both terrible homesick.

And I couldn't hardly wait to get home and make things right with Annie.

TWENTY ★ ONE

BLACK BUCK PROVED BETTER THAN his word. The coast around Apalachicola was crawling with soldiers, he told us, so he would show us a safer way west to avoid 'em. Next morning at sunrise we set out in his skiff, Black Buck pulling hard on the oars agin a stiff west wind. Me and Jeff sat in the stern to balance the jugs of corn whiskey and barrels of smoked mullet Mister Buck planned to sell in Apalachicola after he got shed of us.

The rising sun had set the horizon on fire, and a flock of seagulls looked like black specks agin it. To the south I seen the outline of coastal islands. Somewhere amongst 'em was the Union outpost at St. Vincent Island. We had stopped there for a spell on the way to Cedar Keys when me and Jeff first joined up with the Yankees. That thought near made me shudder. I was some glad we'd made the acquaintance of Mister Black Buck, that's a fact.

We was about halfway across the sound when Black Buck turned the skiff north, putting the town of Apalachicola on our left. It was a incoming tide, and it carried us along so that Black Buck went to steering more than pulling on them oars.

It weren't long till we was past town. Soon the wide mouth of the Apalachicola River come into view. Black Buck turned the skiff west and pulled hard agin the current till we was inside the river's mouth. Then he made for the south bank where the current run slower.

Tall cypress trees and marsh grass growed thick along the riverbank. Here and yonder, there was paths tromped through the grass leading to wallering holes. I knowed from back home that this was prime gator country. Overhead, bald eagles and ospreys circled, hunting for their morning meal. A time or two we spooked a big heron that went squawking off to find other fishing grounds.

The sun was well over the trees and the morning mist had burned off, turning the sky blue when we come to a branch in the river running north. Black Buck rowed past the north branch another twenty minutes or so till the river took a sharp bend south. Then he made for the bank and the skiff run aground.

Me and Jeff jumped out and helped Black Buck pull the bow of the skiff onto dry ground. He motioned for us to follow him. I grabbed my quilt bundle and we scrambled up the bank till we come to a trail that run between the river and a thick forest of mixed pines and hardwoods. "This be Bayou Wimico," Black Buck said, pointing west where the river widened and run through a vast swamp. "Keep to this trail, maybe two days, take you to old St. Joseph railroad. Follow it south to St. Joseph."

Me and Jeff give our thanks for his kindness, then set off on the trail. "You boys take to high ground come night," Black Buck called after us. "Gators in them swamps big as my skiff."

* * *

Four-five days of hard walking brung me and Jeff to the shores of St. Joseph Bay. We'd skirted around St. Joseph near sunup and hid amongst the dunes west of the village. St.

Joseph had once been a thriving port town till yellow fever and a hurricane wiped it out twenty-some years back. Weren't much to speak of now, just a few fishing shacks and such, but no sense chancing it. So far our luck had held. We hadn't seen hide or hair of soldiers since Newport, Yankee or Rebel.

We was a mite closer to home now. St. Andrew was forty miles or so west. But we'd have to be extra careful from here on out. Yankees was crawling all over St. Andrew Bay, and there was bound to be patrols between here and there on the lookout for Rebels or saltworks or such. Jeff near throwed a fit when I told him we'd best lay up in the dunes for the day and head out that night.

"Look here," I said, "if the Yankees catch us they'll likely shoot us for being deserters. And the Rebels will send us off to prison camp. Just which one is it you fancy?" That seemed to satisfy Jeff for the time being, so we ate the last of the smoked mullet and cornbread Black Buck had give us, then settled in amongst the dunes to wait for dark.

We watched the gulf swallow the sun, then set out after the last of the gold horizon faded to black. Five-six miles across the bay, somebody had built a fire on Cape San Blas. The cape followed the coast a ways, separating the bay from the Gulf of Mexico. Most likely it was fishermen out netting mullet, but it might've been soldiers. Whichever, I aimed to put a heap of miles between them and us by morning.

We stayed off the coast road and kept to the beach much as we could. High tide had left the sand packed hard, so the footing was good and we made near twelve-fifteen miles, I figured. Would've made more if Jeff hadn't kicked up a dead catfish half buried in the sand. The fins ripped open his foot between his big and first toe. Jeff washed the cut good in the salt water, then I got the bleeding stopped and bound it with a rag tore from the spare shirt I'd bought from the Widow Cordell.

Next morning I decided to leave Jeff resting in the dunes

while I went to look for something to eat and get a better sense of where we was. "I might be gone a few hours," I told him, "so you stay put. Don't leave these dunes."

I had a hunch of where we was from remembering my geography lessons, but it wouldn't hurt none to know for sure. I left the dunes and snuck across the coast road, then headed on north through the big piney woods. Come across a game trail that run roughly the way I was going and followed it. Them woods was full of big diamondbacks. I figured that trail would be a heap safer than tromping through the palmetto thickets, even if it did wind this way and that a mite.

Here and yonder was stands of candle trees, big pines that woodpeckers had bored till the sap run like melted tallow down the trunk to protect their nest holes. A couple of times I come across a big black and silver fox squirrel cutting pine cones which set my stomach to growling. It had been a spell since I'd feasted on a mess of good fried squirrel.

The morning cool soon wore off and it weren't long till I was slapping at pesky skeeters. Through the trees ahead come the laughing call of seagulls. A piece farther on the trail petered out and the pines thinned and give way to marsh grass. Yonder was what I'd hoped to find. The morning sun was dancing sparkles on the waters of East Bay. I knowed then we had made it to East Bay Peninsula, which run between the gulf and the east arm of St. Andrew Bay.

———◆———

I found Jeff right where I'd left him. His foot was hurting a mite, but his eyes lit up when he seen the load of oysters I'd gathered in the bay and toted back in the quilt. We opened them oysters with our jackknives and ate our fill. I broke out the jug of fresh water Black Buck had give us and we finished that up too. I wrapped the rest of the oysters inside the quilt and buried it in the shady side of a dune so they'd keep for supper. We would soon have to find us a creek or spring somewheres and fill up our jug. A body can travel a fair piece with a growling stomach, but lack of water will drain you in a hurry, that's a fact.

We laid up in the dunes to pass the day and wait for dark. Far to the southwest I could barely make out the high sandy bluffs of the north end of Cape San Blas. Towards sunset while we was eating the rest of the oysters a schooner sailed by close enough to shore that I seen it was flying the Union flag. I had seen such sailing the bay during our salt making days, so I figured it was headed for Hurricane Island or thereabouts. I knowed the Yankees was about, but seeing that schooner spooked me a mite. It was a reminder that me and Jeff was still game apt to be snared if we weren't careful.

Night fell. The moon was near three-quarters and lit up the dunes like winter frost. We scrambled down the dunes to the flat sand along the beach and went to walking. Leastways I did. That sore foot had Jeff hobbling at best. After a hour we took to the dunes again. I took the bandage off Jeff's foot and held it up agin the moonlight, squinting for a better look.

"Looks to be festering a mite," I said. Wished then I had some tobacco on me to make a poultice, but I didn't smoke or chew in them days and neither did Jeff. I tore off a fresh rag from the spare shirt, then run down to the beach and soaked it in salt water. Cleaned the cut best I could, then tied a clean bandage around Jeff's foot, taking care to wrap in-between his toes to keep the sand out. Then I hiked up the road and searched around in the moonlight till I found a stout sapling that would make Jeff a fine walking stick.

A good hour passed before we set out again. Jeff done the best he could, but I knowed that foot was paining him a heap. I'd have to somehow doctor it better soon, or Jeff would be in a heap of trouble. It was a struggle and we stopped for Jeff to rest ever now and then, but we made another ten miles or so before the sun come up. I give Jeff my shoulder and we struggled through the deep sand to rest in some low dunes covered in sea oats.

I scooped up enough sand to prop up Jeff's sore foot a mite, then covered him with the quilt. Weren't long till he was in a fitful sleep. I laid awake, staring up at the sky and wondering just how I was going to get us out of this fine fix we was in. Went to feeling sorry for myself knowing how close to home we was, yet being near helpless as a sack full of kittens somebody had throwed in the creek. I weren't no doctor, and Jeff sorely needed one. If only we was home. Aunt Nettie would know what to do for Jeff. She was a healer, kept all kind of leaves and berries and roots and such at hand for divers ailments.

But Aunt Nettie weren't here, and Jeff was ailing. I'd got him in this fix and it was up to me to get him out. There was a little village name of Farmdale a few miles farther on, but I weren't sure I could trust the folks there, not knowing if they was of Union or Confederate bent.

I knowed there was a settlement of free nigras near the end of East Peninsula at Redfish Point. José Massalina lived there on St. Andrew Bay with his wife and brood of young'uns. I had met him years ago when I was eight-nine years old. My daddy had took me and Daniel down to the bay for a week to help out on the spring mullet run. One morning, this nigra man and a boy near Daniel's age come sailing up in his ketch. Me and Daniel and the boy went to catching blue crabs and such while our daddies spent a goodly part of the day jawing and sharing a jug. That was near all I recollected, except that the man talked funny and Daddy said José Massalina was a good and trustworthy man.

Only thing was, Redfish Point weren't but a half mile or so from Hurricane Island. It would be risky, but the more I pondered it the more I figured it was my best chance to get Jeff help. My mind was made up. Come morning I would strike out for Redfish Point and look for Mister José Massalina.

TWENTY ★ TWO

AT FIRST LIGHT, I TOOK the empty jug and set out down the coast road looking for fresh water. The East Peninsula was full of cypress swamps, but they couldn't be seen from the beach. Figured I had to chance traveling the road a spell till I found some, because Jeff was feverish and would be needing water while I was gone to fetch help.

Weren't long till I spied a stand of cypress maybe a quarter mile off the north side of the road. I headed for it, pushing through thick wire grass and palmetto bushes, glad I still had my high-top boots. Soon as I could I found myself a stout limb to fend off any snakes I might come across. It weren't much protection agin a rattler or moccasin, but having it made me feel a heap better.

I soon made the swamp, and was mighty relieved to see it held water. I poked about the water with my limb, than leaned over and scooped up a handful to taste. It weren't the sweet spring water from home, but it was tolerable and I was thankful for it. I filled the jug and drank my fill, then topped it off and headed back.

Before I left the road for the dunes, I gathered up a good armload of dead pine branches, and stacked them up in a rough pyramid between the road and dune line. It was a mite risky, but I reckoned it looked natural enough. Figured I might need a marker of sorts to find where I left Jeff hid.

Jeff was moaning when I got back. He was feverish and his foot was swole up near twice its size. Poison was streaked up far as his ankle. There weren't no food, but he had a full jug of water and the quilt to guard agin the chills when they struck him. "I'm going for help," I told him. "You stay put right here. I'll be back shortly." Least I hoped to be.

When I had made Jeff comfortable as I could, I drug up a big log that had drifted ashore and pointed it towards the dunes. Then I set off down the beach, walking hard. The sun was struggling to shine behind a low bank of clouds and I heard thunder rumbling far to the north. Overhead the sky was still blue and there weren't a cloud to be seen. Beyond the surf, a big flock of pelicans was resting up after their morning meal. Sandpipers kept scooting down the beach ahead of me, staying just out of reach.

It was risky business traveling in the daylight, but there weren't no choice. I planned to keep to the beach till I was past Farmdale and caught sight of Hurricane Island, then I'd cut across the coast road and take to the woods till I reached Redfish Point. Figured it wouldn't be much trouble finding it. When I run out of peninsula, that would be Redfish Point.

Near noon I seen a few shacks and the roofs of other buildings above the dune line. Took that to be Farmdale, so I kept to the foot of the dunes and hurried on by fast as I could. A short piece farther I caught sight of Hurricane Island. Far out in the bay I seen three small boats, but they was too distant to make out if they was Yankee vessels or just fishermen going about their business.

I walked on down the beach a ways till I seen the Union flag flying above a clutch of buildings near the bay on Hurricane Island. I recognized that as the Yankee outpost near where we had camped the night before setting out on the Econfina raid. I left the beach and cut through the dunes till I come to the road. Then I hunkered down behind some bushes for a spell to give things a good look-see.

Near half a hour or so passed but nothing stirred, man nor beast, so I left my hideout and hoofed it on down the road. After a ways, the fine coastal road turned hard north and narrowed into a rough sandy rut. The woods thinned out to spindly scrub oaks and scattered pine saplings growing amongst stumps. Weren't nothing fit to hide behind, so I give up my plan of keeping to the woods. Soon after, the rut road petered out in a clearing of wire grass and clumps of young palmettos. Looked to me that somebody had once growed crops there a few years back, but give it up.

I knowed Redfish Point had to be close now, and sure enough I soon spied smoke rising above the trees and brush to my left at the far side of the clearing. Figured that must be what I was looking for, and made for it. I come across a wagon road leading from the clearing through the thin woods and followed it. A short ways farther and there before me was the blue waters of St. Andrew Bay, shining beyond a passel of cabins and barns and smokehouses and such.

I looked around and seen a couple of twin young'uns over by a live oak. They was dressed in short breeches and rough cloth shirts and was laughing while scratching in the sandy dirt with sticks.

"Halloo there!" I called. Them little fellers looked up with saucer eyes and their mouths fell open wide but mum. "Halloo," I said again, and they dropped them sticks and hightailed it around the corner of the nearest cabin like they had seen a ghost or such.

Figured I'd best stay put for the time being. No sense coming closer and making myself a easier target in case somebody was bent on shooting first and asking questions later. A mockingbird went to calling like a jay in some tree behind me, then turned itself into a laughing seagull. I took that bird's call personal, like it was mocking me for getting into yet another fix.

I had near talked myself into backtracking when a thin nigra woman come walking out the back door of that cabin. Them two young'uns was clutched fast to her red skirt, peeking out from either side. She was young, near my age, I figured. She was light-skinned with high cheekbones so I figured she weren't pure African.

I held my hands out, palms facing her as a sign I meant no harm. "I'm looking for Mister Massalina," I said. "Would he be around?"

She shook them kids from her skirt, said something that sent 'em scurrying back inside the cabin. When they was safe inside she turned back to me and straightened the blue checkered bandana tied about her head like she was primping to receive company. "Who a-wanting to know?"

She didn't look unfriendly, just a mite suspicious, which I couldn't fault her for. "My name is Eli Malburn, from up Econfina way. My daddy knowed Mister Massalina from mullet fishing yonder across the bay."

She turned her head a mite like a hawk checking out a field mouse, looked me up and down, said, "Ain't heared of no Econfina, and you don't look to be no fisherman. Where you boat?"

I shook my head. "Ain't got a boat, ma'am. My friend is down the coast a ways, hurt bad. I was hoping Mister Massalina might help us."

She looked me over a mite longer. The wind had picked up and thunder growled across the bay towards the northwest. "Mister José gone to St. Andrew for salt, be back soon," she said.

"My man Hawk over at the salting shed. He Mister José's son. We go see him."

———•———

Well, sonny, turns out Hawk Massalina was the very same boy me and Daniel went crabbing with that day our daddies spent jawing a few years back. Course, he was growed up now, with a wife and them twin boys and a baby girl still on the tit. He was a friendly sort, said he recalled the day we'd spent playing together and such. Seemed genuinely grieved to hear that brother Daniel and our daddy had passed.

When I told Hawk about the fix me and Jeff was in, he told me not to fret. Soon as his daddy got back from St. Andrew with the load of salt they'd see to Jeff. Weren't nothing more could be done till then, so I grabbed a knife and went to helping Hawk split and salt the heap of mullet he had netted that morning.

It was midafternoon when José Massalina come sailing up in his two-masted ketch. I followed Hawk out on the dock and helped him tie up the boat. Then the three of us unloaded four heavy salt barrels and rolled 'em up the dock where we heaved them onto a wagon. When the salt was safely stored under the shed, Hawk told his daddy who I was and the fine mess I was in with Jeff and all.

José Massalina was a man of few words. He looked from his son to me, said, "You papa oncet he'p me and my people. Now we he'p you."

Well, sonny, I had no earthly idea what he was talking about. I never knowed my daddy to have business with José Massalina except that one particular day I recollected, mind you. But I weren't about to look no gift horse in the mouth. If my daddy had done his people some kindness I weren't aware of, that was fine by me. Jeff sorely needed help and these folks was offering it.

Hawk and his daddy went to jawing for a minute amongst

theirselves, then Hawk told me to stay put under the salt shed while they made ready to leave. A few minutes later they was back. Mister Massalina put a bundle he was toting in the wagon bed while Hawk checked the mule's harness and tack.

I started to climb onto the wagon but Hawk stopped me. "Papa say you best stay here. Could be so'jers about. We get you boy, bring him back."

I figured they was right. Weren't no sense me bringing them grief with either side in this hogwash war. So I give 'em directions best I could. Told 'em to keep to the coast road past Farmdale, maybe four-five miles. Look for the pile of limbs I'd left that morning. Jeff should be resting somewheres in the dunes nearby.

I give my thanks to Hawk and his daddy, then Hawk flicked the reins and whistled to the mule. I watched the wagon till they was out of sight. Being near tuckered, I found myself some shade agin a smokehouse nearby and fell asleep in no time.

Slept like a rock, best shuteye I'd had in many a day. Some time later I slowly come aware of something shuffling next to me. I opened one eye, seen Hawk's twin young'uns standing there looking down at me. They backed off when they seen I was awake. Then one of the boys pointed back towards the cabins, said, "Poppy coming wid de wagon," or some such.

———◆———

Maria Rose Massalina proved to be ever bit as fine a healer as Aunt Nettie, maybe even better. She had give her husband José a poultice for Jeff's foot to start drawing out the poison, and by the time they got back to Redfish Point Jeff was already feeling a mite better. Once they got Jeff inside their cabin, she made him drink a potion made from different roots and herbs and whatnot.

Weren't long till Jeff drifted off to sleep. Then Maria Rose took a knife she had heating in the fireplace and lanced Jeff's foot. I near throwed up when I seen all the bloody puss and such spurt out of that cut. Then she went to massaging the foot from above the ankle till all the poison was drained. When she was done, she packed the wound with a wet poultice and wrapped Jeff's foot in clean bandages.

While Maria Rose was putting away her doctoring things, she looked at me and smiled. "He be fine now. Lord be praised you got him here. 'Nother day or two, he lose the leg, maybe die."

I was near speechless. I knowed Jeff was ailing, but I hadn't figured him to be near to dying. Reckon that fish poison was some powerful stuff, that's a fact. I thanked the Massalinas, told 'em I'd work hard to earn our keep till Jeff was fit to travel, promised I'd return soon as I could and pay 'em whatever they seen fit for saving Jeff's life.

While I was rambling on José held up a hand to stop my jabbering. Know what he said then? I'll tell you. He shook his head, said, "Done tol' you, you pappa he'p my people, so we he'p you. Christian folk not beholden fo' doing God's work."

And that was that.

TWENTY ★ THREE

JEFFERSON PROVED TO BE A quick mender. He was hobbling about on his feet in three-four days, and before two weeks was up he was doing more'n his share to earn our keep. My daddy was right, José Massalina was a good man. The whole family growed on me and Jeff till we felt we near belonged amongst 'em. Fact is, the whole Redfish Point settlement was fine folk. If others was wanting for anything, they was quick to share, and if a helping hand was needed, there was a passel ready to do what they could.

Ever morning when the weather was fit Hawk and his daddy would set out in the ketch and spend the day catching loads of snapper and grouper by hook and handline. Most days they carried their catch over to Hurricane Island or on to St. Andrew to sell or trade for goods. Me and Jeff spent the days doing whatever chores needed doing about the place.

Near ever night we feasted on fried grouper jaws or snapper throats or tail meat from the gators Hawk trapped in the swamps nearby. Most nights after supper, José would break out a jug and we'd sit around a fire outside drinking good corn whiskey while Hawk played the banjo and his daddy blowed tunes on his harmonica. Most the womenfolk and young'uns would clap their hands and dance around the fire, singing and laughing and having a high ol' time of it.

When it got towards bedtime the Massalinas would strike up some hymn or such and near the whole bunch would stop their dancing and go to singing. That was always Jeff's favorite time. He'd break out with the biggest grin and join right in with the others. Reckon it reminded him of the good times singing with Preacher Jubal and Nebo back at the salt camp. Seemed like a hundred years had passed since them days.

Weren't long till Jeff's foot was good as new. I knowed we would miss our new friends, but we sorely missed our families and it was time for us to get on home. It had been near a month since we'd got to Redfish Point. That night at supper I told Mister Massalina it was time that me and Jeff be moving on, and asked would he kindly give us a ride across the bay to where we could pick up the Marianna road.

His thick eyebrows raised up under his wrinkled forehead as he took another puff on his pipe. After a minute he shook his head, said, "Too many so'jers thereabouts. Hawk here, he take the ketch, take you up to Bayhead."

Well, sonny, I knowed better than to argue. José Massalina had done drove that point home more'n once. These good people had saved Jeff's life and took us in and treated us like their own. Now they was going to see to it we got dropped off practically on our own doorstep. I near teared up thinking about all the kindness them folks had showed me and Jefferson.

Said before how José Massalina was a man of few words, so I figured following his ways would be best. I swallowed the lump in my throat, said, "Much obliged, sir."

Two days later, at daybreak, we set out in the ketch for Bayhead after saying our goodbyes and shedding some tears, a few of my own amongst 'em, I ain't ashamed to say. Hawk soon had the sails fit to the wind and the ketch cut across the bay like a galloping horse. He worked the tiller this way and that, keeping us midway between Hurricane Island and the town of St. Andrew. We soon left both behind and sailed through the pass into North Bay.

Me and Jeff kept low while helping Hawk keep a eye out for any Union vessels that might be about. We was carrying a few barrels of salt mullet in case somebody took a mind to stop us. Hawk had fixed up a hiding place between the barrels and the bow of the ketch where extra sails was stored. If somebody come snooping me and Jeff would sneak underneath that canvas. Hawk would show 'em the load of mullet he was taking up the bay to sell. Since the Massalinas done regular trade with the Yankees, it weren't likely we'd be found out.

It was as fine a spring morning a body could hope for. Don't reckon I ever seen a bluer sky. Knowing we would soon be home didn't spoil matters none. We was done with this dern foolish war. I was near giddy inside, knowed Jeff was too. More'n once I had to hush him up from singing. "We ain't out of this stew pot yet," I told him.

Well, sonny, our luck held. Shortly after noon Hawk steered the ketch into the mouth of Bayou George and it weren't long till Mister Enfinger's fish camp come into view. Most of the camp was still burnt ruins, but it done my heart good to see a couple of new cabins had been raised, and a new general store partly framed up.

When we got near to shore me and Jeff ducked down while Hawk give the place a good look-see. Weren't no sign of soldiers about, Union or Confederate, and being it was Sunday there weren't none of Mister Enfinger's workers around either. Hawk give us the okay and we helped him ease the ketch up agin the pier. Then I jumped onto the pier and tied the bow line to a piling while Jeff done the same with the stern.

Hawk come ashore to do his business and stretch his legs for a spell. Short time later, he checked the sun, said, "I best set sail. Make St. Andrew afo' dark, maybe sell them mullets."

Handshakes turned into hugs, then Hawk climbed back aboard the ketch. Me and Jeff untied the lines and give it a good shove away from the pier. Hawk pulled on the oars to turn the ketch about and get it going, then fiddled with the sails till they caught the wind. When he was done he turned and held up a hand. We waved back and watched until the ketch disappeared around a bend.

Well, sonny, me and Jeff might never've made it home at all if it weren't for the kindness of them fine God-fearing Massalina folk. I swore right then and there that when this war and all its nonsense was over I would return to Redfish Point to visit José and Hawk and their families. Did just that too, only unfortunate things come up and it took a few years longer than I figured on. I visited with 'em several times down the years. Them good people are living there yet, Hawk and his daddy, though both their wives has passed. Mister José is a mite feeble these days, being he's near a hundred and ten now. You can go see for yourself if you a mind to.

Best I could figure, it had been near two months or so since the fight at Natural Bridge. Me and Jeff hadn't seen home or family since October of 'sixty-three, and we was powerful homesick. We was so close to home we could dern near smell it. But I knowed this sure weren't the time to let down our guard. We was still some fifteen miles from the farm, and there was bound to be Confederate home guards or such about. Figured by now it was common knowledge in these parts that I had joined up with the Union army. And somebody at the Watts' place might have recognized Jeff being amongst the colored soldiers that burnt them out. Getting caught could mean prison camp, or worse. Things was going hard agin the Confederacy, last I'd heard. Way I seen it, they couldn't hold out much longer. So I aimed to sneak home and stay hid best I could till the whole mess was over and done with.

Jeff throwed another fit when I told him we'd best wait for dark. "Look here," I said. "There's most likely Rebels about. We cain't be moseying down the road like we was going fishing or such. You fancy getting shot or going to prison?"

Jeff pouted and looked near to crying. "But we ain't soldiering no mo', Eli. I wants to get home, see Mama and Daddy."

It took some jawing, but Jeff finally seen it my way. So we hid out in the woods behind the cabins to wait. Seemed like the sky had turned to molasses, slow as the sun sunk. When it was finally dark enough we took off up the road towards Ard's Ferry.

Jeff stretched out them long legs of his till he near walked me in the ground. A time or two I grabbed a-hold of him to slow him down. Mister José had give Jeff a pair of boots after his foot healed, and our clomping sounded like a team of mules in the still night.

Judging from the moon I figured it was near midnight when we made the ferry. We stopped and took off our boots. Mister Ard's nigras would be in their cabin sleeping. His hounds was most likely fast asleep on the porch, but I didn't want to chance them hearing us and go to barking. I had done told Jeff we'd have to swim the crossing. Weren't no way I was risking taking the ferry. Me and Jeff could likely handle it ourself, but it would be noisy. Besides, Mister Ard would be a mite bothered finding it across the creek come morning. And getting to the canoe would likely set his hounds to howling.

We snuck up to the clearing near the ferry and watched for a spell. Weren't nothing stirring, so we headed down to the landing, toting our boots. Jeff's feet was a mite tougher than mine, so the crushed oyster shells didn't bother him none. I hadn't gone barefoot much since being in the army. Crossing them shells felt near to walking on broke glass.

We made the creek just fine. Getting across might not prove so easy. Bear Creek growed some awful big gators back in them days, that's a fact. Here and yonder, bulls was bellowing in the cypress swamp the creek run through. I strained through the dark best I could, didn't see no red eyes shining. Took that as a good sign, but there weren't much light from the moon to speak of. I waded in up to my waist. Stood there a minute, looking and listening.

Well, sonny, wishing weren't going to get us across that creek, so I gritted my teeth and pushed on in. That cold water near sucked the breath right out of me. Kept my boots high and dry best I could, and went to kicking and side-stroking agin the current. Looked back and seen Jeff doing the same. Couldn't shake the thought of some bull gator's big, tooth-filled jaws chomping me in half at any time. Seemed like that creek had growed three times wider, but we finally made it to the other bank. We crawled up the landing a piece, then put our boots back on. Figured we'd best walk ourselfs dry than sit there freezing, so we set right out for home.

A couple of hours' hard walking brought us to Vicker's Ford. We stopped to rest a spell while I pondered whether to cross the ford or keep to the Marianna Road. Williford Road would be quicker, and we'd be less likely to come across people. But that would mean crossing the Watts' farm to get to the bridge. I sure didn't cotton to running into Yerb.

Keeping on the Marianna Road meant we'd have to pass through Bennet. Weren't likely many folks would be stirring about before light, but Confederate home guards was apt to be patrolling the road anywheres between Marianna and St. Andrew. I chewed on it a spell longer, then we set out up the Marianna Road. Figured I'd rather chance running across a home guard patrol than Yerby Watts.

The moon had just set and the sky was graying up a mite when we reached Marianna Crossroads at the edge of Bennet. There was a lamp on inside Hutchins' General Store, but on down the street that run through Bennet nobody seemed to be stirring. Figured the safest way to get through was to just walk right on down the main road like we belonged. It was dark enough that nobody was likely to recognize us from a distance. So that's what me and Jeff done.

We got on past town without nobody noticing, except for a dog that went to barking from a alley and a couple of roosters having a crowing contest. A short spell later we come to the road that led down through the woods to our farm. I was mighty relieved when we turned onto it, that's a fact. Jeff went to singing some spiritual or such, and this time I didn't bother to hush him. We was on Malburn property now, almost home!

Weren't long till Jeff's cabin come into view. It was getting light now, though the sun still weren't up above the trees. Uncle Nate's corn crop was already waist high, and there was still a heap of cabbages and collards and such growing in Aunt Nettie's winter garden. Smoke rose from the chimney, and a lamp shined through the window. Figured Aunt Nettie was fixing breakfast. I dern near smelt bacon frying and biscuits baking. My mouth went to watering. Jeff was fixing to have hisself a fine welcome home feast, that's a fact.

Jeff was so excited I figured I'd best go with him to the cabin to help explain things to his folks. Maybe have a bite to eat too, before I went on to the home place. We left the road and set out across the field. Hadn't made twenty foot when a voice called out:

"Well now, if it ain't the traitor and his Yankee nigger!"

Me and Jeff stopped dead in our tracks. I held up my hands and turned around slow, squinting into the poor light. My eyes told me what my ears already knowed. It was Yerby Watts, armed and mounted.

Daniel Malburn
Freedom
1865–66

TWENTY ★ FOUR

IT WAS MIDAFTERNOON WHEN the prison wagon rolled through Rock Island and onto the wharves south of town. They'd give us a choice of taking the train back east or a steamboat heading south. Most of the boys chose the train. Me and a handful of others that lived farther south figured a riverboat would be quicker. So we stayed on the wagon till it come to a stop at the waterfront.

That's when I got my first good look at the Mississippi River, though I'd spent the last year on a island surrounded by it. I looked across the river towards Iowa. The Mississippi was nearbout a mile wide at that point. The buildings in the town of Davenport looked like match boxes. Weren't no wonder only a handful of prisoners had managed to swim it, what with the strong currents and all.

We got off the wagon and the guards marched us up a gangplank where we boarded a paddlewheel steamer bound for St. Louis. Didn't know whether to laugh or cry when I seen the boat's name painted on the bow: *Victory*. Well, sir, the Confederacy was gone up, but I'd made it through the war alive and was headed home. Reckon that was a victory of sorts. Figured I'd take it as such, anyhow.

The guards herded us onto the stern amongst stacks of cordwood and said we'd best mind our manners if we knowed what was good for us. Told us where we was welcome to move about on the boat and where we weren't. We was to sleep on the stern deck and take our meals there, too. I picked out a spot good as any next to a big stack of wood and unrolled my blanket to stake out my territory.

A hour later the steamer's whistles commenced blowing. Deckhands cast off the lines and pulled up the gangplank and we was underway, heading south and leaving Rock Island Barracks behind forever. I walked over to the starboard rail and stared out at the river. Some of the boys was trying to catch sight of the island as we steamed downriver, but I kept my eyes ahead. I'd had a bellyful of that place, and if I never seen it again, it would be too soon.

Well, sir, you wouldn't think it would take a good month to travel three hundred-some miles by river, but it did. The *Victory* weren't no passenger steamer that run from city to city taking in all the sights. It was a river freighter, and there weren't many towns, big or small, betwixt Rock Island and St. Louis where we didn't stop for a spell. Seemed we was always pulling ashore here and yonder to take on water or wood or cargo. Once we docked at some town for a few days whilst they fixed a boiler that had sprung a leak. Two or three time we turned around and headed back *upriver* to deliver this or that.

Us newly-freed prisoners weren't allowed to go ashore the whole time, so even if I'd had the means to write a letter home there weren't no way to send it. I didn't have a penny to my name, just the clothes I wore and the blanket they give me. So I bided my time, sleeping as much as I could and conjuring up plans to get home once we made St. Louis.

I kept to myself mostly. Weren't nobody aboard I had

knowed particular well from the prison, and I figured there weren't much sense in striking up a friendship now. Besides, I hadn't had a whole heap of luck with friends lately. Seems they had a way of dying on you.

Then one day, towards evening, the Mississippi widened out where another big river joined it from the west. That was the Missouri, what they called the Gateway to the West. I remembered that fact from my schooling. St. Louis was just around the bend a short piece downriver!

The sun had set by the time the crew got the *Victory* tied up to the wharf and the guards marched us off the steamer and onto the riverfront. They lined us up, then some Yankee officer give us a speech about how the United States government's duty to us was done, we was now free to go on our way home, but we had best behave like upright loyal citizens or else.

Well, sir, like I said, I was flat broke. I aimed to find work and make a few dollars before I struck out for home. My plan was to hire on with one of the steamers that run up and down the Mississippi. I'd watched the deckhands whilst they went about their daily chores. From what I'd seen there weren't nothing they done that I couldn't manage. Figured to work my way downriver to Memphis, then cut east for Chattanooga. I knowed the country betwixt there and home well enough. So I set off down the riverfront looking for work.

Didn't take long to find out I weren't a fit hire for them riverboats. Happened to be that most the captains and crews in them parts was Union men. Seems the war had spoilt their business a mite, and a goodly number of 'em was holding a grudge agin the Confederacy for it. They sure weren't bent on paying good Union greenbacks to no "goddamn Rebel scum," which is how one feller kindly put it. The few that did take the time to talk to me said I looked fit as a broke down mule, that I wouldn't hold up to the work.

I'd been at it for three or four hours and had nearbout give up when this big, stout feller with a beard the color of dirty cotton took me aside.

"So, ye looking for work, eh?" he says with some thick tongue. He took a big draw on his pipe, blowed the smoke into the night air and pointed inland towards town. "Go down that street three blocks, lad. Tucker's Tavern. See the barkeep, Henry. Tell 'im Mike MacGrew sent ye."

"Much obliged," I says, and took off down the narrow street. My shoes clomped agin the bricks like hoofbeats. It was darker here, not lit up like the waterfront. Here and yonder, groups of sailors was making their way up and down the street, laughing or singing or cussing up a storm. I was a mite scared, and done my best to keep out of their way. Didn't have nothing worth stealing, but I sure weren't looking for trouble.

I found Tucker's Tavern easy enough. It was on the corner just like Mike MacGrew had said. There was a street lamp out front which lit up the sign. The whole street was shining bright as day. The boardwalks that run up and down in front of the establishments was crowded with boat crews and longshoremen and other fellers looking for a good time. Piano and banjo music rolled through the open doors onto the street. I stood outside the tavern, gawking. I ain't never seen the likes of such a place before. Army life and prison camp had got me used to crowds, but this was different. Truth be told, I was a mite spooked by the whole kettle of fish.

Well, sir, gawking weren't going to put food in my belly or money in my pocket, so after a spell I pushed on through the swinging doors and went inside.

———◦—◦———

I don't recollect exactly why, but Henry Tucker took to me right off. Might've been because his younger half-brother Tommy had fought for the Confederacy under General Sterling Price. Lieutenant Thomas Tucker had been kilt at Pea Ridge in sixty-two whilst leading his men in a charge. A portrait of him hung on the wall behind the bar.

Anyways, Henry Tucker hired me on the spot for a dollar a day plus a room inside the lean-to out back of the tavern. My duties was to clean up the barroom ever morning before it opened at ten o'clock, and to help keep the storeroom in order. It weren't no glorified work, but it beat toting a rifle and getting shot at all to hell. The pay was fitting too.

Mister Tucker give me a couple of dollars in advance to see to my needs, so the first thing I done after I got settled in was to buy a pencil and some paper and send off a letter home. Figured none of my letters had got through whilst I was in prison, but I was a free man now, and antsy for my family to know how things stood. Wrote my mama that I was alive and well and would be home soon as I could. To save money I put a note for Annie in the same envelope. Figured the folks would see she got it.

I spent my days sweeping and mopping floors, cleaning tables and polishing mirrors and spittoons and such. Unloaded the whiskey wagons and kept Mister Tucker's shelves stocked proper. I found a café down the street where the owner was willing to swap meals for my dishwashing services. The weeks passed quick, and it weren't long till I had thirty-some dollars saved up. I was eating good and putting on weight and gaining back my strength. Ten dollars would buy my fare to Memphis. With what money I'd saved, I figured another week's pay would see me the rest of the way home. So that morning when I come in to work I told Mister Tucker I'd be leaving come next week.

Two or three days later I'd just laid down for the night when somebody commenced knocking at the door of my room. Figured it was Mister Tucker needing some chore or the other done come morning, so I got off my cot and opened the door. Last thing I remembered was staring out into the dark, trying to make out who it was. Then something cracked agin my skull and snuffed me out like a candle.

TWENTY ★ FIVE

WHOEVER WAYLAID ME STOLE MY money, ever last dime of it. But that weren't all that goldamn thief took, no, sir, not by a long shot. Whoever done it took away the next four months of my life, gospel truth. When I come to my senses I weren't in St. Louis at all, I was in Paducah, Kentucky, living in the home of one Mister Randolf Avery and his wife Priscilla.

One morning I woke up, figuring on moseying down to the café to take breakfast before I commenced my chores at the tavern. Of a sudden I sensed something was wrong. Looked around and seen I was in a strange room, laying in a big bed on a stuffed mattress. Outside the window it was snowing to beat all hell. That's when it struck me—there weren't no window in my room inside the lean-to!

I seen my clothes draped across a chair near the bed. Leastways I reckoned they was mine. They weren't the same ones I'd had on before, and for the life of me I couldn't recollect where I might have got 'em. I put 'em on anyways and found they fit proper. Then I opened the door and stepped out into a hallway. There was a flight of stairs nearby, so I walked on down to find out just where I was and how I come to be there. I was more'n a mite confused.

There was a queer feeling in my gut as I come to the end of the stairs. Last I remembered it was the middle of summer, and now it was snowing? I knowed my name, knowed I was in St. Louis working for Henry Tucker at his tavern. Knowed I had saved up close to forty dollars and was fixing to catch a steamboat to Memphis in a day or two.

I smelled something good cooking. Walked on down a hallway covered by a fine rug till I come to a room on the left. A plump, silver-haired woman wearing a house dress and a apron was busy cooking over a fancy wood stove. Reckon she heard me coming because she turned around and smiled.

"Morning, Daniel," she says, waving a spatula at me.

Well, sir, I had no earthly idea who this woman might be. I knowed it weren't my mama, and this weren't my house. "Morning, ma'am," I says, trying to figure out what was going on.

"Breakfast will be ready in a minute," she says. "Sit yourself down and have some coffee."

I took a seat at the table whilst she poured a cup of coffee and brung it to me. There was a pitcher of cream and a bowl of light cane sugar on the table. I hadn't used sugar or cream to cut my coffee since before the war. Figured I'd have myself a spoon of sugar so I reached for it. My hand was shaking so much I spilt a goodly part of the sugar before I got it to the cup. Dumped the rest in my coffee and give it a stir, then set the spoon on the table. By then I was nearbout to tear up.

"Pardon me, ma'am," I says, my jaw a-quivering, "but I need to ask some questions of you."

———•———

Well, sir, this is what I come to find out. When I didn't show up for work at the tavern the next morning, Henry Tucker went looking for me. He found me laying just outside the lean-to with my head cracked open. There was so much blood puddled up he figured I was a goner, but of course I weren't.

Mister Tucker sent for a doctor and they toted me to his office where I spent most of the next month, that being July, whilst they nursed me back to health. I'd come to for a spell, then slip back into a deep sleep for days at a time. By early August I was keeping awake mostly, had recollected my name and who Henry Tucker was, and remembered that I'd been working for him at the tavern.

Soon I was fit enough to leave the doctor's care. Mister Tucker didn't have the time to tend to his business proper and see to my needs, so he arranged for me to go live with his sister, one Priscilla Tucker Avery and her husband Randolf, downriver at Paducah, Kentucky. Paducah is situated on the Ohio River, not far from where it joins the Mississippi.

Happened to be that Mister Randolf Avery owned a towboat company that carried coal from the Kentucky mines and red bricks from the factory in Paducah upriver to St. Louis and points north. Amongst his boat captains just happened to be one Mike MacGrew, the same feller that got this whole shebang started in the first place!

I'd been earning my keep doing chores around the Averys' house and odd jobs at Mister Avery's towboat business. According to what Miz Avery told me that morning, I knowed who I was all along but couldn't recollect my family or where my home was. "Somewheres up in Georgia," is what I'd told them, which of course weren't true, but I didn't know it at the time.

Well, sir, when I woke up that particular morning, I couldn't recall any of what she told me of my time with the Averys. The past few months was blank as a clean sheet of writing paper. I knowed my name, but I had plumb forgot nearbout everthing else. I was still confused about where I come from and where I was headed. Reckon that blow to the head had give me another case of the fugues. But I had a powerful yearning to move on. Figured I'd strike out for Georgia soon as the winter weather broke. The way I seen it, doing such just might spark my memory the closer I got to home.

By late March of sixty-six I had got my strength back again, thanks to the Averys' kindness and the work I'd been doing. I felt fit in body but knowed I was still a mite touched in the head. But staying put in Paducah weren't going to get me home, wherever that was. The war had been over for nearbout a year. My family was out there somewheres, and I was bent on getting home to them soon as I could. So one night at supper I told the Averys I'd be moving on in a few days.

I'd studied the big map in Mister Avery's office. Figured it would be going out of my way to take a boat down to Memphis, so I decided I'd head southeast across country towards Nashville, then on to Chattanooga from there. The roads was mostly good, Mister Avery told me, and well traveled by freight wagons transporting goods betwixt Paducah and Nashville. With any luck it weren't likely I'd have to wear out much shoe leather along the way.

Well, sir, that morning in April when I struck out on the road for Nashville there was many a tear shed. The Averys had come to look on me like a son, and I felt nearbout the same towards them. Miz Avery packed me enough food to last a week, and just as I was leaving Mister Avery handed me fifty dollars in greenbacks. Course, I made a show of refusing this kindness, but he commenced lecturing me as to how I'd more than earned my keep, and he owed me ever dollar of it for the work I'd done.

So, with my belly full and pockets fat, I said my goodbyes and headed east on the road towards Nickelsville. "Godspeed, Daniel," I heard Miz Avery call out, but I didn't look back.

TWENTY ★ SIX

IT TOOK TWO DAYS OF hard walking to make Nickelsville, a little village just across the Tennessee River. From there I turned south onto Between the Rivers Road, that run along a ridge betwixt the Tennessee and Cumberland rivers some forty miles south to the state of Tennessee. Made camp that night just outside of town in a grove of oaks. It come close to freezing, so I kept a fire going to keep warm.

The third day out I hitched a ride with some kindly farmer and his son that was returning home after selling a wagonload of late winter produce in Nickelsville. Their home was near the town of Fenton, which would save me some twenty miles of shoe leather. I sat in the wagon bed agin some grain sacks, resting my feet and taking in the sights whilst we rolled along. Between the Rivers was some jim-dandy country. There was small farmsteads scattered here and yonder alongside the rivers, cut out of stands of great oaks and other hardwoods. A body would never run out of firewood or fence rails or lumber in such a place. And that river bottomland made for some fine farming. Weren't nothing like the sandy soil around the Econfina.

"Years ago this here trace was a buffalo trail, yessir," the farmer says after a spell. "Every winter thousands and thousands of them critters would make their way down this very road, heading for the salt licks and winter feeding grounds on south."

"It is fine country, sir," I says, not wanting to seem a unfriendly sort.

"Then come the Injuns, after the buffalos," he says, paying no mind to my compliment. "Then come the white man, after the land. My own people's been settled here nigh on a hundred years now, yessir."

The farmer rambled on about this and that and the other the whole day, whilst his boy took turns blowing tunes on a tin whistle and shooting at birds and squirrels and such with his slingshot. Never hit nothing as I recollect, but that whistle growed downright annoying after a spell.

Towards evening we come to the crossroads that led west to Fenton. The farmer pulled his team to a halt. "This here's as far as we go," he says. "I wish you luck getting home, yessir."

I thanked him for his kindness and commenced walking south whilst he turned his wagon for home. Weren't long till I come on a fitting place to make camp a short piece off the road. Gathered up enough wood for a fire and settled down for the night.

———◆———

Woke up the next morning feeling a mite ill. Had one of them ripsnorting headaches that had been plaguing me ever since I'd got whopped across the head and robbed back in St. Louis. I looked through my belongings and found the bottle of laudanum the doctor had prescribed for me. It shames me to say it, but I was nearbout hooked on the stuff. I took to it like a drunkard to whiskey. Kept telling myself I was just taking my medicine like the doctor ordered, but deep down I knowed better. I looked hard at the bottle for a spell, then uncorked it and took a swig. Figured it was better than suffering, least that's what I told myself.

It was slow going that day. A few wagons passed me by, but nobody offered a ride and I weren't going to beg. Truth be told, I weren't fit for company. Around noon I finished the last of the laudanum and took a nap to rest a spell. Woke up feeling a mite better and made the stateline before dark. There was a sign post drove into the ground beside the road that read *Tennessee* on one side and *Kentucky* on the other. I walked on a short ways into Tennessee and camped for the night.

Next morning I woke up with the shakes. Figured I was just shivering from the cold, being as the fire had burnt out during the night. But when the sun got up higher and I was still shaking like a leaf I knowed better. It weren't the cold at all. I needed laudanum, much as it pained me to admit it.

Around noon I come to a little settlement name of Bass. I commenced asking around was there a doctor or drugstore nearby. Learnt from the postmaster I could find both in the town of Dover, some fifteen miles on down the road.

That was some disheartening news to hear. Truth be told, I weren't sure I could go on that far without my medicine. I was plumb whipped, and my gut was aching. But being as I had no choice, I struck out for Dover. Reckon the good Lord was watching out for me, because I hadn't gone a mile before some young feller come along in a wagon and asked if I wanted a ride.

"Much obliged," I says, and climbed up on the wagon seat. He looked to be near my brother Eli's age, though it had been four years since I'd laid eyes on him. The war had made it hard for me to judge a body's age.

The boy, whose name I don't recollect, clucked at the mule and the wagon jerked ahead. After a spell he give me a look. "Ain't seed you around afore. Wherebouts you live?"

"Georgia," I says, not knowing better at the time.

The young feller's eyes lit up when he heard that. "Didn't take you for no Yankee. Say, was you in the war?"

"I was. Got took prisoner a spell back. Been up at Rock Island."

"Never heared of it. Hit's right shameful, them Yanks keeping you shut up so long."

I didn't bother telling him I'd been released some months back. Figured my recent troubles weren't none of his affair.

"My brother Amos was in the war," he says. "Fourth Kentuckians. He got kilt somewheres near Atlanta. Say, ain't that in Georgia?"

That's when it struck me. The Kentucky boys had been with us when we attacked at Dallas, the very day I was wounded and took prisoner. Of a sudden, my best pard Joe Porter come to mind, then the Sixth Florida. Why, I weren't from Georgia at all, I was a Florida boy!

"Say Mister, ain't Atlanta somewheres in Georgia?" he says again. "Ain't that where you said you's from?"

"It is. I'm real sorry about your brother." I'd nearbout forgot my ills, my mind was racing so, trying to recollect things.

"I was a-going to join up, but my pa wouldn't let me," the boy says. "Hit near kilt my ma when we got word about Amos. Pa said losing one boy to the war was aplenty, he weren't going to give us both up."

I give him a good look then, seen the hurt in his eyes. "Your pa done right."

* * *

Late that afternoon we come to the end of Between the Rivers Road, where the Tennessee and Cumberland rivers part ways. Happened to be the boy had business in Dover, so we turned east at the crossroads. Four or five miles later we rolled into Dover. It was growing dark by then. The young feller pointed me towards a fine hotel, then we said our goodbyes and he went on his way.

I didn't much feel up to another night sleeping on the cold hard ground, which is why I got me a room in the hotel. It cost two dollars for the night, but I had the money to spare and knowed I could use the rest. After I signed the registry the clerk give me directions to Pearman's Apothecary & Sundries which he said would be open for business for another half hour yet.

Well, sir, I didn't waste no time getting over there. I explained my situation to the druggist and showed him the empty laudanum bottle to prove the doctor had ordered it for me. He sold me two bottles, which I figured would last a spell.

Back in my room I took a goodly dose of medicine and slept like a dead man that night. Next morning, after a fine breakfast at a nearby cafe, I crossed the Cumberland River and headed east for Clarksville, thirty-some miles away. It took two days to get there, and I made it just before a big storm struck at sundown.

Well, sir, I never seen such a ripsnorting storm before. The sky turned a queer blackish green, and the air growed cold of a sudden. Then come thunder and lightning that sounded like a thousand drums a-beating and lit up the sky bright as day. The wind commenced howling and blowing powerful as any hurricane.

I seen a boardinghouse sign down the street just off the town square and made for it. I no sooner run up the stairs onto the covered porch when it commenced raining hail big as quail eggs. I opened the screen and pounded on the front door loud as I could. Porch chairs and tables and tree limbs and other such was tumbling across yards and down the street.

I knocked again and the door opened. A prim slip of a woman, not more'n five foot tall stared through the screen door at me.

"How do, ma'm," I says. "I'd be much obliged if you'd let me in whilst this storm blows over."

"I swan!" she says, looking past me at the howling storm. "Come in, come in."

She stepped back and held the door open. I walked in and stood on the rug in the foyer. "Thank you kindly," I says, mopping myself dry best I could with my blanket roll.

"I have a room, if you'll be a-needing one," she says, adjusting the blue checkered apron she wore over a plain house dress. Her silver-steaked hair was pinned agin the nape of her neck. I took her to be forty or so, and a right smart looker. "Rooms are a dollar a day, five dollars by the week. Meals are a dollar extra a day."

The storm was still caterwauling, and I sure weren't antsy to weather it outside. "Yes ma'am," I says, "be pleased to have a room for the night." Then I caught the smell of tasty cooking drifting in the hallway and my mouth commenced watering. "And I'll be having supper too, if it ain't a bother."

Well, sir, the Lord does move in mysterious ways, His wonders to perform. Weren't no way of knowing it then, but Miz Mildred Barfield opened up a whole heap more than her door to me that stormy evening, gospel truth.

Elijah Malburn
Back Home
1865

TWENTY ★ SEVEN

"HOW-DO, YERB," I SAID, after I found my tongue. "What you up to?"

Yerby kneed the fine bay mare he was riding and left the shadow of the woods and come out onto the road. He was dressed in Confederate garb. Had a peg leg strapped to the stump of his right leg. "Home guard business," he said.

Well, sonny, this was some fine fix I'd got us into. Dern if I hadn't managed to run slap into Yerby Watts *and* the home guard. I give Jeff a quick look. He was shaking and had turned near ash gray, but had his hands up. I lowered my arms real slow, said, "We ain't armed."

Yerby looked me up and down with them mean eyes of his. "Where's your bluebelly uniform?"

"Got shed of it. Got shed of the whole dern mess."

Yerb spit a stream of tobacco juice and give a little whistle. Two more riders come easing out of the woods and joined him on the road. I didn't recognize either of 'em, but couldn't help wondering if they'd been amongst them that had chased me during the Econfina raid a spell back. Yerb turned to the one on his right. "We got us a couple of Yankee deserters. What you reckon we ought to do with 'em, Luke?"

Jeff went to mumbling the Lord's Prayer while Luke took off his slouch hat and scratched at his scalp. He was a tall, mean-looking sort, with long brown hair and a stringy beard to match. His eyes was narrow behind a big hooked nose, giving him a hawk look. He looked me and Jeff over. "Was you boys with them what attacked Marianna last summer?"

I hadn't heard of that fight. My mama hadn't mentioned nothing about a Marianna fight in her letters. So I looked Luke straight in the eye, said, "No, sir. Last time we was in Marianna we was hauling salt for Big John Anderson."

Well, sonny, that seemed to catch his fancy. Luke leaned over close to Yerb and them two went to jawing amongst theirselves for a spell. They was talking too low for me to make out what they was saying. I seen Yerb spit and nod a time or two, then Luke stared me down again.

"You two was with them Yanks what raided this valley last spring?"

I nodded towards Yerb. "He knows I was here. And he knows what I done."

Luke kept them hard narrow eyes locked on mine a spell, then walked his horse around Yerb and whispered something to the other rider. That feller kicked his horse and took off down the road towards Bennet. Didn't know whether that was a good sign or bad. After a minute Luke walked his horse a mite closer towards us. Pointed at Jeff, said, "What about the nigger?"

Jeff went to shaking so hard I could hear his teeth chattering. I grabbed a-hold of his arm so he wouldn't bolt. "Jeff just done what he was ordered, like any soldier's duty. We didn't want nothing to do with this war, Mister, Yerb knows that. It cost us both a brother. But what's done is done. All me and Jeff want is to go home and get back to farming."

Luke and Yerb went to jawing again. Yerb seemed near ready to throw a fit a time or two but Luke shut him up quick. Reckon he was in charge. Know what he done then? I'll tell you.

Luke turned back to face me and Jeff, said, "Go on, then. War's good as over anyhow." Then him and Yerby wheeled their horses and trotted off towards Bennet.

Well, sonny, me and Jeff had ourself a joyous homecoming all the same, that's a fact. I thought Aunt Nettie weren't ever going to stop crying and praising God. Then she went to kissing us so much I felt like a kitten after its mother give it a good licking. After he near hugged the life out of us, Uncle Nate grabbed his fiddle off the wall and filled that cabin with joyful music. Then him and Nettie went to dancing a jig till I thought me and Jeff weren't never going to get fed.

After all the hoopla settled down and our bellies was full, the four of us walked on up to the big house and the whole affair took up again. My mama cried herself dry and my sisters Ruth and Naomi carried on for near a hour dancing and singing with Jeff and his folks.

Later on when things had settled down I learnt from Mama that General Lee had surrendered his army a month ago up in Virginia. And just two weeks back General Joseph Johnston had done the same with the Army of Tennessee somewheres in North Carolina. None of the local boys had made it back home yet, least not that she had heard of.

But Tom Gainer was home. Mama had wrote me last fall how Tom had caught some shrapnel in his back and legs at Jonesboro during the fight for Atlanta. He had made it home in time for Christmas, and sister Sara was taking great care and delight in nursing her husband back to health up at the Gainers' place.

Joe Porter had wrote his ma and pa a letter they received

some time in February. There had been a big fight with the Yankees up in Tennessee at a town called Franklin, and another scrap at Nashville. Joe weren't one to worry his folks, but them fights had near took the life out of the army. That's the last the Porters had heard from their son, but no news is good news is what Miz Porter had told my mama.

Now I don't recollect the exact date me and Jeff got home, but it was towards the end of the first week of May, eighteen and sixty-five. I was hankering to see Annie, but figured I'd best give it a few days. Brother Daniel had been kilt near the end of May the year before, or so we all believed at the time. Annie would still be mourning him official-like for another three weeks or so, which was the custom folks followed back in them days. Way I figured, it wouldn't hurt none to visit with her a spell, seeing how we'd knowed each other our whole lives and was such good friends. So about a week later, after I had helped Uncle Nate and Jeff finish up the spring plowing and such, I took off to pay Annie a call.

I was antsy to see my Annie, but I was a mite troubled with how the Gainers might take to me. My mama had sent word that me and Jefferson was home from the war, but no answer had arrived as yet. By now most everbody along the Econfina knowed I'd been in the Yankee army. I hoped word had got out about what I'd done when the Yankees come raiding, but I weren't sure if that would be enough to unruffle feathers or not.

Turns out I ought not to've fretted none, leastways with the Gainers. Mister William Gainer and his missus welcomed me into their home like I was a long-lost son. They went to thanking me over and over for sending word about the raid, said it give 'em time to hide most of their valuables and such, and to get many of their people hid out, though the Yanks did make off with a goodly number of slaves and livestock and other whatnot.

Tom weren't holding no grudges neither, though I cain't say I felt the same. I still blamed him some for what befell Hamp.

He come hobbling up on his walking cane and hugged me like a brother, which I reckon he was of a sort. Told me how sorry he was about Daniel, and how he was glad I'd made it home safe. Sara made a big to-do over me of course, hugging and kissing me till I was near wore out. Then she told me I was fixing to be a uncle, come fall. Seems Tom weren't that crippled-up after all, the scoundrel.

One of their house nigras brung a tray with coffee and tea and we sat in their fancy parlor and jawed about folks and crops and the weather. Talked about near everthing till my ears was ringing. So after a spell I said, "Where is Annie?"

Miz Gainer, who was always the proper sort, went to squirming like she had bugs in her bloomers. She give a polite smile, said, "Why, Annabelle is up in her room, napping. I'm sure she'll be down directly."

Sara reached over from the settee where her and Tom was sitting and touched my arm. "Now don't you go expecting too much of Annie," she said, quiet like. "It's been a hard year for her."

Well, sonny, I was just a touch befuddled. Seemed Miz Gainer and Sara was being a mite protective of Annie, like I was some hungry fox come to raid their henhouse or such. I knowed Annie was in mourning. She hadn't even bothered to answer none of the letters I'd wrote her from Cedar Keys, but I took that to be part of her mourning duties. I'd come there to visit as a old and dear friend. Leastways, I hadn't give nobody reason to think my intentions was otherwise. I'd took great pains to keep my feelings for Annie shut up inside.

Then there come a shuffling on the winding staircase that led up to the second floor of the Gainer's home. Yonder stood Annie in front of the portrait of her folks, like she somehow had knowed we was talking about her and decided to come hear things firsthand.

Reckon sister Sara was on to something, because even from

where I sat, I could see the spark had gone out of Annie's eyes. She was pale as a ghost. Her skin was a sick milky white, like she ain't been out in the sun in a blue moon, nothing like the tanned tomboy that used to run with me and Hamp Watts. Them big purty eyes of hers was sunken, with dark shadows beneath 'em. And that wrinkled black dress couldn't hide the fact that she was near skin and bones.

Annie stood there staring down at us for a minute, then she give a little wave and near hollered, "Eli!" and come bounding down the rest of the stairs like a doe heading for a field of spring clover. "Eli!" she said again, then come running over and give me near the biggest hug you ever seen.

Well, sonny, I hugged her right back and it felt some good, that's a fact, like I was truly home at last. We kept at it for a spell till I come to my senses and realized her folks was sitting right there staring at us. My face went to burning, so I pushed away easy-like, said, "It's mighty good to see you."

Annie raised up a hand and touched her pale cheek. "I must look dreadful," she said, her smile gone, "not fit for company." Then she busted out crying, turned and run back up the stairs. I stood there with my jaw dropped open, dumb as a tree stump, till I heard Annie's door slam shut. I felt sick in my belly, near to puking.

"Poor dear, hasn't been herself," I heard Miz Gainer say, then Sara went to spouting something or the other, but it was like I was lost in a thick fog and her voice sounded all muddled up.

After a spell I turned to Annie's folks, said, "I'm powerful sorry I upset her so. I never meant to." Then I said I had best be going if I hoped to make it home by dark. So I took my leave, my heart near to breaking.

TWENTY ★ EIGHT

I WORKED HARD ON THE farm, helping Uncle Nate and Jeff finish the spring planting. When that was done I went to fixing the hog pens and whatever work needed doing on the barn and other outbuildings. Most evenings after chores I took a jug of whiskey and headed for the creek to do some fishing before supper. Done more thinking than fishing, mostly about Annie.

Things sure hadn't turned out the way I'd pictured. Seems brother Daniel's dying had took the very life out of Annie. Reckon her heart belonged only to him all along. All my highfalutin plans and dreams for me and Annie building a life together had come crashing down that day in the Gainers' parlor.

Still, Annie had seemed right pleased to see me, leastways at first. She'd give me that sweet smile and come running downstairs to hug me like she never intended to let go. Then, like somebody blowed out a lamp, she went dark on me. Backed off like I had the pox, then run back up them stairs. Things sure was befuddled, that's a fact.

Then one morning in the middle of June, Annabelle Gainer

come riding up to the house on her Appaloosa gelding. I was in the barn fixing a plow harness when I heard the clopping of hoofbeats coming up the lane. Wiped my hands and headed towards the house to see who was calling, hoping it weren't Yerby Watts looking for trouble. I hadn't seen hide or hair of him since the morning me and Jeff got home, and I sure weren't looking forward to the next time.

I near fell over when I seen it was Annie. She was tying the reins to the hitching post when I come around the corner. She looked up and smiled, said, "Hey there," just as friendly as could be. She weren't near as pale as before. Her cheeks was even a mite rosy and her eyes was near shining. Best of all, she'd shed the black mourning dress. She was all gussied-up in a gingham riding outfit, with bloomers and boots.

"Hey yourself," I said, grinning like a egg-sucking possum. "You look a sight better."

Annie turned back to the Appaloosa and fetched a package wrapped in brown paper out of the saddlebags strapped back of the saddle. "Could be I'm feeling better," she said, then sidled right past me onto the porch. "I've got a present for Mama Malburn. She inside?" Annie opened the door and went inside without looking back or waiting for a answer.

I went back to my business in the barn, hoping she wouldn't leave without saying goodbye. It had turned hot, and I'd raised a sweat working that leather and awl. I was thinking how good the creek was going to feel when Annie strolled up to the barn, leading her horse.

She stopped just inside the doorway, hands on her hips. "We've got some talking to do," she said in that bossy voice she sometimes used when me and her and Hamp palled around.

My belly went cold. "Do tell?" I weren't sure I wanted to hear what Annie had to say. If she was aiming to put me in my place, well then, so be it. My heart was already broke, and if there weren't no place in Annie's for me, I'd just soon hear it now and be done with it.

She nodded and brushed back a curl that had strayed across her cheek. "It might take a while. Can we go for a walk?"

I unsaddled the Appaloosa and fetched him some grain and water, then we set out across the cornfield towards the creek. The rains had been good: the stalks was already head-high and green as spring clover. Some ears was already tasseling. Annie followed me through the rows, neither one of us saying much. We come out on the far side and turned downstream along the path that followed the Econfina. Walked another fifty yards or so to one of my favorite fishing holes. The limestone bluff jutted over the shady creek where it took a sharp turn west, cutting a deep hole that held good fish. I stepped to the edge and sat down. Annie done the same.

The west wind sighed cool agin our faces. Clouds was building to the north, promising another afternoon shower. We sat quiet a few minutes, listening to birds chirping and scratching amongst the leaves, the creek gurlgling below.

"Joe Porter is home," I said after a spell. "Him and Charlie Hutchins. Uncle Nate run into Joe's daddy at the general store a couple of days ago."

Annie didn't answer. When I looked, she was crying. She wiped her cheek, said, "I'm glad for them."

My throat tightened and dern if I weren't near to tearing up my own self. Them that was coming home from the war was home. Tom and Joe and Charlie and a few others from the Econfina Valley. But there was a passel more that weren't never coming back. Them poor souls lay moldering in some unmarked grave far from home and family, my brother and best friend amongst 'em. It near tore up what was left of my heart to think of it.

I swallowed the lump in my throat. "What was you wanting to talk about?"

Annie sniffled, fiddled with a loose thread on her skirt. "Us, or me, I guess."

Another minute passed. "Well, go on then," I said.

She sighed, stared down at the creek. "When word arrived about Daniel..." she said, then stopped. A skeeter hawk buzzed over the creek, flashing green when it caught the sunlight. "When we heard Daniel had been killed, I took to bed for the longest time," Annie said. "I didn't leave my room for weeks. I hardly ate, except for broth Mother pestered me to drink."

I looked into her eyes. "I was right sick my own self. Fact is, I felt guilty."

With that, Annie swung around to face me. Her eyebrows arched, and she had that *And just what does that mean?* look she used to get when me and Hamp kept a secret between us to vex her. I knowed she was waiting for a answer. Figured I'd best get it out.

"Thing is, I was jealous, you being sweet on Danny and all. I mean, you was my friend, and Hamp's. Then one day you up and took to Danny like a bee to clover. Then, when Danny was kilt, it was like I'd done him wrong somehow." That ain't exactly what I intended to say, but it's what come out.

Annie give a hint of a smile. "My being fond of Daniel didn't mean I wasn't still friends with you two. It's just that I was growing up some, I guess."

I picked up a stick laying nearby and tossed it into the creek, watched it swirl in the eddy a spell, then float downstream. Looked Annie in the eye and shook my head. "That ain't it. What I meant was, when Danny got kilt I felt eat up with guilt, because for the longest time I'd been thinking of how to get you to love me instead of him."

Well, sonny, that set Annie to crying again. She went on and on till I felt like jumping into the creek and drowning myself in that deep hole. Because right then and there I would've rather been dead than cause her more grief.

After a spell she looked at me with them red, swole-up eyes, sniffled a few times, said, "I'm just awful," then buried her face in her hands and went to shaking.

I was a mite confused when she said that, mind you. Didn't have the foggiest why she would say such a thing. So I edged closer and took one of her hands in mine. "You're talking nonsense, Annabelle Gainer." I pulled her other hand away from her face.

Annie looked away. "But I *am* awful. I loved Daniel, but I loved you too. There, see?"

I near fell over when I heard that. My mouth opened, but no words come out.

"I hated wearing that horrid black all that time," I heard her say like she was far off, "hated not answering your letters. But Mother said it wouldn't be proper even if we were just good friends, that it might give others the wrong impression.

"And then I'd feel so guilty, like I'd betrayed Daniel. But I hadn't really, you see? I did intend to marry him after the war, I truly did, but I still had feelings for you. But Mother wouldn't understand. She said I must do what's proper and expected of a lady in mourning.

"And then, when you came to the house that day, I felt truly alive again. I couldn't help myself. Daniel was gone, but we were *alive*, Eli, we were alive, and I loved you!"

Next thing I knowed we was holding tight and kissing like when I'd come home from hauling salt to Marianna and learnt about Hamp. Only this time when we finally come up for air Annie didn't hightail it for the house like I'd slapped her. Them big doe eyes burnt into my own, then we went at it again.

TWENTY ★ NINE

I COME CALLING ON ANNIE often as I could the rest of that summer. Most of our courting took place at the Gainer place. We took things slow, which suited her ma just fine, Miz Gainer being such a proper sort. Her daddy seemed pleased as a pig in slop to see his daughter happy and enjoying life again after that long year of hurt she'd been through.

Once or twice a month the Gainers would host a barbeque and dance or other such sociable get-togethers. Seems there was always somebody looking after me and Annie, Tom or Sara or one of her folks lurking nearby. Ever now and again we'd manage to slip off by ourself for a spell, but weren't nothing improper happened, being as how I had too much respect for Annie to give in to my devilish urges.

Me and Uncle Nate and Jeff worked hard that summer, harvesting the late crops and plowing the fields for winter planting. There was feed corn aplenty stored in the bins to see the pigs and chickens through till spring. We carried several wagon loads to Porter's Mill, which had been rebuilt since the raid, for grinding into meal and grits. Mama and Aunt Nettie and the twins put up a passel of canned goods to see us through the winter.

Most of the farm work being caught up, come early autumn I had more time to spend with Annie. So one afternoon in early October I saddled up the mule that Uncle Nate had broke to saddle and headed for the Gainer place. Not wanting to chance a run-in with Yerby Watts, I took the Bennet Road and crossed the creek at Williford Bridge which had also been rebuilt.

It was a fine day for a ride, a cool breeze drifting out of the north and cottony clouds floating south. Flocks of blackbirds wheeled this way and that, looking for leftovers on harvested fields. Maples and sweet gums was showing the first signs of fall color, and squirrels was busy storing nuts and cutting leaves for their winter nests.

I was happy as a bee in honeysuckle when I rode up to the Gainer's house towards evening and seen Annie sitting on the porch swing. I had a big surprise planned for after supper, and was antsy to get to it. Annie run down the stairs while I was tying up the mule and give me a big hug and a quick peck on the cheek.

"Sara's in labor!" she said, grinning and clapping her hands and dancing from one foot to the other like she was standing on hot coals.

"Do tell?" I wondered why it was women always made such a big to-do over babies. "How's poor Tom holding up?"

"She started having contractions this morning, then her water broke while I was helping her upstairs," Annie babbled on, paying no mind to my question and telling me more'n I wanted to know. "Lord, that like to have scared the life out of me. Daddy sent for Doctor Haygood. He should be here directly."

We went inside. Annie hurried upstairs, saying she was going to check on Sara and that I might as well sit a spell with Tom and her daddy in the parlor. I'd no sooner sat down with the glass of whiskey Mister Gainer offered me than here come Doctor Haygood clomping down the hallway and into the parlor toting his bag of doctoring tools.

"Would one of you boys see to Elvira?" the old white-haired doc said, following Mister Gainer upstairs. "We been on the go since sunup."

I told Tom to sit tight in case the baby was to come and went outside to tend to the doc's horse and surrey. The gray dappled mare was standing near my mule in the fading light, swishing her tail back and forth more out of habit than shooing flies. Doc Haygood had owned that same horse long as I could remember.

He hadn't bothered to tie her up. I went to the barn and fetched a bucket of oats and a pail of water. Loosened the halter and dropped the bit so the old mare could have supper. Give a bit of oats to the mule while I was at it, then went back inside to keep Tom company.

Well, sonny, the night crawled by like a snail through spilt molasses. Me and Tom and his daddy bided our time in the parlor, working on a second bottle of Mister Gainer's fine whiskey. Near ten o'clock Annie come running out to the balcony. "It's a girl!" she shrieked, clapping and dancing that jig again.

We shook hands and swapped congratulations, then the new daddy and granddaddy went upstairs to welcome the newest member of the Gainer clan. I stayed put, figured they could use some family privacy. Fact is, I'd drank so much whiskey I weren't sure I could make it up the stairs without falling and breaking my fool neck.

After a spell Annie come down and sat beside me on the settee. We held hands a minute, then she laid her head agin my shoulder. I felt her shudder, seen a tear roll down her cheek. I give her a gentle hug. She looked up, said, "They named her Daniela."

Weren't long till Annie fell asleep. I eased her agin the padded arm of the settee, then slipped out of the house quiet as I could. Tightened the halter on Doc Haygood's mare, then led my mule out to the Gainer's barn where we bedded down for the night.

Took me a spell to get to sleep. Kept thinking about Annie, how she'd cried over the baby's name. She was still carrying Daniel's memory in her heart, I was sure of it, and that vexed me some. What I wondered was, was there enough room in her heart for both me and my brother?

I fished in my coat pocket, found the gold ring I'd ordered from Mister Hutchins' fancy catalog. Couldn't see the ring in the dark, but I knowed ever detail etched in it, ever heart and diamond, and the words on the inside: *Forever, Eli.* I'd planned on giving it to Annie that night after supper, just when the big harvest moon was climbing over the treetops, romantic fool that I was. But Sara having her baby had went and spoilt my highfalutin plans, or was it Daniel's ghost haunting Annie that done it?

I laid on that pile of hay fighting sleep long as I could, thinking ever bad thought I could conjure up and feeling right sorry for myself. It might only have been a few minutes, or maybe hours, but the whiskey finally won out. Next thing I knowed a rooster was crowing me awake.

———◆———

The sun weren't up yet, but dawn was coming on. I walked over to the stables and splashed the sleep out of my eyes with water from the trough. My head pounded from the whiskey, my mouth tasted like a herd of goats had shat in it. I chewed on fresh sweet hay and rinsed my mouth out till it felt clean, then I walked back to the house.

Doc Haygood's surrey was gone. I tiptoed across the porch and inside the house quiet as I could, not wanting to wake folks or set the baby to crying. Annie was curled up on the settee where I'd left her. Somebody had covered her with a quilt.

I knelt down and shook her gentle as I could. She give out a little groan, then stretched and opened her eyes. She smiled, said, "Good morning," yawned and sat up.

"Look here," I whispered, slipping the ring from my pocket. "I meant to give you this last night, only the baby come and all." I took her hand, turned it palm up and laid the ring in it.

Annie stared at her hand and blinked two-three times. When she finally seen what it was, her eyes growed wide. Her mouth dropped open but nothing come out.

I looked her straight in the eye. "I want you to marry me. Will you?" It weren't the fancy romantic words I'd planned on saying, but it's what come out at the time.

Annie stared at the ring again, went to fanning herself with her other hand like she was feeling faint. Her fingers closed over the ring. "Oh Lord, Eli. Yes!"

We got hitched that coming spring, on the second of April, eighteen and sixty-six. It was as fine a day for a wedding a body could hope for, and my Annie was some sight to behold, that's a fact. Annie's ma had the dress special made by her sister, a dressmaker up in Eufaula, Alabama. The ceremony took place on the Gainer's fancy front porch which they gussied-up with flowers and ribbons and other such finery. The guests, which there was a passel of, sat on chairs and benches on the front lawn. Me and Annie stood at the top of the steps, with Sara standing with Annie and Tom with me, which was mostly to keep peace in the family. Naomi and Ruth made the dandiest flower girls you ever seen in their matching pink dresses. They was twelve or thirteen then, as I recollect, and was turning into right smart young ladies their own selves. Wouldn't be long till some feisty colts was bound to come a-courting.

Joe Porter, who had took up preaching when he come home from the war, did the honors of marrying us up. I was shaking like a plucked duck in winter when Joe had us join hands and recite all them vows and such. Somehow I managed to mumble my way through it.

When it come time for me to slip the ring on Annie's finger, it galled me some to see her wearing the ring my brother had give her on her other hand. We'd had ourselfs a argument or two about that, but I'd finally seen things Annie's way. She'd promised Daniel she would wear that ring for the rest of her life, and a promise is a promise, like it or not. And she done just that, which in time I come to tolerate though I ain't ashamed to say I never cared much for the idea. Leastways it was *my* ring on her marrying finger.

After all the formalities was done, Mister Gainer throwed the biggest barbeque and party the Econfina Valley ever seen. There was music and singing and dancing, food and spirits aplenty. You never seen such a spread. Course, me and Annie done the wedding cake thing, and the first dance and all the other hoopla that's expected at such a big affair.

The celebrating went on till late afternoon. When all the guests finally went their way, me and Annie climbed into the Gainers' fancy surrey for the ride home. It was decorated up right nice, with a big *Just Married* banner across the back and a long string of tin cans trailing behind. My mama and sisters had arranged to visit with the Gainers for a couple of days to give me and Annie a chance to "settle in," as Mama put it. She'd moved her belongings and such into Daniel's old room, and give me and Annie the big bedroom her and my daddy shared for so many years. It was only fitting, she said, being as I was now head of the Malburn household.

Me and Annie waved and hollered our goodbyes and such, then set off down the road in the fading light towards our new life together. We was happy as a couple of bear cubs paw-deep in honey, that's a fact. Halfway home thunder went to rumbling in the north, then a short spell later it come a-raining. I hopped out of the surrey and quick-like put up the top. Let it rain, I went to thinking. Weren't no storm could put a damper on the happiness me and my sweet Annie was feeling that evening.

Well, sonny, a body ought to be careful what he goes to thinking. There was a storm brewing all right, a big one, and it would be blowing in soon.

Daniel Malburn
The Trek Home
1866

THIRTY

WHEN I WOKE UP THAT early May morning after the big storm, I looked out the window of my room to see what damage it done. It was bad as I'd figured. In ever direction, trees was uprooted and blowed down, yards and streets plumb covered with branches and clapboards and roof shingles and such. Miz Barfield's boarding house weren't spared, either. A big sycamore tree was leaning agin the house a ways down from my room, and even from there, I seen the roof would need a heap of work. No telling what other damage might've been done. Carpenters living around Clarksville was bound to stay busy for quite a spell.

I got dressed and went downstairs, aiming to have myself some more of Miz Barfield's good food before setting out on the road for Nashville. Despite the storm, she'd set a fine table at supper the night before. And except for that jackass Yankee, who I will get to directly, I had a dandy time listening to her and the boarders jawing about this and that and the other. I'd spent nights a-plenty with only myself for company. Truth be told, I was also hoping to see one Miz Francine Waters again before moving on.

Happened to be that Miz Waters was Miz Barfield's niece, and like her aunt, she was a widow woman. Learnt at supper that her husband had been kilt at Chickamauga, though I sure weren't the one that asked about the tragic circumstances of her early widowhood. That had come from what I took to be a Yankee peddler down from Chicago, shopping his wares betwixt there and Atlanta.

"How unfortunate," he says to Miz Waters after she answered his rude question concerning her late husband's untimely passing. "The late Rebellion was such a tragic affair for our nation."

Well, sir, my hackles was raised a mite after hearing him ask the young widow such a indelicate question. Weren't none of his business. But when he kept spouting how he'd come to help out the needy people of the South after the "late Rebellion," as he called it, I'd had a bellyful of him and his jabber.

"No need you going farther than Chattanooga," I says. "I hear tell your General Sherman didn't leave much standing south of there. Folks won't have the money to spare for your truck."

That wiped the pompous grin off his face. He set his fork down and dabbed his mouth with his napkin. "Quite the contrary, young man. Why, opportunity abounds. Even as we speak, the government is hard at work setting up agencies to help the citizenry of the South get back on their feet."

I stared at him a second or two. "Just what is it you selling?"

The peddler put down his knife and fork and fiddled with his napkin. "I am in land speculations, my good man. My company purchases and resells delinquent properties to those needing a hand-up after the recent unpleasantries."

I nearbout choked on my food when he said that. My ears was burning. I drank some water to cool off and took a minute to choose my words. There was ladies present, and I didn't want to offend them. "If your company and the Yankee government wants to help, they ought to go home and leave the South alone, which is all we wanted in the first place."

Miz Waters give a little smile, looked down at her plate and fiddled with her food a mite. Nobody said a word for a spell. The peddler tugged at his collar and flushed like he'd been out in the sun too long, then excused hisself to Miz Barfield and the other guests, saying he had early appointments come morning. He never give me so much as a sideways glance.

Weren't no way of knowing then, but I had just met my first goldamn carpetbagger. He wouldn't be the last, not by a long shot.

———•———

It was early, not yet six-thirty. Breakfast was served at seven. I moseyed into the empty dining room to wait. Through the open door that led to the kitchen I seen Francine Waters puttering about. She was taller than her aunt, maybe five foot three or four, and fuller of figure. A handsome woman, gospel truth, with chestnut hair and green eyes that sparkled when they caught yours. I took her to be my age or thereabouts. Her hair was pinned back in a comely bun. She wore a apron smudged with flour dust atop a cornflower-blue dress.

My stomach commenced growling when I caught the smell of frying ham and fresh coffee. I stuck my head through the doorway. "Morning ma'am, am I too early for coffee?"

Miz Waters smiled and give a little wave with the fork she was using to turn the ham slices. "Good morning, Mister Malburn," she says, pointing the fork at a big porcelain coffee pot. "It ought to be ready by now. Help yourself."

I grabbed a cup and poured the coffee. "My friends call me Dan, or Danny. That ham smells mighty good."

She turned and smiled. "Then you must call me Franny," she says, flipping a slice of ham. "Franny and Danny. How odd."

She went back to cooking whilst I sipped the hot coffee.

"Ham's ready," she says a minute later, putting the last slice on a big platter atop the others. "There's grits and drop biscuits and eggs-to-order. How do you like yours?"

"What?" I says, realizing I hadn't paid attention after her telling me to call her Franny. Of a sudden I had the queerest feeling, like something stirring inside my head.

"I asked how you like your eggs cooked. I'm caught up, so I can fix yours."

"I ain't particular, scrambled's fine." I walked out to the dining room and sat down, still trying to figure out what was jostling about inside my head.

A few minutes later Franny come toting my breakfast plate in one hand and the coffee pot in another. She set the plate down in front of me and refilled my cup, then fished in her apron pocket for silverware that was rolled tight in a white cloth napkin.

I thanked her and commenced eating. She disappeared into the kitchen and come back out directly with a dish of butter and a can of cane syrup which she set on the table.

"Much obliged," I says.

"Welcome." She stood by the table another few seconds, then says, "Mind if I sit a spell?"

I looked up from my plate, swallowed what I was chewing. "No ma'm, suit yourself." Then I remembered my manners and stood as she sat. For some reason I was a mite troubled by all this. Miz Francine Waters was a fine looking young woman, and I admit I was drawed to her like most fellers would natural be. But there was something that vexed me. I weren't sure if it was her or me. It weren't the fact that she'd been widowed. Come September, Chickamauga would be three years past, plenty more than the customary grieving time.

Franny sat across from me with her hands in her lap all proper-like. After a spell she says, "I wanted to thank you for coming to my rescue last night."

I had just sopped my biscuit in some syrup and took a

bite. I nodded whilst I hurried to chew. "That feller was a mite unmannerly, way I seen it. Like most Yankees I've come across."

Franny tilted her head. Her eyebrows lifted and scrunched together, them green eyes sparkling. "I believe you are a good judge of character, Danny Malburn."

We jawed a spell longer till other boarders come strolling into the dining room and Franny got up to see to their breakfast. I learnt she was twenty-two years old, been born and raised in Springfield, a piece east of Clarksville. She'd been married less than a year when her husband, a lieutenant with the First Tennessee Regiment, fell at Chickamauga. That's when she come to live with Miz Barfield, her late mother's sister. Franny worked days at a dress shop on the town square. She helped her aunt run the boarding house, mostly cooking breakfast and helping with the cleaning and such when she weren't working at the dress shop.

I told Franny most of what I remembered about myself, how I had been wounded and took prisoner, and about how my memory weren't all back as yet. "Somewheres in Florida," I told her when she asked where I was headed. "Reckon I'll know it when I get there."

Franny was still working in the kitchen when I was done eating, so I went back upstairs and fetched my bedroll. Walked downstairs past the dining room. Give a quick look but didn't see Franny anywheres about. Figured that was that, and headed out the front door. Halfway down the porch steps the door opened behind me and Miz Barfield called my name.

"Might I trouble you a minute?"

Well, sir, I'll spare you the details and get right to it. Miz Barfield told me times was hard and she needed help with cleaning up her place and fixing whatever damage the storm had caused and would I be interested in the job. "I can't pay much," she says, "but you'll get room and board plus two dollars a day."

I was right antsy to be on my way, but I figured there was a good week, maybe ten days of work to be had from what I seen of the place. I stood to make twenty or thirty dollars if I took Miz Barfield's offer, which would come in mighty handy once I got home. Another week or two with a warm bed and good food might just help jog my memory some, too.

Then there was Miz Francine Waters. Talking with Franny that morning had stirred a hunger in my gut I ain't felt in a long spell. I weren't sure, but it just might be she'd took a liking to me, too. Figured staying put another week or so wouldn't do no harm, so I might as well take Miz Barfield up on her offer. So that's just what I done.

THIRTY ★ ONE

I SET RIGHT TO WORK. First thing I done was to haul limbs and other such littering the grounds to a pile and get it burning. Feeding that fire took most of the first day. The next morning I fetched a ladder and saw and ax from Miz Barfield's shed and went to work on the big sycamore tree that had blowed over agin the roof. That took three or four days, as I recollect. I covered the damaged roof with a tarp till I could get around to fixing it.

It took a couple of days after I give Miz Barfield the list of lumber and shingles and nails and such for the roof before the hardware store got around to delivering it. Near ever building in the area had suffered some sort of damage, and supplies was short. Meanwhile, I done what I could to stay busy. Miz Barfield said a deal was a deal, and paid me for them slack days.

It weren't all work and no pleasure. The morning after Miz Barfield hired me, she asked would I mind escorting her niece to and from her job on the square. Seems a passel of laborers had come to town for all the work that needed doing, and she was a mite concerned how ungentlemanly some amongst that crowd might be.

The dress shop weren't but fifteen minutes from the boarding house, but them two walks a day give me and Franny plenty of time to get better acquainted. Franny would have my breakfast ready at six-thirty, then I'd work till eight o'clock when she left for the shop.

The days passed by quick. Me and Franny took to sitting out on the front porch nights after supper, watching lightning bugs and listening to crickets serenade us whilst we talked. Weren't long before we was holding hands, then late one evening when things was quiet and nobody was stirring about the boarding house, we kissed a time or two.

A few nights later I walked Franny back to her room, kissed her goodnight, then went on to my room. Laid awake a good hour or more, torn betwixt staying put with Franny or heading home. My work here was done, but I weren't quite ready to leave just yet. Fact is, I had paid for my keep the past three or four days, like any other boarder.

Weren't no telling what I might find waiting for me back home, if I ever remembered where home was. My memories was still scrambled. I knowed I had family. I knowed Joe Porter was my best pard, or had been. I knowed we had fought with the Sixth Florida Infantry. But my memory was like roads inside my mind that kept petering out or dead-ending before they took me to where I needed to go.

I laid there struggling with my thoughts, trying hard to shut them out and get to sleep. Finally I got up and took me a dose of laudanum. I'd been feeling better lately, what headaches I'd had weren't near as bad as they had been, so there was plenty of laudanum to spare. But I knowed it would help me sleep, and that's just what it done.

That very night the dream come.

Me and Franny was sitting on a limestone shelf that hung out over a bubbling spring. The full moon was just rising over the treetops. It was a cool evening, and Franny pulled her wool shawl tighter about her shoulders to ward off the chill. We sat there watching the big silver moon rise, listening to crickets and whippoorwills calling from the woods. Here and yonder, lightning bugs lit up like stars, twinkling over the spring.

I reached inside my coat pocket for the fancy felt box, opened it and took out the ring. Reached for Franny's hand and slipped the ring on her finger. "I was hoping we could get married," I says.

Franny's mouth dropped open. She gasped and stared at the ring. "Oh my, it's the prettiest ring I ever saw!"

I leaned over to give her a kiss, only it weren't Franny staring back at me with them big doe eyes. It weren't Franny at all—

I woke up with a start. My heart was pounding and I was gasping for breath. It felt like my head was going to bust wide open. I sat up and rubbed my temples, trying to get a-hold of myself. "Annie!" I says out loud. "Annie!"

———————

Well, sir, I recollected nearbout everthing then, all my family and friends, where I come from, everthing about the war—and Annabelle Gainer. It all come back in a rush, clear as the springs that fed Econfina Creek back home. My Annie, my bethrothed.

Didn't sleep a lick more that night. It had been more'n two years since my furlough home in January of 'sixty-four, and going on two years since I'd heard any word from home. Was things still the same with me and Annie? I loved her and I knowed she loved me, but by now she might well think I was dead. I remembered then that I had sent a letter from St. Louis whilst working for Henry Tucker at his tavern. Surely the folks back home got that one.

What in tarnation was I going to tell Franny? *How* was I going to tell her? We was sweet on each other, maybe even in love. The war had took her husband, and now she stood to lose me too, if I went home to Annie. It was a downright miserable mess I'd found myself in. And whatever I done about it, there would be devil to pay.

THIRTY ★ TWO

I WENT DOWN TO BREAKFAST that morning, told Franny I felt off my feed and would just have coffee. Truth be told, I couldn't stomach food just then. I was plumb sick in my gut. I'd left my bedroll in the foyer next to the front door. Planned to hit the road soon as I told Franny what I'd come to say.

After a spell Franny got caught up on her cooking, poured herself a cup of coffee and joined me. It weren't no time till she seen something was wrong and asked what was troubling me. So I told her about the dream, how I come to remember it all now, and how I reckoned I had best be on my way. "I cain't rightly break my word to Annie," I says, my voice choking, "much as it pains me to leave."

Well, sir, Franny's chin commenced quivering. I seen tears well up in her eyes, then come rolling down her cheeks. She buried her face in her apron and sobbed a spell, then looked up, them purty green eyes framed in red. Told me it hurt, but she understood. She reached over and squeezed my hands in hers, then got up and hurried into the kitchen without looking back.

I sat there another minute or so, wondering if I was doing the right thing, almost hoping Franny would come back out and ask me to stay. But it weren't to be. Directly, other boarders come moseying into the dining room for their breakfast. I took one last look towards the kitchen, then walked away.

The railroad run from Clarksville to Nashville, but at the time it rolled north into Kentucky before looping south back into Tennessee. Weren't no way I was heading north again, so I asked directions from some feller on the town square and set out for the Nashville Pike. Figured it would take me three days to make Nashville, forty-some miles away, maybe less if I could hitch a ride with a freight wagon or such.

It was a fine, sunny morning in mid-May. The warm weather and the blue sky soon helped ease the pain and gloom I felt leaving Franny behind. That, and the thought of soon being home and seeing Annie.

I struck the pike, and after a hour of hard walking I left the farms outside Clarksville behind. Trees along the road was leafed out and birds was singing and flitting about. Here and yonder a wagon passed, or some feller riding horseback, but pleasantries was all they offered.

I was a mite footsore towards late afternoon when I hitched a ride with a man driving a big coal wagon headed for Franklin. Said he'd be glad to carry me as far as Nashville where I could catch the train to Chattanooga. I don't recollect his name, but I ain't to this day forgot his kindness. That night, we camped along the pike and I shared his supper. The next afternoon, we crossed the Cumberland River and rolled into Nashville. He pointed me towards the train depot, then turned his team onto the Franklin Pike.

The next morning I boarded the train for Chattanooga and points south. I'll spare you the details, but it was a bittersweet journey, truth be told. Conjured up a heap of memories from the war, not all bad. We rolled past Chattanooga, then through Tunnel Hill that cut through Missionary Ridge into Georgia. That's where the gallant General Cleburne and his boys had held off the Yankees till the Army of Tennessee could make good its escape south to Dalton.

Later, when the train stopped at Resaca to take on coal and water, I tried not to think of poor Orville Cowart and Billy Yon and the other souls that laid buried just north of town in the mass grave we'd dug. Instead, I set my thoughts on the time me and Joe Porter had passed through there on our furlough home. Recalled how Joe remarked what fine country it was, not like the steep mountains where we spent that long cold winter.

I figured on traveling by rail to Columbus, then catching a boat downriver to Chattahoochee, same as me and Joe done in January of 'sixty-four. The train rolled on through the long days and nights, the weather growing warmer the farther south we got. I done my best to shed my mind of what I'd left behind up in Tennessee. Kept busy reading ever newspaper or magazine I could get a-hold of. Slept as much as I could and kept mostly to myself. It weren't that I was the unfriendly sort, but I was tussling with a heap of thoughts and feelings. I weren't the same person that had marched off to war with the others back in March of 'sixty-two, so full of grit and spoiling to fight. I knowed I'd never be that person again. I had seen and done too much.

When the train finally chugged into Columbus, it struck me for real that at long last I was going home. Before then it had seemed like a dream of sorts. There was still a boat to catch, and a horse to buy for the ride down to Econfina.

But home was in sight now. Truth be told, I found that thought a mite bothersome. Couldn't help wondering if I'd fit in, or find I was a stranger once I got there.

Malburn Brothers
Reunited
Spring 1866

THIRTY ★ THREE

WELL, SIR, RECKON I WON'T never forget the morning I rode down the lane that led up to our house. It was late May and warm, sweat was already trickling down my neck and it weren't yet noon. I passed the last bend and yonder just ahead the house come into view. I pulled the old nag I'd bought in Chattahoochee to a stop. Sat there a spell, taking it all in. I was home!

Weren't nobody stirring that I could see, so I kneed the horse on ahead. Stopped at the gate, got off and swung it open. I walked the mare up to the house and tied her to the post out front. Just then I heard footsteps shuffling, looked up and seen Aunt Nettie come around the corner of the porch, broom swishing back and forth, chasing what little dust might've settled since her last sweeping. Aunt Nettie always was a stickler for clean floors.

I watched her a minute, then give a "bob white" whistle like I done when I was little. The broom stopped in mid-sweep. Aunt Nettie looked up and seen me standing there, stared a spell like she didn't recognize who it was. Then the broom dropped from her hands and clattered on the floor. She cut loose a scream, turned and run into the house, her hands waving over her head like she was swatting off a swarm of bees.

It weren't exactly the greeting I figured to get from Aunt Nettie, but then I reckon my showing up the way I done might've startled her a mite. I took off my hat and swept back my hair, dusted off my clothes best I could, then walked towards the porch. I hadn't made it to the steps yet when the front door flew open and Annie of all people come running out to see what had upset Aunt Nettie so. She stopped in her tracks when our eyes met, like she'd been pole-axed. Her mouth dropped open, then she slumped to the floor, fainted dead away.

"Annie, who is it?" my mama says, coming out the door wiping flour off her hands with her apron. When she seen Annie laying sprawled on the porch she hollered for Aunt Nettie. Before she got to Annie, Mama looked up and seen me. Her eyes growed wide, both hands flew up to her mouth. "My Lord!" She dropped to her knees beside Annie like her legs had plumb give out.

I run up the steps to help Mama tend to Annie. Annie's eyes was fluttering. Mama had turned pale as one of them fine china plates she used to set out for Sunday dinner. I seen Aunt Nettie stick her head out the doorway, all wide-eyed and mumbling something about haints or such.

"Bring water, Nettie!" Mama says at last, wiping at Annie's brow with her apron. "And my smelling salts!" Then she looked up at me, her chin a-quivering. "My Lord, is it really you, Daniel?"

I knelt down and put my arm around her. "Yes ma'am, I finally made it home," I says, just as Annie give a little groan. I touched her shoulder. "Why is Annie here?"

Before Mama could answer, Aunt Nettie come creeping towards us like a whipped pup, toting a bowl of water. "It's all right Nettie," Mama says, "Our Daniel has come home."

Me and Jeff and Uncle Nate had spent most of the morning in the cornfield, hoeing weeds and checking the crop for earworms. We was walking up to the house for the noon meal when we heard Aunt Nettie screaming bloody murder. I took off running, Jeff hot on my tracks. Weren't no telling what had happened, but from the sound of things it couldn't be good.

I come around the corner of the house and seen Annie laying on the porch, with Mama and Aunt Nettie and some man leaning over her. "What happened?" I hollered, taking the steps two at a time.

Well, sonny, when that feller looked up and I seen who it was, you could've knocked me over with a feather, that's a fact. My dead brother, in the flesh, fanning Annie with his slouch hat while our mama wiped Annie's face with a cool wet cloth. Her eyes was half open, but she was still groggy.

"She fainted," Mama said. "Your brother give her quite a fright."

"Like to scairt the life out o' me, he did," I heard Aunt Nettie say. "Lawd, I thought he a haint, I did."

Things was a blur, and I don't recollect everthing that was said. Uncle Nate and Jeff was on the porch by then, holding onto Aunt Nettie. Mama still had Annie's head cradled in her lap. Daniel stood up and give me a hug. Reckon I was more'n a mite shocked to see him standing there after counting him for dead the past two years. He was thin as a rail, had a ugly red scar on the left side of the head that run like a furrow from his temple past his ear. After a spell I found my tongue. "Joe Porter wrote, told us you was dead."

He nodded. "Mama told me."

"How come you didn't write?"

Daniel looked near to tears. "I wrote from prison. Wrote again from St. Louis after the Yankees turned us loose."

Annie was sitting up now, holding the cloth agin her pale forehead and taking deep breaths. Mama looked at Daniel. She was crying. "We never got no letters, son, not a one."

"Figured as much," was all he said.

I knelt down beside Annie and looked Mama in the eye. She wiped at the tears with the apron and shook her head. I felt Annie's clammy cheek, then stood up to face my brother. It had to be done. Figured I'd best get on with it. "Did Mama tell you about me and Annie?"

Daniel stood tall and shook his head, but I seen in his eyes he knowed what was coming.

THIRTY ★ FOUR

WHEN ELI TOLD ME HIM and Annie had got married the month before, it felt like I'd been gutted with a dull knife. All the wind went out of me. A bullet in the head would've been a heap more merciful, way I felt then. It was all I could do to make it to the porch steps and sit down. I kept hoping it was a dream, that I would wake up where I'd camped last night north of the Porters' place.

But it weren't no dream, and no amount of wishing would ever make it so. I was home, but life had moved on and left me behind. Annie and my brother was married. I felt all empty inside, like everthing I'd hoped for and dreamed about all them long years was dead and gone. I reckon it was, truth be told.

I heard voices behind me, but they was muddled. After a spell Annie come to her senses. Mama and Aunt Nettie got her to her feet and back in the house to rest. Uncle Nate and Jeff went inside to eat so me and Eli could have our say. Eli sat down next to me, arms resting on his legs, staring out across the yard.

"I don't rightly know what to say, Danny. Nobody knowed.

Me and Annie, we—"

"I got to see to my horse." I got up and walked over to the hitching post, leaving Eli on the steps. I led the mare to the barn, took off the saddle and tack and brushed her down. Give her a bucket of feed and water, then put her out to pasture. Whilst doing all that I kept thinking how if I had only come directly home, not dillydallied them weeks in Clarksville at Miz Barfield's boarding house acting like some moon-struck young'un, I might've got home in time to stop them two from marrying up. If I hadn't of met Miz Francine Waters, if I would've remembered things just a mite sooner, if, if, if.

Well, sir, I was doing one jim-dandy job of making myself feel downright miserable. After a spell I come to my senses enough to know there weren't a goldamn thing I could ever do that would make this mess go away. I was just going to have to live with things the way they was. Me and Annie was gone up, like the Confederacy and all them poor souls that had died fighting for home and hearth and the dream of Southern independence.

Eli and Annie. I loved them both. So how could I hate 'em or hold it agin 'em for what they done? After all, I had been dead for two years, far as they knowed. Them two had been best pals as young'uns, along with Hamp Watts. It weren't hard to understand that they'd be drawed back to each other, knowing I weren't ever coming home from the war. So right then I swore I would play the cards I'd been dealt, I would try my goldamndest to be happy for Annie and Eli.

But it was a bitter thing to swallow, gospel truth. Bitter as the dose of laudanum I fished from the saddlebags and swigged down to stop the pain in my head.

———•———

Right away Mama sent word throughout the valley that Daniel was back from the war, alive and well. That weren't exactly so, but that's the way she seen it. With the Gainers' help, she throwed a big welcome home to-do for Danny down by the creek the weekend after he got back. Joe Porter and Tom Gainer and Charlie Hutchins and a few more of their army pards had a high time of it. Even Yerby Watts showed up. Him and Daniel made their peace over a jug of corn whiskey. Well, sonny, that there was the first of what come to be the Malburn family reunions. They've been held ever year since, last weekend of May, but you know all about that.

Me and Annie took to walking on shells whenever Daniel was around. He never had much to say to either of us, but he was mannerly enough and never give us no cause for grief. After a week or two things got back to normal, of a sort. But my brother had changed, that weren't hard to see.

He took to running with Yerby Watts, staying out till all hours of the night drinking and carrying on. More'n once he come home stinking drunk with skinned knuckles and a black eye or busted lip. I tried talking to him a time or two for our mama's sake, but he weren't having none of it. Told me I ought to mind my own business if I knowed what was good for me. And he wouldn't sleep in the house with the rest of the family neither. Instead, he fixed hisself a room in the barn loft.

Now, Daniel done his fair share of work helping us keep the farm fit, I'll give him that, but it weren't hard to tell that his heart weren't in it. Most nights he'd take his supper out to the barn where he always kept a jug handy. In his spare time he wouldn't go fishing or such with me or Jeff or Uncle Nate. When he weren't off raising cain with Yerb, he spent most his time fixing up the old two-room cabin our daddy had built when him and Coleman Watts first come to the Econfina Valley. It stood near the Econfina on the south section where our property fishhooked west into the creek. Weren't but sixty acres or so, but there weren't a finer piece of rich bottomland in the whole valley. It had stood fallow since Daniel had joined the army and went off to war. Near four hundred acres was plenty enough for me and Jeff and Uncle Nate to handle.

The days come and went till summer was used up and the woods took on the first flush of fall color. Reckon me and Annie was happy enough, though it weren't all blue skies and clover like we'd felt before Daniel come back into our life. Annie would get to brooding now and again, and sometimes she could be a mite testy. I figured she was troubling over my brother, and done my best to be understanding about it. I knowed things had to be hard on her, Daniel coming back from the dead the way he done. After all, she had loved him, had planned on marrying him when the war was over. The way I seen it, a body couldn't just snuff out feelings like a candle wick. It would take some time, was all. Time would set things right. Least I hoped it would.

Then one evening after supper, not long after the first frost, Daniel come in from the barn. Told me we needed to have ourself a little talk. We walked back out to the barn. I took a seat on the workbench while my brother fetched his jug. We sat there drinking and jawing about this and that and whatever till weren't neither of us feeling much pain.

After a spell, Daniel looked at me real serious-like, said, "I want Daddy's cabin and them south acres deeded to me. And one-third of the stock. You and the twins can have the big house and the rest of the farm to work out however you see fit."

Well, sonny, that took me back a mite. That was a mighty fine house and more'n four hundred acres he was giving up claim to. Always figured we'd find a way to split it up even between the two of us when the time come, the way our daddy had talked about. Uncle Nate had his cabin and twenty acres. Ruth and Naomi was bound to marry-up sooner or later and make their own way with their husbands, the way sister Sara had done.

It didn't sit fair with me, so I shook my head. "That ain't right. You worked this farm all your life. It's rightly half yours, you know how Daddy used to say such."

Daniel lifted the jug and took a swig. Wiped his mouth with

his sleeve and handed me the jug. "I got no use for it no more. The cabin is plenty big enough for me, and I aim to work that bottomland. We got a deal or not?"

The wind gusted and blowed open the barn door we'd left ajar. I looked towards the house, seen Annie and my sisters bustling about in the kitchen. My brother had lost his beloved to me, now he was giving up claim to most of the farm he'd been born and raised on. The firstborn, giving up his birthright. But if that was what he wanted, I was game. I held out my hand, said, "Deal."

Daniel stared at my hand, then reached past it and took the jug out of my other. "Deal," he said, and lifted the jug.

Malburn Brothers
1867

THIRTY ★ FIVE

WELL, SIR, IT WEREN'T LONG after the war before the Yankees had took over ever state government in the South. They done this by giving the freed nigras the right to vote, and taking away the vote from them that had fought for the Confederacy, leastways for a spell. The Yankees sent troops to oversee the elections, making sure the nigras voted the proper way, which meant the state governments would all have a Republican majority to see that business was done the way the bigwig politicians up in Washington wanted.

In towns of proper size, Marianna being the closest, government officials set up what was called the Freedmen's Bureau, and the Union League. Their purpose was to look out for the rights of newly freed nigras and carpetbaggers that come south to leech off what was properly ours. The Yanks had finally whipped us, but that weren't enough for the goldamn North. They aimed to make us suffer and pay till ever drop of blood was squeezed out of the Southern turnip, gospel truth.

Eli come riding up to my cabin one evening in April. I'd done ate supper and was sitting on the porch smoking my pipe and watching the sun paint the evening sky red. He dropped the reins and waved a paper at me whilst running up the steps.

"You seen this?" He looked madder than a cornered rattler. "Them scoundrels up in Tallahassee's wanting three hundred dollars in taxes!"

Course I hadn't seen the tax bill yet. Eli had just picked it up from the post office in Bennet that very afternoon. We hadn't yet gone through all the formalities of deeding the cabin and south section to me, so there weren't no separate notice for my place.

He handed me the tax notice and I give it a good looking over. It was for two hundred, ninety-four dollars and sixty-five cents to be exact, to be paid in full by June thirty, eighteen sixty-seven, or "... *said property shall be subject to foreclosure and seizure by state authorities, Department of Marianna, Jackson County, Florida.*"

"You got that much money?" I says, handing the bill back to Eli and reaching for my jug.

"Maybe I do, maybe I don't, but that ain't the dern point! That's more'n twice what they took last year. Last I looked, this farm ain't growed none."

I handed Eli the jug and he took a swig. "Now don't go getting a burr in your breeches. What you figure my share to be? Seventy, eighty dollars?"

Eli sat down on the top step and leaned back agin the porch rail. He thought about it for a spell. "Reckon that's fair. But I don't cotton to paying them thieves a dime. It ain't right, but they got us by the short hairs."

A owl hooted from the woods near the creek. I drawed on my pipe, blowed the smoke and watched it drift downwind. "I don't see where we got much choice about it. Yerb's going to lose his place."

Eli took another drink. "Reckon that's so."

Coleman Watts had took ill over the winter and died. Lung

fever, old Doc Haygood said. Truth be told, Mister Watts had worked hisself to death trying to build a cabin and barn and keep up with all the farmwork. With his slaves gone and Yerb being crippled up, it had proved too much for him. Yerby couldn't run a farm that size by hisself, and there weren't no money to hire help. Times was tough all over the valley. Me and Eli had offered to help out what we could, but Yerb was too goldamn proud or stubborn to take us up on it. The Watts' place was roughly the same acreage as ours, and there weren't no way for Yerb to survive. Come summer, the Yankees would run him off and sell the place to carpetbaggers or uppity Union League nigras or other trash.

———————•———————

I didn't want to burden Annie with worrying about the taxes we would have to pay come June. She had plenty enough to fret over, what with the baby coming and all. Seems Annie and Mama and the twins was forever sewing or knitting or some such these days. Tom and Sara's new baby, a boy they named William James after our daddies, had come in February. Now ours was on the way, due sometime late summer.

Daniel took the news of the tax bill better'n I thought he would. Seems I was a heap more upset about it than he was. Course, when I give it some thought, I reckon my brother had seen and suffered things that made taxes seem not all that bothersome.

That night after supper I fished the ledger from Daddy's desk drawer and went to ciphering. I was near to falling asleep at the desk before I finished with all them numbers and went upstairs to bed. I eased under the covers quiet as I could. Annie give a little groan and snuggled her backside next to me. I put my arm around her, felt the swell of her belly agin my hand.

A cool breeze drifted in through the window. Outside, the near-full moon painted the ground like frost. Crickets was chirping, and a pair of whippoorwills went to calling back and forth. Laying there beside Annie, the problems of running the farm seemed a thousand miles away, that's a fact. We weren't rich, but there was money enough to pay them ungodly taxes and see us through to harvest. If Daniel come up with his share, so much the better. The spring crops was in and faring well. The cow herd was growing, and the pigs was rolling fat. If things held, we ought to make out just fine.

Of a sudden a gunshot split the night calm, then right quick come two more. Annie give a little shudder, but didn't wake up. Yerby Watts, drunk and raising cain, I figured, from the direction they sounded. After a spell the crickets started up again, and I drifted off to sleep.

THIRTY ★ SIX

A FEW DAYS LATER I was out in the cornfield checking the crop when my sister Naomi come calling for me. "The sheriff wants to talk to you," she said, brushing back a strand of hair that had blowed in her eyes. "He's got some soldier man with him."

Well, sonny, that set my skin to crawling. Right then and there I figured the army had somehow caught up with me for deserting. Wondered who might've sold me out. Yerby Watts come to mind as I followed Naomi back to the house. I give the barn a quick look when we walked by. Thought about saddling my horse and hightailing it for the woods. I sure didn't cotton spending time in some Yankee prison, or getting shot or hung. But I couldn't leave Annie and my family, not when times was hard and promising to get worse. Figured I'd best face up to what was coming.

When I got to the house I found my mama jawing with Pete Abbott, sheriff of Washington County, and some Yankee major. I was a mite relieved that I didn't recognize the officer as being from the Second Florida Cavalry, but figured I weren't out of hot water yet. They was all sitting in the shade of the porch, drinking coffee and carrying on like old friends when I walked up.

When he seen me, the major stood up, all proper like. Sheriff Abbott and my mama kept their seats. Pete Abbott was a big man, near as round as he was tall. He'd been too old to go off to the war, but had served in the home guard a spell. He'd been sheriff since I was knee-high to a cypress knee. "Good day to you, Eli," he said.

I nodded, trying not to look edgy.

"This here is Major Simpson," Sheriff Abbott said, tilting his balding gray head towards the major, "provost marshal with the Freedmen's Bureau, over in Marianna."

"That so?" I turned and nodded to the major. "Major."

My mama made a fuss about leaving us men to our business and pardoned herself. I took a seat on the porch rail. Major Simpson kept to his feet. "What's this about?" I said to Sheriff Abbott. "If it's taxes, they ain't due yet." I knowed it was one of the sheriff's unpleasanter duties to kick folks off their place when the taxes weren't paid.

The sheriff give a little laugh. "No, no," he said, fanning hisself with his hat. "It seems one of the major's associates has up and gone missing, but I'll let him tell you about it."

The major was a short, wiry man with a thin moustache and a sneer that seemed to be stuck fast. His dark hair was graying a mite on the sides. I took him to be forty or so. He stood with his hands behind his back, looking hard at me. "Mister Malburn, are you familiar with Mister Rupert Holden?"

I knowed the scoundrel all right, knowed him for the thieving snake he was. Knowed he worked with the Freedmen's Bureau somehow, buying up property with Yankee money from poor folks who couldn't pay their taxes. But I kept my poker face. "Holden? Believe I've heard the name. Say, ain't he the feller who bought the Widow Tuller's place a spell back?" Poor old

Widow Tuller had lost her farm last year when she couldn't scrape up the money to pay the blood tax.

"One and the same," Sheriff Abbott said. "You seen him about lately?"

"Hmm. I seen him in town a couple of weeks ago, best I remember. Hutchins' store, I believe it was."

Major Simpson went to pacing, his heels clacking a steady beat across the porch floor. "Have you seen or heard of any disturbances in the last few days. Gunfire, for instance?"

I shook my head. "Cain't say as I have, Major."

"I see." The major looked at me like I was lying, which I was, but he couldn't of knowed it. "Do you know of anyone who might have wished Mister Holden harm?"

I near busted out laughing when I heard that. Near everbody in this valley, I wanted to say, but held my tongue. "No, sir. Why, what did this feller do?"

The major didn't answer, just grabbed his hat off the arm of the rocker and put it on. "That will be all," he said, huffing past me and tromping off the porch to his horse. "Sheriff!"

Old Sheriff Abbott struggled to his feet, said, "You let me know if you hear anything, you hear?" and give me a wink.

———◆———

When I told Yerb I'd ride with him that night, I never figured it to turn out the way it done. "We rob the son-of-a-bitch, give him a good thrashing as a warning, then turn him a-loose," Yerb told me before we set out from his cabin.

I cain't say that Rupert Holden didn't deserve it. That goldamn carpetbagger was in cahoots up to his ears with the Yankees and their Freedmen's Bureau. He had took the Widow Tuller's place several months back, turned her out with nothing but the clothes on her back, then sold her farm and everthing she owned on this earth to a family of uppity nigras from over Jackson County way. Now, word was Holden had his eyes on

Ben Hayes' farm over on Williford Road south of Yerb's place. Mister Hayes' boy Earl had died fighting with me at Missionary Ridge. Be damned if I'd let that happen to Earl's family.

Me and Yerb was both nearbout shitfaced by the time we rode north up Williford Road. The moon was full, so we made sure to keep well back in the woods by the bridge where we planned to wait for Holden. Yerb had learnt earlier in the week that Holden would be traveling back to Bennet after checking out the Hayes' place and other farms down Williford he aimed to steal come tax time. Yerb's own place was on the list.

It was a mite chilly that night. We hunkered down under blankets and shared the bottle I'd packed in my saddlebag whilst we waited. Two or three hours passed. I figured Holden weren't going to show, told Yerb that maybe he'd crossed the creek somewheres south and was taking the Econfina Road back to Bennet. I handed Yerb the bottle, said I was going to get a little shut-eye, and commenced to doze off.

Seemed like I'd just got to sleep when Yerb elbowed me in the ribs. "Mount up," he says real quiet, "he's coming."

The moon was high overhead and it was nearbout bright as day. Looked like frost was covering the ground, but it weren't that cold. Down the road I seen a rider coming at a trot. When he got closer I recognized the long frock coat and top hat that Holden wore when he was out doing business. He was alone.

I slipped the hood Yerb had give me over my head, put my hat back on. When Holden was some thirty yards away, Yerb kneed his horse and trotted out onto the road ahead of him. I kept to the edge of the woods, eased my horse a piece south and come out onto the road behind Holden. Yerb had his pistol drawed. I felt for mine, but kept it tucked inside my belt. It was the same Colt's I'd took off that dead Yankee officer at Chickamauga. Joe Porter give it back to me not long after I come home.

Holden reined in his horse when he seen Yerb pointing that pistol his way. "What's the meaning of this?" he says in a high and haughty voice.

"I'll take that money belt you wearing, is what," says Yerb, his voice muffled a mite underneath the hood.

Holden turned, seen me blocking the road behind him. "Now see here, sir," he says, turning back to face Yerb. "I am on official government business. If you don't stand aside I'll have no recourse other than to report this to the provost marshal in Marianna."

Yerb's horse shied at some moving shadow or such. He yanked the reins tight to calm him. "And if you don't hand over that belt I'll have no recourse other than to blow your brains out."

Yerb had tried to keep his good leg towards Holden, but when his horse shied I reckon Holden caught sight of his wooden one.

"Why, I know who you are, young man." He eased a hand towards his belt. "That hood may hide your face, but it can't hide your—"

Them was the last words Rupert Holden ever uttered this side of Hell. Yerb's bullet caught him square betwixt the eyes. That carpetbagger was dead before he ever hit the cold hard ground, but Yerb put two more in Holden's chest for good measure.

THIRTY ★ SEVEN

I KNOWED SOMETHING WAS UP when I rode over to Daniel's cabin that night after supper to let him know the law had come snooping around. There was three horses tied loose to the bushes beside the cabin. Even in the poor light I recognized Yerby Watts' big black stallion. Weren't no telling who the others belonged to. Figured I'd best play it safe, so I sat my horse and hallooed the cabin.

The door creaked open. Daniel stood like a shadow in the doorway staring out at me, pistol in hand. Behind him a couple of fellers was sitting around the table but I couldn't make 'em out. "That you, Eli?"

"Course it is. We need to talk."

Daniel waved me inside, then shut the door. I tied my horse to the rail, walked across the porch and opened the door. Right off I recognized Luke, the mean-eyed home guard with the hawk nose who was riding with Yerb the morning me and Jeff come home. He was sitting between Yerb and some skinny young redheaded feller I ain't seen before.

Daniel was standing by the cookstove, fetching a cup from the shelf. "You weren't born in no barn," he said, "shut that door."

I closed the door and give a nod to them sitting at the table. Weren't a one of 'em looked the least bit neighborly.

Daniel tossed me the cup and pointed to the jug sitting on the table. "You wanting to talk, pull up that chair." He sat down next to Yerby. "You know Yerb. This here is Luke Long and his brother Matthew, from over Calhoun County."

"We met," I said, giving Luke a quick look. "Howdy," I said to his brother, who mumbled something back I didn't catch.

Well, sonny, the air inside that cabin was so thick you could've cut it with a knife. Yerby Watts was his usual surly self. Luke Long looked friendly as a coiled cottonmouth, and his brother weren't exactly the sociable sort. I was near afraid to breathe wrong, lest I set one of 'em off.

I poured myself a drink. "Pete Abbott come by the house today. Had some Yankee major from Marianna with him. Simpson, I think his name was."

Daniel give Yerb a quick look. "What was their business?"

I took a swig, felt the whiskey burn down my throat. "They was asking about some Holden feller, had I seen him and such. Seems he's gone missing."

Yerb grabbed the jug, poured hisself another drink. He leaned forward and locked eyes with me. "And just what did you tell 'em?"

I took another sip, let it slide down my gullet. "Told 'em the truth, Yerb. Said I seen Holden at the general store a couple of weeks back, and I ain't seen him since."

Things got real quiet inside that cabin, so quiet you could've heard a mouse run across the floor if one chanced to do such. I took another drink, heard a owl calling in the distance.

After a minute Daniel set his cup down on the table. "What else?"

"That major wanted to know if I'd seen or heard anything out of the ordinary hereabouts. Like gunfire or such."

Ever eyeball in the cabin was burning a hole in me.

"Or if I knowed anybody that might wish Mister Holden harm."

Yerb near come out of his chair.

I held up a hand, said, "Course, I told him I ain't seen or heard a thing."

I turned to my brother. "Sheriff Abbott seemed fine with things, but I ain't so sure about that major. He might aim to do more snooping. Figured I'd best let you boys know."

———•———

"Lord A'mighty, Danny, that sounds awful risky," says Joe Porter. "Besides, what business is it of ours? That's Jackson County."

"There you go, taking God's name in vain again," I says, "and you, a man of the cloth." Joe had been preaching for over a year now, but still hadn't shook off using the Lord's name a mite loose now and again. I give him what-for about it ever chance I got.

It was a hot muggy night in late June. Me, Joe and Goose Hutchins was sitting on the porch of my cabin, sharing a jug and having a informal meeting of the Econfina Regulators. Young Men's Democratic Club of Washington County was our official name, but that was more'n a mouthful.

The Union League and Freedmen's Bureau was planning a big Fourth of July jubilation in Marianna. Highfalutin Yankee politicians and other government officials would be strutting and crowing like a flock of barnyard roosters, stirring up the Unionists and carpetbaggers and freed slaves to no good. We aimed to make a little show ourselves, give them carpetbaggers and uppity nigras a thing or two to chaw on.

"I know it's Jackson County," I says, slapping at a skeeter biting my neck, "but what's happening in Marianna is bound to spill over here. Hell, it already has. You ain't forgot about Rupert Holden, have you? There's more like him coming."

"My pa says some carpetbagger done paid the taxes on Ben Hayes' farm," says Goose Hutchins. He spit, pushed the wad of tobacco to his other cheek and took a drink. "Pa says he aims to sharecrop it out to a bunch of niggers from Jackson."

"Wiley Ferguson sold out too," I says. "Yerb seen him last week down at Ard's Ferry. Said there weren't no way he could keep up the farm, what with both his boys lost in the war." The Ferguson boys had been captured at Missionary Ridge. Word was both took sick and died at Camp Douglas up in Chicago.

"Some goddamn Yankee officer come in the store the other day," Goose says, refilling his cup from the jug, "tells Pa he's requisitioning cornmeal and flour for the colored troops in Marianna. When they was done loading their wagon, weren't fifty pounds of either left. All Pa's got to show for it is some paper with that Yankee's name scrawled on it."

I finished filling my pipe and commenced to light it. "It ain't all going to the troops, truth be told," I says, betwixt puffs. "Luke Long says the same is happening over in Calhoun. The Yanks is robbing the stores for the Freedmen's Bureau and giving it to all them nigras they got on their hands. It's a goldamn shame. The bluebelly bastards went and freed the slaves, and now they cain't fend for theirselves."

"Hell yeah," says Goose. "The way I see it, it's just a matter of time before they start taking what they want straight from the farmers. Even if a feller's got money for taxes, he cain't eat it."

Joe scratched his head, thought it over a spell. "That's a fact. Okay boys, count me in, Lord willing."

"Good," I says. "I'll tell Yerb to get word to Luke and his boys. We ride for Marianna, night of the third."

———◆———

I was walking the woods along the creek, checking on the

cattle, when I seen my brother and Yerby Watts riding on the far side of Daniel's cornfield, headed for the road. Figured right off they couldn't be up to no good. Weren't the first time I'd seen them two riding off near dark.

I was a mite worried about Daniel. Ever since he'd took up at that cabin of his, seemed he was always rubbing elbows with a jug of whiskey or Yerb or both. I'd sooner trust a cornered diamondback than Yerby. He was bad news, had been ever since he come back from the war. I hated that him and Daniel was like body and shadow of late.

It didn't take a heap of brains to figure out Yerb and Daniel was likely neck-deep in that carpetbagger Holden disappearing the way he done. How else could Yerb have raised the money to pay his taxes? I didn't believe for a second him telling folks it was money his daddy had buried when the Yanks come raiding back in the spring of 'sixty-four. Course, I held my tongue about it. Didn't wish Yerb no harm, and I sure didn't want my brother caught up in a murder or such.

Now, I didn't give a tinker's damn for none of them two-faced carpetbaggers, sonny. Highfalutin Yankees coming south, buying up poor folks' land for taxes they couldn't pay, then sharecropping the land to freed nigras weren't one bit different than slavery, way I seen it. Fact is, it was worse. Ever slave holder I knowed seen to it their people was took good care of and treated proper. But them poor nigra sharecroppers was left to fend for theirselves, barely scratching up enough to eat. It was dern shameful what the Yankees done to them people.

I watched Daniel and Yerb till they was out of sight, then headed back towards the house. Just as I come out of the woods, Ruth come busting out the end of our cornfield.

"Eli!" she hollered. "Eli, come quick—it's Annie!"

THIRTY ★ EIGHT

JOE, GOOSE, AND THE OTHER boys was waiting at the Moccasin Creek bridge north of the mill when me and Yerb rode up. Amongst 'em was a handful of pards that had served in Company K.

Jed Hicks come armed with the Spencer repeating rifle he took off a dead Yank the first day at Chickamauga. Jed's twin brother Jeremiah had lost a leg in the fight on Missionary Ridge and died later of gangrene poison.

The Miller boys was ready to ride, too. Jim's left arm dangled useless from a ball he caught in the shoulder at Franklin. Gil come through the war without so much as a scratch. When the Army of Tennessee was surrendered up in North Carolina, he'd made the long journey home with Joe and Goose.

Bobby Yon was antsy for the chance to ride with us agin the Yankees. His younger brother Billy had died in the trenches at Resaca. Bobby's club foot had kept him out of the war, but he could sit a horse and pull a trigger good as the next man.

There was a dozen or so of us regulators in all, but time has took its toll and I cain't recollect the others. We had a long ride ahead of us, some thirty miles, so we struck out for Marianna right away. Not wanting to wind the horses, Yerb set a easy pace. There weren't no moon to speak of, but the road was good and there was stars aplenty to guide our way. We stopped a few times to rest and water our mounts, but still made Marianna before sunrise. We holed up in a grove of oaks off the road a couple of miles west of town to get some sleep and wait for the festivities.

Luke Long and his band of regulators from Calhoun County rode north from Abe's Spring that same night and camped southeast of Marianna. The Federals had confiscated a couple of big plantations east of town. Carpetbaggers bought 'em at the tax auction, then let the land to sharecroppers. One of the places had belonged to Luke's uncle. Luke and his boys planned to burn the northern bloodsuckers out.

"Eye for a eye, tooth for a tooth," is how Luke put it when we was planning the raid. "Them Yankee bastards took from mine, now I aim to make 'em pay."

The Calhoun boys would strike the plantations at two o'clock on the fourth, whilst the parade and other festivities in town was commencing. The ruckus they raised would draw most of the Yankee troops out of town.

Then us Econfina boys would hit fast and hard from the west. Our targets was the Union League and Freedmen's Bureau headquarters, both located downtown on Lafayette Street. If things worked out the way we planned, the golddamn Yankees would have theirselves a Fourth of July they weren't soon to forget.

We ate a cold breakfast, then passed the morning playing cards or resting in the shade. Towards noon Bobby Yon and Gil Miller rode into Marianna. Them two was to keep their eyes peeled on things in town, make sure the Yanks cooperated once Luke's boys struck the plantations east of town. If they smelled a skunk, Gil would ride hard to warn us. Otherwise, the rest of us would hit town ten minutes after the shooting started.

By two o'clock we was spread out just west of town, keeping hid best we could in twos or threes. In town a band had struck up a lively tune, but a steady south wind was blowing and I couldn't make it out. Of a sudden distant gunfire commenced to the east. Them Calhoun boys was right on time!

"Hoods on, boys," Yerb hollers, "let's ride!"

I swung into the saddle, checked to see my Colt's was fast inside my belt, then kneed my horse to a trot. A minute later we hit Lafayette Street at full gallop and charged into town.

We rode hard in two columns, raising Hell and dust down both sides of the road. The crowd commenced scattering like a passel of cottontails with hounds snapping at their hind parts. A couple of the boys fired their pistols in the air and cut loose with the Rebel Yell. The rest of us took it up, screaming for all we was worth, hoping to put the fear of God in what colored troops was left behind to guard the town.

East of town black smoke was rising and drifting north. Luke's boys was making a good show of things. Down Lafayette some colored troops fired off a few wild shots, then turned tail and skedaddled. Jed Hicks raised a racket with his Spencer, making sure them Yanks was retreating proper. I pulled my Colt's and cut loose a couple of high shots to help keep 'em on the run whilst me and Joe headed for the Union League headquarters. Yerb and the Millers was seeing to the Freedmen's Bureau at the far end of town.

We found the place and pulled up in front. Joe stood guard whilst I swung down from the saddle and grabbed the bottle of coal oil out of my saddle bag. I pulled my Colt's and tried the door. It was locked. The place looked deserted but I weren't taking no chances. I kicked in the door, pistol cocked and ready.

Weren't nobody home, which was jim-dandy by me. I poured coal oil over what files and stacks of papers and ledgers was handy, then struck a match and set it afire. When things was burning good I run outside, grabbed the reins from Joe and we skedaddled back down Lafayette Street. The raid had took no more'n fifteen minutes, start to finish.

"Whoowee, Joe Porter!" I says when we was safe out of town and heading for the oak grove where we was to meet back up. "I ain't had that much fun in a coon's age!"

———◦———

Jed Hicks was standing guard a couple of hundred yards from the grove, his repeating rifle at the ready in case some brave souls was fool enough to follow us. He was still wearing his hood.

"Y'all the last in, 'cept for Yerb and the Millers," he says. "Let me know soon as they show up." After sacking the Freedmen's Bureau, Yerb and the Miller brothers had took the south road out of town instead of backtracking down Lafayette.

"Anybody hurt?" I says.

Jed give a laugh. "Only them damn Yankees' pride."

Ten minutes later Yerby and the Miller brothers come riding into the grove. Right off I knowed something was up. Yerb and Gil Miller was cussing each other for all they was worth. Then they dismounted and commenced scuffling.

I sent Bobby Yon to fetch Jed, then hurried over to see what had Yerb and Gil so riled.

"There's a whole heap of Yankees east of town if you two peckerwoods is antsy to fight," I says, pushing my way betwixt 'em, "but right now we best be making tracks out of here."

Gil backed off and picked up his hat, dusted it off agin his breeches and put it on. His face was flushed beet red underneath all them freckles. "He kilt two niggers, kilt 'em in cold blood!"

Even with his wooden leg it was a struggle to hold Yerb back. I hollered at him to get a-hold of hisself. After a spell he calmed down a mite.

"I shot two goddamn Yankees, is what I done," says Yerb.

"Two Yankees that needed killing."

"One weren't even armed," Gil says, pointing a finger at Yerb. "He was sitting behind that desk when you shot him down."

"I told him to get his hands up. Ain't my fault the bastard didn't listen."

Well, sir, I finally got 'em both cooled down enough to where we could ride. I sent the Millers and the other boys off ahead of me, Joe and Yerb. Figured we'd guard the rear and keep them two hotheads from each other's throat a spell till this kettle of fish simmered down.

We give the others maybe five minutes, then mounted up and rode hard. Kept a sharp eye behind us the first few miles, but there weren't no sign of trouble following.

Trouble was bound to come calling sooner or later though. Yerb had shot dead two of their own right in the middle of town. The Federals weren't likely to take that lightly. And there weren't no telling what all grief Luke's boys had caused east of town.

"We looked for peace, but no good came," says the Good Book, *"and for a time of health, and behold trouble!"*

Well, sir, it was coming all right, I could feel it in my bones.

THIRTY ★ NINE

THE BABY COME IN A rush, and there weren't no saving it. Weren't no saving *him*, reckon I ought to say, being it was a boy. Aunt Nettie and Mama done their best, but it was born near three months early. Poor Annie was bleeding like a stuck pig. It was all they could do to save her. Uncle Nate went to fetch Doctor Haygood right away, but by the time they got back, there weren't nothing much Doc could do that Aunt Nettie and Mama hadn't already done.

This all happened on a Wednesday evening. We buried the baby that Friday. July fifth, it was. Being the middle of summer, we would've buried him on Thursday, but Daniel hadn't yet come home from wherever him and Yerby had rode off to. Mama insisted we wait for him, said it wouldn't be proper not to. First thing Friday morning I rode over to Daniel's cabin and told him about the baby and the burial. Told him I'd be much obliged if he could find the time to be there.

Aunt Nettie seen the body was took care of proper. Uncle Nate and Jeff built a fine casket out of cypress planks which they sanded real smooth. Them two also served as pallbearers with me and Daniel. Joe Porter showed up to do the preaching and such. Doc Haygood had ordered Annie to stay in bed for a week, so we moved the bed to where she could watch from our bedroom window.

We laid little Adam to rest that afternoon under a clabbered sky. Annie picked out the name. It was fitting to call him Adam, she said, being he was our firstborn. Said it weren't proper for him to be buried without a name, so Adam it was.

Well, sonny, I ain't ashamed to say I shed a few tears that day. Reckon near everbody done their share of crying. All the Gainers was there, and the Porters, Doc Haygood and his missus. Cain't recollect who all else, but I do remember that Yerby Watts weren't.

Joe Porter give a little prayer and spouted some words, then opened his bible and went to reading from Psalm One hundred and three. Of a sudden from the big magnolia nearby, a mockingbird cut loose with the sweetest warbling song a soul ever heard. Sounded like a angel from Heaven itself. I took that as a good sign, and found some comfort in the words Joe read:

"Like as a father pitieth his children, so the LORD pitieth them that fear him. For he knoweth our frame; he remembereth that we are dust. As for man, his days are as grass; as a flower of the field, so he flourisheth. For the wind passeth over it, and it is gone; and the place thereof shall know it no more. But the mercy of the LORD is from everlasting to everlasting upon them that fear him, and his righteousness unto children's children..."

When Joe was done preaching and praying, Jeff sung one of them fine spirituals him and Nebo used to sing. Then we lowered little Adam into the ground, not far from his granddaddy.

I weren't home more'n a good hour or so when somebody commenced knocking on the door. The sun was barely up. I rolled off the bunk and put my breeches on, then opened the door. Soon as I seen Eli's face I knowed something was wrong.

"Annie had the baby," he says before I could ask. "It died. Mama wants you at the burying this afternoon if you can make it." Then he walked back to his horse and rode off without another word.

Well, sir, I was stunned. First thing that come to mind was Annie. Felt like hurrying over to the house to see how she was faring, but decided I'd best not. I still loved her, but it weren't none of my affair now. Figured she must be all right, else Eli would've said so.

I boiled up some coffee, poured a goodly shot of whiskey in the cup and sat out on the porch to gather my wits. I had my good suit to wear, but I'd need a bath and a shave after all that riding we done the past two days. I was nearbout played out, but figured I'd ride over and tell Joe. He'd done their wedding, figured they'd want him to see to the burying. I'd best leave Yerb be. He was blind drunk when we got home anyways.

I could've saved myself the trip out to the Porters. Jefferson had showed up at the mill the day before and left word with his folks about the baby, and requesting Joe's help. I rode back home and commenced getting ready for the burial.

Well, sir, it was a sad affair, gospel. Must've been thirty or forty people gathered and there weren't a dry eye amongst 'em. Poor little soul, gone before he even had a chance to live. Least he didn't suffer none. Lord knows I'd seen a heap of that the last few years.

Right off I noticed Annie weren't there. When Eli weren't looking, I asked Mama about it. She told me the doc ordered her to bed, and they had moved the bed over to the window so she could watch. Nearbout broke my heart thinking about Annie laying up there by herself, looking on whilst we laid her poor dead baby to rest. Course Annie weren't exactly alone. Aunt Nettie was there to see to her needs and such. I was glad for that.

Joe preached a right fine service, read from one of the Psalms, as I recollect. I tried not to think of what us two had been up to just yesterday. Weren't sure how Joe managed to hold a pistol in one hand and the Good Book in the other. Figured that was betwixt him and God.

Ever now and again I'd sneak a look up at the window, hoping to catch sight of Annie. Done just that a time or two. Poor Annie's sad, sweet face looking out that window stirred me. Made me want to run up there, hold her tight and comfort her. That shamed me, truth be told. Felt like I was intruding on her privacy when it weren't none of my business doing so.

When the burying was done we had a big dinner outside back of the house. Times was hard, but nearbout everbody had brung a covered dish and them tables was heaped with food. I jawed with folks a spell, then fixed myself a plate and looked for Joe. We found ourselves a shady spot and sat down to eat.

"You done a fine job preaching," I says, "I'm obliged to you. I know Eli and Annie appreciate it."

Joe nodded, finished chewing a bite of ham. "It's a sad thing, but the Lord will see 'em through it. Cain't say the same for Yerb."

I put down my fork and stared into Joe's eyes. "What you getting at?"

"That business yesterday is what," says Joe, looking around. "The killing. Lord A'mighty, Danny, I think he enjoys it."

I shook my head. "That ain't so. Yerb said he had to do it, or the feller was going to—"

"Do what?" says Joe. "Do like them poor souls he butchered that night at Chickymauga after Hamp got kilt? Was them fellers fixing to shoot Yerb too?"

I stared down at the ground, knowing Joe was right but not wanting to believe it. I watched a ant toting something twice his size through the grass, struggling with his burden like I was struggling with mine.

"You seen that poor feller's throat well as I did. You heard them others crying out too, same as me."

I lifted my head, stared across the yard at nothing in particular. "I know it, but I figured he was shed of all that."

"Well, you figured wrong," says Joe, forking up some butterbeans. "Weren't nobody supposed to get hurt yesterday, you know that as well as me. I'm done with it. I'm done riding with Yerb."

"I'm sorry to hear it," I says. "But I reckon you got your reasons, your calling and all."

Joe swallowed the beans. "It ain't that. I reckon riding agin them carpetbaggers is ever bit as noble as the cause we was fighting for. It's Yerb. He's gone bad, like a chicken-killing cur. He's full-up with evil. You best steer clear of him, Danny boy, else he'll bring you down too."

FORTY

ONE MORNING ABOUT TWO WEEKS after the burial, Sheriff Pete Abbott and that provost marshal, Major Simpson, come calling again. I walked out and joined 'em on the porch. The sheriff took off his hat and give his condolences for our recent loss, then got down to business.

"The major here has reason to believe that some of our local boys might have been party to some trouble they had up in Marianna on the fourth."

"Do tell," I said, "what trouble would that be?"

"Murder, and destruction of federal property," said Major Simpson, without a grain of politeness in his voice.

I looked at the major. "That so? I ain't heard nothing of it." Which was the truth, but right then and there it set me to thinking about my brother and Yerby Watts.

The good major strutted a mite closer, looked me hard in the eye. "Where were you that day, Mister Malburn?"

Pete Abbott's nostrils flared when he heard that. He quit fanning hisself with his hat, said, "Now see here, Major, I already told—"

I held up a hand. "It's okay, Sheriff, I'll answer his question."

I give Major Simpson the coldest stare I could muster. "I was right here, tending to my sick wife and getting ready to bury our dead baby."

The major looked more disappointed than sorry that he'd asked such a unseemly question. He looked away, mumbled, "Yes, well..."

The sheriff fished in his breeches pocket, pulled out a plug of tobacco and a jackknife. Cut hisself a hunk. "Witnesses says them boys was all wearing hoods, but one of 'em had a wood leg."

I knowed what the sheriff was poking at. Figured I'd best pepper Yerby's trail to throw the hounds off, seeing as how Daniel had been riding with him. "Reckon there's a passel of fellers short a leg since the war," I said, "but if you're talking about Yerby Watts you barking up the wrong tree, Sheriff. I seen him and Danny both that morning, down by the old cabin."

"That morning... do you mean July the Fourth?" the major said.

"Yep," I said, knowing it was a dern lie.

The major scratched his chin. "Can anyone else in your household vouch for your brother's whereabouts?"

I shook my head, turned to Pete Abbott. "Mama and Aunt Nettie and the twins was tending Annie. Uncle Nate and Jefferson was busy building the casket. I went to Danny's cabin around nine that morning to tell him what time the burying would be. That's when I seen him with Yerby."

We jawed a spell longer, the good major doing his best to poke holes in my story. Finally, he got his fill of me. Him and the sheriff mounted up and headed for Yerb's place. I waited a minute or two, then run out back to make sure they took the bridge to the Watts'. When I seen 'em disappear into the woods, I haltered one of the mules and hightailed it for the cabin. I figured Yerb would give them two the slip, if he was home. That ought to give me enough time to get word to Daniel before they showed up at his place. I had lied to the law for him and Yerb. That put me right slap in the stew pot with them and whatever tomfoolery they'd been up to. And if the sheriff and major seen me riding the mule to Daniel's? Why, I was just taking the mule to my brother so he could get to plowing the winter hayfield he planned on putting in.

———————

I was weeding a corn row when Eli come riding up on one of the plow mules. I hurried towards the cabin, hoping it weren't bad news about Annie. She was doing better, Mama had told me a couple of days ago, but still had a ways to go from feeling fit.

Eli was waiting for me in the shade of the porch. "What is it?" I says, when I got within earshot.

"Trouble. That Yankee major just left the house. Him and Pete Abbott's headed for Yerb's place. They'll most likely be coming here next."

I took off my hat, wiped the sweat off my face with my handkerchief. "What they wanting now?"

"Was you and Yerb in Marianna on the fourth?"

"It ain't none of your affair," I says, not wanting him tangled up in our mess.

Eli's jaw clenched tight as a snapping turtle's. "It is now, seeing how I just went and lied for you two."

"How so?" I says.

Eli looked towards the creek, checking for company, I figured. "I told 'em I seen you and Yerb here at the cabin Thursday morning. Said I come around nine to let you know when the burying would be. You best find Yerb quick and let him know. It won't do to have our stories contrary."

Eli left the mule and took to the woods along the creek. Said it wouldn't do for the law to see him cutting across the field from my place. I put the mule in the barn out back, then went inside the cabin to whet my whistle and get my thoughts together for when the sheriff come a-calling.

Grabbed my jug and a cup off the shelf and poured a snort. Kept thinking what my brother had said, how he was in this mess now. He hadn't done a goldamn thing, but me and Yerb had drug him into it anyways. Yerb still had it out for Eli, thought of him as the enemy in his own twisted way. Yet Eli had gone and lied to cover his hide. Reckon he'd done it mostly for me, truth be told, but Yerb owed him, all the same. And I aimed to tell him just that.

———◆———

Two days later Eli come riding towards the cabin again. I was sitting on the porch, tipping my jug and watching the sun sink below the trees along the creek. I went inside and fetched another cup. Eli was tying his horse to the rail when I come back out.

"Here," I says, handing him the cup. I didn't care at all for the look on his face.

He took the cup and sat in the rocker next to the door. Tilted back his head and swigged the whiskey down. He held out the cup for more. "You get word to Yerb?"

I shook my head whilst pouring him another drink. "Ain't seen him. He ain't been home."

Eli drained his cup again. "Figured as much," he says. He reached for the jug and poured till the cup was half-full. "I just come from town. We got real trouble."

Well, sir, my gut went cold like I'd swallowed a bucket of ice. With Yerb gone and Eli bearing troubling news from town, I figured something bad was up. "What is it?"

Eli took a big swig, coughed and wiped the dribble off his chin. "That Yankee major, Simpson? Somebody bushwacked him on the Marianna Road. Kilt him and two of his men."

FORTY ★ ONE

AFTER I HAD MY SAY, Daniel fessed up and told me how he'd been riding with Yerb and the other regulators in the valley. Said they only aimed to scare the sharecroppers from working the farms the carpetbaggers had stole for unpaid taxes. If the land couldn't be farmed proper, then the carpetbaggers might not be so quick to rob folks out of what was rightfully theirs.

But scaring folks weren't enough for Yerby. Daniel had been with him the night he waylaid that Holden feller.

"I thought Yerb only meant to rob him, but then Holden reached under his coat. That's when Yerb shot him."

They toted the body north along the creek and dumped it in a sinkhole. Wouldn't nobody ever find it, them sinkholes is so deep. Yerb give the horse and such to Luke Long over in Calhoun County.

The raid on Marianna had changed everthing. Gil Miller swore Yerby shot that one feller in the Freedmen's Bureau for no good cause. The other had gone for his rifle when he seen his friend shot down in cold blood. Joe Porter and the Miller boys and most of the others had flat-out quit the regulators after that. Only Jed Hicks had stuck by Yerb, best Daniel knowed. Neither of them had been around for a spell. Word was, they had joined up with Luke Long and his gang.

"You can bet the seed money Yerb was in on them killings," Daniel said after we'd finished off the jug and I was fixing to ride back to the house. "And you can bet the crops that I'm done riding with him."

<hr>

Well, sir, Eli weren't wrong when he said we had real trouble coming our way. The killing of that major and his two aides brung the bluebellies down on us like the plague of locusts on Egypt. The week weren't out before a squad of cavalry and a company of colored infantry was dispatched from Marianna to Bennet. Their mission was to... *restore order and complicity to the laws and statutes of the state of Florida and the government of the United States of America...* which is how the handbills they posted all over town put it.

A body could hardly go anywheres without running across a Yankee patrol. They commenced searching such homes or farms they took a mind to, Fourth Amendment be damned, and it weren't unheard of for them bluebellies to confiscate whatever caught their fancy. "Contraband, or items of unlawful or suspect nature," they called it. Weren't nothing of the kind. Didn't take folks long to start hiding what they didn't want stole by the Yanks.

People liked to have drove Sheriff Abbott plumb harebrained with all the complaints of person and property being violated by the Yankee occupiers. Weren't long before the whole valley was riled to boiling over. The sheriff talked to the Yankee commander, one Major Samuel Parnell, till he was blue in the face, but it done no good. Seems the Yanks was out to make us pay.

Then the Union League come to town, recruiting members

and generally stirring up trouble amongst the freed nigras in the valley. They took up shop in what had been Miz Eliza Harper's dry goods store before she was forced to give it up for unpaid taxes. Well, sir, it's been many a year since them days, but here's what the League business was as I recollect it.

Most was run by haughty northern politicians or southern Unionists. They come south and set up chapters all over the occupied states. They'd come to a new town and commence spouting all sorts of fancy nonsense to whatever nigras' ears they could turn.

"You all must band together, and stand together, against your former white oppressors," is how one such speech went. "And you must vote Republican to ensure that those who once ruled over you with an iron hand shall never have that opportunity again."

It went on to say that if the Republicans could maintain power, then one day the confiscation of all former Confederate properties would become a reality, and every man amongst them would receive forty acres and a mule, and other such nonsense.

Them Union League organizers commenced traveling all over Econfina, jawing with nearbout ever nigra that lived in the valley, filling their heads with their goldamn trash talk. Weren't long before it took root. Most the colored men in these parts commenced attending meetings and organizing theirselves into chapters. They even took to marching and drilling like a local militia, with talk of ever man amongst 'em someday being armed.

Worse of all, many of 'em took to disrespecting white folks, acting uppity to man and woman alike. And the soldiers was always nearby to take their side and back 'em up. Well, sir, that didn't sit well with folks, didn't sit well at all. I figured no good could come of it, and I figured right.

———◆———

Well, sonny, the Yankees didn't waste no time sending troops to Econfina after the killing of Major Simpson and his two men.

By the end of summer things had growed more'n a mite dicey around these parts. Seems the Yankee soldiers went out of their way to goad folks and make life miserable ever chance they got.

A short spell later, the Union League come to town, and it weren't long before a goodly number of nigras in the valley took to acting like they was better than white folks. Near ever week there was trouble of some sort between whites and nigras over some nonsense or the other. By fall the situation growed bad enough to where the local regulators went to riding again, mostly at night. Weren't sure if Daniel was amongst 'em, but I had my suspicions.

One chilly morning in mid-October I hitched the mules to the wagon and headed to Bennet for supplies. The Yankees had set up checkpoints at both ends of town to make sure folks weren't carrying guns or other weapons into town. I come to the checkpoint north of town and pulled the mule to a halt. It galled me to have them devils treating me like I was some lowlife outlaw. I gritted my teeth and held my tongue while the sentries went to searching me and the wagon. When they was satisfied I weren't armed and dangerous, I flicked the reins and drove on into town.

I done my business at Hutchins' store, then headed home. On the way out of town I'll be derned if them Yankees didn't stop me again. "What's this about?" I said to the sergeant in charge when he told me to halt. "You boys done checked me on the way in."

The sergeant was a ornery, bowlegged sort with a greasy beard and pocked cheeks. Way he acted reminded me a mite of that scoundrel, Sergeant Bullard. "Just keep your mouth shut and raise your hands," he told me.

While one of his men frisked me, the others went to rummaging through the sacks and boxes and whatnot in the wagon bed. One of the soldiers give a whistle, said, "Halloo, look what I found, Sergeant."

I turned to see what all the hoopla was about. The sergeant walked to the back of the wagon, reached down and picked up two burlap bags. Give me a sneer, said, "What have we got here?"

"Why Sergeant," I said, "I'd of figured a man of your high position would be able to read." I pointed to one of the bags. "That there is buckshot, the other one is powder."

Well, sonny, the good sergeant didn't take too kindly to that. His eyes narrowed-up and he turned near red as a beet, said, "I can damn well read, smartass. Now get off that wagon. You're under arrest!"

"What for?" I said, feeling my hackles rise. "Last I heard, talking ain't no crime."

Next thing I knowed I was staring down the muzzle of his pistol. "Step down off the wagon, and be easy about it."

I figured that revolver didn't much care one way or the other what was a crime and what weren't, so I done what the sergeant said. He kept that pistol on me while another feller jerked my arms behind my back and handcuffed me. Then the sergeant mounted his horse and herded me back into town like a stray bull.

I kept my mouth shut while we walked through town to the sheriff's office. Pete Abbott was sitting behind his desk drinking coffee and reading the Marianna newspaper when we walked through the door. His bushy eyebrows raised up when he seen who it was. He put down the paper, said, "What's this all about, Sergeant?"

The sergeant poked me in the back with his pistol. "This man was trying to smuggle ammunition out of town. He's to be held in your custody until the provost marshal can investigate the matter."

"I bought buckshot and powder at Hutchins' store," I told Sheriff Abbott. "Me and Danny aim to do some deer hunting shortly, or go hungry." Which was the truth. With taxes being high as they was, and most goods costing a arm and a leg since the war, near everbody done their best to store up venison for the winter. Pigs and cows and such was best sold to raise tax money.

"Regulators have been seen carrying shotguns, Sheriff," the sergeant said. "Major Simpson was killed by a shotgun blast."

Pete Abbott turned to me. "That's a fact, Eli. Now, I don't for a minute think you had anything to do with that or any other regulator business, but I'm afraid I'll have to hold you here until Major Parnell gets back from Marianna. The sergeant here has brought charges, and I'm bound by army regulations."

He slid open the desk drawer and pulled out a key ring. Walked over to the heavy wood door with bars over the window and unlocked it. "Take those cuffs off," he told the sergeant.

I walked into the cell, shaking the blood back into my fingers. The door shut behind me and I heard footsteps walking away. I looked through the bars, hollered, "Since when is it a crime to buy shot and powder for hunting? I never heard of such a dern fool thing."

Nobody answered. I heard the front door open. The sheriff and sergeant stood outside jawing a spell, but I couldn't make out what they was saying. Then the door shut and Pete Abbott come walking back towards the cell. "I'm sorry about this, Eli, but my hands are tied."

I grabbed the bars. "Look here, you know I ain't done nothing wrong. That feller took offense at something I said. He arrested me for back-talking him, is all."

Sheriff Abbott shrugged. "I figured as much. Still, I got my orders, and I'm obliged to do what the army tells me."

I looked the sheriff in the eye. "And I'd sooner burn in Hell."

———————

Pete Abbott took another drink of whiskey from his cup. "Major Parnell is due back tomorrow," he says. "According to that lieutenant he left in charge, he'll be bringing another squad of cavalry with him. You boys might want to lay low for a while."

It had been three days since Eli got arrested and locked

up. The sheriff had been down to Ard's Ferry on business and decided to stop by on his way back to Bennet to jaw a spell and pass on the latest news about the Yankees. I finished packing my pipe. "What about Eli? Think they'll turn him loose?"

Pete turned his head and spit a brown stream off the porch, wiped his mouth with the back of a hand. "They got to. I looked into it. There's no federal ordinance says a person can't buy or possess ammunition. That fool sergeant was just looking to cause trouble." Then Pete give a little laugh. "That is, unless that brother of yours decides to cuss out the major or cause some kind of ruckus at the hearing. I swear, Danny, he's every bit as hotheaded as your daddy could be at times."

"Gospel truth," I says. "When is the hearing? Figure I best be there, see that Eli gets home without pissing off any more Yankees."

Pete laughed again. "Reckon you should, at that. I expect it'll be a day or two after the major gets back. I'll send word as soon as I know."

After the sheriff left I rode over to the house to let the folks know that Eli was doing fine and would probably be home in a couple of days. Annie had nearbout worried herself sick over it, thinking they might send Eli off to prison. She'd be happy to hear what the sheriff had to say about the hearing.

I had my own reasons for wanting my brother back home as soon as possible. There was something I needed to tell him, something that I didn't want him fretting over whilst locked up in jail. Weren't nothing he could do about it inside that cell, so I hadn't told Eli when I'd gone to visit him the evening he got arrested.

There weren't no sugarcoating such news. Eli wouldn't be wanting to hear it, and I didn't fancy being the one to tell him. But he had to know that Jefferson had up and joined the Union League.

Malburn Brothers
1868

FORTY ★ TWO

WELL, SONNY, FOR THE LIFE of me I couldn't figure who or what finagled Jefferson into joining up with the Union League. I know he'd done a heap of growing up the last few years, us working at the salt camp, then all the soldiering we done. That had opened Jeff's eyes to a wider world other than the farm he'd always knowed, and give him a hankering to make his own way in life.

That weren't necessarily a bad thing. But all the hogwash them scoundrels at the Union League meetings kept filling his head with was. Weren't long till Jeff went to putting on airs and acting highfalutin around his folks and mine. Me and Uncle Nate talked to the boy till our jaws near fell off, but Jeff weren't having none of it. Seems the more we jawed at him, the more time he spent in town at them meetings with his new friends.

Real trouble broke out at election time in November of 'sixty-seven. The local Union League went to parading up and down the streets of Bennet, spouting all sorts of nonsense in support of the Republicans, harassing anybody that happened to speak their mind agin 'em. Many a time, jawing turned to brawling, and the Yankees was always johnny-on-the-spot taking up for the League. When election day come, Union League members lined the street near the polling station, some bearing arms. It pains me to say it, but Jeff was right there amongst 'em for everbody to see.

Come spring, Uncle Nate had a time getting Jeff to do his share of work around the farm. Jeff would take off and stay gone for two-three days at a time. Figured that couldn't be a good thing, and it weren't.

That spring the Union League formed up their own militia and took to bedeviling ex-Confederates and other folks all over the valley who they figured had caused them grief of some sort or the other. Well, sonny, the local regulators weren't about to let that go, so they dusted off their hoods and went to riding again, mostly at night, giving back whatever dose of trouble the League's militia dished out. Sad to say, it weren't long till blood was spilt on both sides.

When I learnt that Jeff was marching with the League's militia, I done my best to talk some sense into that thick skull of his, but it weren't no use. The way he seen it, the Union League was part of God's army, raised up to save his people and set things straight once and for all.

Then one night in early summer a wagon pulled up in front of Uncle Nate and Aunt Nettie's cabin. Laying in the wagon bed moaning in pain was their boy, shot through the right shoulder, the bones busted.

Turns out the militia had been over to the Wheeler farm, aiming to pay young Johnny Wheeler back for the thrashing he'd give one of their own outside of town a spell back. Johnny was home by hisself when them League boys jumped him. They tore the shirt off Johnny's back and was fixing to lash him with a whip when a regulator patrol come to the rescue. Gunfire broke out, and the militia hightailed it back towards town. That's when

Jeff caught a ball in the shoulder and went down. Gil Miller was riding with the regulators and recognized Jefferson right off. Knowing Jeff had once been our slave, he seen no more harm come to him. Then Gil borrowed the Wheeler's wagon and brung Jeff home to his folks.

Soon as Uncle Nate come running up with the news, I rode into town and fetched Doc Haygood. He give Jeff some ether to knock him out, then dug the pistol ball out of his shoulder blade and patched him up. Jeff would live, Doc said, but he weren't sure that arm would ever be good for much more than hanging a sleeve on.

Now, it might sound a mite unkind, cruel even, but fact is I weren't all that sorry it happened. Uncle Nate and Aunt Nettie had their boy back, and Jeff was alive and safe from further harm. Jeff was shed of the Union League and their high jinks for good.

Leastways that's what I figured, till the day in late August when Luke Long and his bunch of cutthroats come riding into the Econfina Valley, Yerby Watts amongst 'em.

FORTY ★ THREE

I'D JUST COME BACK TO the cabin from checking on my hogs when I heard riders coming. I grabbed my Colt's and my jug and stepped out onto the porch. There was two of 'em, riding out of the woods from the west. The sun had set and they was just shadows agin the trees, but when they got closer I seen it was Yerby Watts and Luke Long. It took me a minute to recognize Yerb. It had been several months since I'd last seen him. His hair had growed down to his shoulders. He'd lost some weight and growed a scraggly beard. But his eyes was as cold and hard as ever.

"Evening Yerb, Luke," I says, whilst they dismounted and commenced tying their horses to the hitching post. "Good to see you two's still amongst the living. But you best move them horses around back if you plan on staying that way."

Yerb give a grin. "Still looking out for your pards, just like during the war, huh, Danny?"

"There ain't no Yankee bullet what's got my name on it," says Luke, as him and Yerb led their mounts to the back of the cabin.

"We could use some of that whiskey," Yerb says, following me inside the cabin.

"Grab a cup and pull them chairs agin the wall. It's too goldamn hot to shut the door. What brings you two here?" I says, pouring whiskey all around.

"Things was getting a mite hot over in Calhoun and Jackson," says Luke. "Besides, from what we been hearing we figured you Washington County boys could use some help."

Well, sir, the last thing we needed was more trouble in the valley, and trouble followed them two like a shadow. "Just what is it you heard?" I says. "We doing just fine in these parts."

Yerb took a drink, leaned forward and rested his arms agin his thighs. "We got some business to see to," he says, ignoring my question.

I grabbed my pipe and pouch from the table. "What you got is trouble. There's wanted posters for you two posted all over the valley."

Luke laughed. "How much reward they offering? I'm a mite short in the pocket. Hell, I might just turn in ol' Yerb here if the Yanks make it worth my trouble."

I kept a straight face, didn't find it one bit funny. "Five hundred apiece, last I seen. You boys got yourselves quite a reputation. Best keep your eyes peeled. There's lots of folks hurting for money."

"Them goddamn posters is up all over West Florida," says Yerb. "Ain't nobody took 'em up on it yet."

I poured myself another drink and passed the jug to Yerb. "Sorry about your farm. I would've paid the taxes if I'd of had the money. Barely had enough to keep this place."

Yerb nodded as he filled his cup. "Who bought it?"

I finished packing my pipe, reached for a match. "Feller name of Robertson. Agent with the Bureau, if I ain't mistaken."

Then it struck me what business Yerb had been talking about. "Look here, don't go doing nothing foolish, Yerb. Your place ain't doing him no good. He don't live on it, and we done run off ever sharecropper he took on. Likely he'll be selling it before long. You get the money, I'll buy it and tend to things till all this trouble blows over."

Yerby grinned and took another drink. "Much obliged, but I ain't got no use for the place. Once my business is done here, I aim to move on. I hear tell Texas is right fine country."

"I wouldn't know," I says. Then I turned to Luke. "Where you fellers holding up?"

"Oh, the boys is scattered about, few here, few there."

I puffed on my pipe, nodded. "That's good. Best tell 'em to watch their back. There's two squads of Yankee cavalry patrolling the valley now, plus that company of colored infantry posted in Bennet. They liable to show up anywheres, day or night."

Luke reached for the jug. "You boys interested in riding with us? Together we could give them damn Yankees the fits."

I throwed back the rest of the whiskey in my cup and set it on the table. Looked at Luke, then Yerb. "I told you, it's been quiet around here for a spell," I says. "I'd like to keep it that way. We done run most of the carpetbaggers and their sharecroppers out of the valley. The Union League seems to be keeping their hands clean for a change. I'm hoping you boys will think twice before you go stirring up trouble."

For a minute nobody spoke. Then Yerb says, "And if we do?"

I locked eyes with Yerb. "What you do is your business, but my boys won't take kindly to having trouble dumped on 'em."

———•———

Well, sonny, after the ruckus at the Wheeler farm, things quieted down across the county. Seems both sides finally had a bellyful of trouble. By the time the dog days set in, it seemed peace had come to the Econfina Valley at last.

Jeff was healing up good as could be expected. Weren't long till he was up and about, doing what he could to help out around the farm. That arm of his weren't never going to be right again, but with time and hard work Doc Haygood figured he'd have some use of it. Best thing was, the old Jeff was back. Seems getting shot had knocked all the haughtiness clean out of the boy.

It had took near a year, but Annie was back to her sweet self again. The long months had eased her grief. She was strong as ever. The color was back in her cheeks, and the sparkle was back in them big eyes. They'd lit up like sparklers the warm July evening she told me she was with child again.

Things was prospering on the farm. We had ourself a fine corn crop. I sold enough to Mister Porter to dern near come up with next year's tax money. Cousin Vernon Cox had contracted with the army to keep them in pork, and he give me and Daniel a fat price for our hogs. The winter crops was planted, and the smokehouse would be full come cold weather and hog-killing. The womenfolk put up jars aplenty of corn and beans and field peas and such. It was near sinful how good things was going.

Then Daniel come by one morning with news that spoilt it all.

FORTY ★ FOUR

"YERBY WATTS IS BACK," DANIEL said, "and he aims to make trouble. Him and Luke Long come by the cabin yesterday around sundown."

"Dern," I said, the coffee I'd been enjoying turning bitter. I tossed what was left off the porch and set the cup on the rail. "You got to talk to him then, make him see there ain't no sense in stirring things up again."

Daniel rocked back and forth in the chair. "I'd just as soon jabber with that tree yonder. Cain't nobody talk sense to him."

"Did you tell him about all them wanted posters? If he shows his face around here—"

"I told him. He thought it was funny, him and Luke both. Hell, they joked about it."

"What about Pete Abbott?" I said. "Reckon if he talked to—"

"Yerb don't trust nobody, other than hisself and maybe Luke. Ain't too sure about Luke. Yerb sure don't trust me no more."

"Well, we got to do something," I said. "We cain't just let them dern fools ride in here and ruin things for everbody." I'd just got them words out when I seen Daniel staring past me towards the road. I turned and seen a rider coming down our lane. From the size of him I knowed it was Pete Abbott. My belly went cold.

Daniel stood up, said, "I'm guessing we too late," and walked down the steps.

———•———

Well, sir, Henry Robertson was dead, shot through the head inside his room at Wilson's Boarding House. I felt a mite responsible, knowing I'd been the one that give Yerb his name. According to the sheriff, whoever done it had shot through Robertson's pillow. Weren't nobody seen or heard a thing, leastways nobody was owning up to it if they did. Henry Robertson was the Second Bureau agent murdered in the valley in as many years, and I'd of bet my last thin dime it was Yerb that kilt him. Course, I didn't tell Pete that.

"I'm warning you boys," Pete says when he was done giving us the news and mounted up to leave, "this won't sit well with the Federals. The cavalry's already got patrols out. They'll be rounding up anybody they even suspect might be a regulator. Ex-Confederates especially. You got anything you don't want found, you best see to it quick."

I hurried back to the cabin to fetch my regulator hood before company come calling. Pulled it out of the mattress ticking where I kept it hid. Tucked the hood inside my shirt, then grabbed a hoe from the toolshed and headed for the cornfield. I was done with harvesting, but hadn't yet plowed the stalks under. Figured the cornfield would make as good a hiding place as any, so I scraped out a hole and buried the hood betwixt the rows. I put the hoe away, then went back to the cabin and sat out on the porch to catch the breeze and think a spell.

Well, sir, it had started. Henry Robertson was dead. Me and Eli hadn't mentioned to the sheriff about Yerb and Luke being back in the valley. I was hoping Yerb would let it go now that he'd kilt the man that took his farm. Just pocket his revenge and ride for Texas or wherever in tarnation he aimed to go. But I knowed a snowball would have a better chance in Hell. Trouble was coming, as hot and heavy as the heat of this August day. I was mighty glad when Eli decided to take Annie and the family up to the Gainers' place.

I felt weary, like all the sap had drained out of my body. I buried my face in my hands, wanting to cry. I was tired of it all. The war was over, but it wouldn't leave me be. I thought of Annie up there in the big house. I still ached for her, but I knowed nothing would ever come of it. She was my brother's wife, carrying his baby. They was happy, so why couldn't I just let it be instead of torturing myself so?

My thoughts drifted north to Tennessee and Francine Waters. I recollected how we sat nights on the porch of her aunt's boarding house, holding hands and sparking. Them was good times. I knowed we'd cared for each other, might've even been love. Course, that was before the dream come when I remembered about Annie. It near broke my heart to leave Franny, but that's what I done and I just had to live with that, too.

For a minute I got a hankering to pack up my things and head for Tennessee. Get away from this whole kettle of fish, try to strike things up with Franny again. But that had been more'n two years back. Weren't no way of knowing if she still cared for me or not. For all I knowed, she might even hate me for what I done. Anyways, as fine-looking a woman as she was, chance was she'd done met some other feller and married up by now.

I was still thinking about Franny and Tennessee when I heard it thundering to the south. Leastways, that's what I took it to be for a minute, till it kept on and on. Then my mind snapped back and I knowed it was gunfire. A heap of it. I walked into the cabin and grabbed my Colt's from under the pillow and checked the loads.

Seems Yerby Watts hadn't lit out for Texas after all.

———•———

After Pete Abbott rode off and Daniel left for his cabin, I went inside the house and told Annie and Mama about the killing in Bennet. "Pack what you need," I told 'em. "I'm taking you and the girls up to the Gainers' till all this blows over."

Mama went to squawking like a wet hen, saying she weren't about to let a little trouble in town run her out of her own home and such. Then Annie threwed in her two bits, saying she weren't leaving me here by myself to get into who-knows-what kind of trouble, that we was man and wife and she aimed to stand by me come hell or high water.

I stood there and let them two burn my ears another minute or so. Then I raised my hand to hush 'em, near shouted, "Now, I'd be obliged if you'd both get to it." Fished my watch out of my breeches pocket and checked the time. "I want to be out of here in thirty minutes. Have the twins tote the bags out to the porch. I'll bring the wagon around front."

I went to the barn and hitched the team to the wagon. It took the womenfolk near a hour to get packed. You'd of thought they was heading for a trip around the world from the number of bags and trunks stacked on the porch. It was another half hour before we was done loading and headed for the Gainer plantation.

I took the long way, north up the Bennet road, and crossed the Econfina at Williford Bridge. Didn't want to risk using our bridge and cutting across the Watts' old place. No sense chancing a run-in with Yerb if he was about. Figured he'd reclaimed his family farm by killing that Robertson feller.

It was a hot afternoon and there weren't a cloud in the sky, so we took it slow on the way up. It hadn't rained in a spell, and the road was potted with loose sand in places. I didn't want to tire the horses, they was pulling such a load, so it was a good three-hour trip up to the Gainers' place.

The Gainers was right tickled to see Annie, and more'n glad to take her and Mama and the twins in for a spell. I helped tote the bags and trunks into the house, then fetched some water for the team. Stayed a half hour or so to visit and rest the horses, then said my goodbyes.

When I got up to leave I asked Tom to follow me out to the wagon. I climbed onto the wagon and grabbed the reins. "You best be on the lookout," I said. "Sheriff Abbott says the Federals aim to question ever Confederate they can find, see if they can link 'em to the regulators." Then I give the team a whistle and set out for home.

———————

The gunfire I'd heard earlier kept up for a good fifteen-twenty minutes before it petered out. A hour or so passed. I was sitting on the porch with my Colt's handy when a rider come out of the woods from the direction of Yerb's place. It was late afternoon, but the sun was still high enough to blind me when I tried to see who it was. I shaded my eyes and squinted agin it, then seen the rider was leading a second horse. When he got closer, I seen there was a rider sprawled forward agin the trailing horse's neck.

Figured then this weren't no social call, so I took hold of the revolver, cocked back the hammer. When they was about fifty yards from the cabin, the first rider hallooed and waved his rifle over his head. Thought I recognized the voice, but I knowed that rifle right off. It was Jed Hicks.

I uncocked the Colt's and stuck it in my belt, waved for him to come on. "We got trouble," Jed says as he swung off his horse and commenced untying the other feller and easing him off his mount.

"Who don't?" I says, walking over to give Jed a hand. When he got the boy down I seen it was Matthew Long, Luke's kid brother. He was out of it. Looked to be shot high through the chest. His eyes had rolled back till there was only the whites showing. Blood kept bubbling out the corners of his mouth with ever ragged breath.

"He's hurt bad," says Jed.

"He is that." I'd seen wounds aplenty like it during the war. "Lung-shot."

"Can you put him up while I go fetch Doc Haygood?" Jed says, looking nearbout ready to cry.

"Don't reckon I got much choice, but I'd say you wasting your time. What happened out there anyways?"

"Ambush. Damn bluebellies opened up and come riding through our camp before we even knowed they was there."

"And just where was your sentries?"

Jed pointed at poor Matthew laying sprawled on the ground by the porch. "You looking at him."

———•◆•———

The sun was sliding behind the trees by the time I made it to the Williford Road bridge. Figured that since I was by myself now, I'd keep south on Williford Road and chance taking the lane through the Watts' farm to our bridge. That would save me a good three miles, and I'd be home before it got pitch black dark. When I got within sight of the Watts' farm I knowed I'd made a bad choice coming that way. Yankee cavalry had videttes posted on the road out front.

Well, sonny, this was a fine mess of cow patties I'd stepped in. If I turned the wagon around, they was sure to see me and give chase. But I sure didn't cotton to rubbing elbows with the Federals just now, not with all the trouble brewing. I eased the team to a stop to mull things over a spell. Decided I'd best go on ahead and try to talk my way out of trouble instead of backtracking for Bennet. Weren't no way my team could outrun a Yankee ball, or cavalry for that matter.

I grabbed the double-barrel shotgun laying on the floorboard and put it in the wagon bed. No need chancing them boys seeing that scattergun within my reach. Might be some itchy fingers amongst 'em. When I got close, three of the soldiers walked onto the road to block my way. I pulled to a halt. "How-do," I said, relieved to see that pock-faced sergeant weren't around.

A lanky feller with chin stubble and a cheek full of tobacco come moseying over to the wagon. He was toting a carbine and sporting corporal stripes. "Evening," he said, friendly enough. Where you headed?"

"Home." I pointed down the Watts' lane. "My farm's yonder, across the creek. I was aiming to use the road and bridge across the Watts' property there."

The corporal looked at me like I was a mite off my rocker. "That property belongs to a Mister Robertson. At least it did. He was murdered last night."

"Do tell?" I said, making like I hadn't heard. "Sorry to hear it. They know who done it?"

The corporal shook his head. Turned his head and spit brown juice. "Nope. Some damned Confederate regulators, they suspect."

"That so? I thought them boys quit riding a spell back."

"They're at it again. One of our patrols shot it out with them this afternoon. You know about the curfew?"

I shook my head.

The corporal tongued his chaw to the other cheek, said all official-like, "Sundown to sunup. Violators will be subject to arrest."

I pointed to the red glow to my right which was fading fast. "I best be on my way then." I flicked the reins and started to turn the team left.

"Hold on there," said the corporal, grabbing hold of a bridle to stop the horses. "You can't use that road. It's on private property."

"Look here," I said, feeling my hackles rise. "My daddy and

Coleman Watts built that road and bridge more'n twenty years back. Now, I know that feller bought the Watts place for taxes, but I don't see the harm in my crossing it, being as there ain't nobody living on the place."

"I got my orders," the corporal said, and spit again.

"And I got maybe twenty minutes or so to get home before breaking that dern curfew of yours, which I ain't heard nothing about. No way I can make it home in time if I got to turn back and go through Bennet."

The corporal scratched at his chin stubble. "That is a problem."

"Yeah, you boys've got me by the short hairs, that's a fact. Look Corporal, you got men here to spare," I said. "Why not let one of 'em ride along with me, see me home? Won't take more'n twenty minutes, and that way you'll know I ain't up to no foolishness."

He walked off and jawed with another couple of fellers for a minute or two. Then he untied his horse from a picket pin, mounted up and waved for me to follow him. It was near dark by the time we passed Yerby's cabin and the Watts' burnt-out house. Lightning bugs was flickering between the chimneys, the only things left standing of that once fine home. They stood like ghosts keeping watch over the place. Things sure had turned upside down for the Watts' family the past few years, that's a fact.

We passed through what not long ago had been fields full of cotton and corn and other fine crops, fallow now, growed over with weeds. A short piece farther we come to the trace leading down to the bridge. Night birds was peeping and scratching amongst the leaves near the creek, crickets and frogs was singing up a storm. The corporal eased his horse to the side of the trail to let my wagon pass.

"Much obliged for the company," I said, waving away a skeeter buzzing my ear.

"You know about the curfew now," he said. "See that you keep it." Then he turned his horse and rode off into the night.

I crossed the bridge, mighty glad to be home. I was some relieved knowing Annie and my family was safe and away from all this hogwash. Soon as I got the horses took care of I aimed to get some food in my belly and have a nip or two before bed.

Didn't make it halfway past the cornfield before gunshots blasted through the dark behind me.

FORTY ★ FIVE

JED HICKS WEREN'T GONE MORE'N a half hour when Matthew Long struggled down a last breath and died. It was a mite cooler outside, so I shut his eyelids, then wrapped the poor soul in a spare blanket and toted him out to the porch. Laid him next to the wall. What a goldamn waste, I remember thinking. That boy weren't no older than Hamp Watts when he was kilt at Chickamauga. At least Hamp died fighting for a worthy cause. Matthew Long died for pure hatred, nothing more, nothing less.

I went back inside to fetch my Colt's and jug and sat on the porch drinking and watching over the body. The sun had set by the time Jed come riding up by hisself.

"The doc weren't in. Some woman north of town is having a baby."

"Just as well." I pointed to the body laying agin the wall behind me. "He died not long after you left."

"Well, goddamn," says Jed, shaking his head. "Luke'll be fit to be tied."

"Reckon he will at that. What you aim to do with the body?"

"Damned if I know." Jed looked awful peaked. "That's Luke's business, way I see it."

"Well, he cain't stay here. He'll be swole up and stinking by morning, hot as it is. Either we bury him or you tie him to his horse and go find Luke."

"How 'bout we tote him down to the creek?" says Jed. "The water ought to keep him cool enough till we can figure out what to do."

I took a slug of whiskey and felt it burn down my throat. "We do that and the hogs'll have at him. You seen such during the war."

"Well damn," says Jed. "Reckon I better see if I can find Luke then."

It was full dark when we got Matthew's body lashed to the saddle and Jed set out to find Luke. He was holed up somewheres down Williford Road along the creek, about a mile south of Yerb's place, Jed thought. I wished him luck and went back inside the cabin to scrounge up some supper.

I fried up a slab of ham and had just sat down to eat it with some cold biscuits when gunfire rung out from the direction of the Watts' farm. Must've been fifteen or twenty shots in all, and from the sound of it a goodly number come from Jed's Spencer. I quick grabbed my Colt's and blowed out the lamp. Eased open the door and took cover at the corner of the cabin. If trouble come, I aimed to take to the woods along the creek. Figured I could shake anybody that tried to follow me there.

Weren't long till hoofbeats come my way in a hurry. I cocked back the hammer and waited. A minute later, Jed pulled his horse to a stop and jumped out of the saddle. He run for the steps but my whistle stopped him.

"Over here," I says, peeking around the corner.

"Yankees!" says Jed. "I rode right up on 'em. Dropped the one that halted me, and two more that come riding up."

"Where's Matthew?"

"Back yonder with the Yanks." Jed was breathing hard as his winded horse. "His horse bolted. I'm hoping the rest took off after him."

He swung back into the saddle. "I got to get. Good luck to you, Danny." Then he kicked his horse and rode hard east towards the Marianna Road.

Well, sonny, I weren't sure what to do after hearing that gunfire break out on the Watts' farm. It hadn't lasted more'n ten-fifteen seconds, but there was a heap of lead fired off in that short of time. Figured it must've been them cavalry boys with their carbines making most of the ruckus.

There weren't nothing I could do back yonder across the creek except maybe get my fool head shot off, so I drove on ahead to the barn. Unhitched the team and seen they was fed and watered, then walked to the house. I'd done lost my appetite by then, so I fetched the bottle from the pantry and went out to the porch to cool off and think. Kept the shotgun handy, just in case trouble come to visit.

Clouds had rolled in, snuffing out the moon and stars. I'd blowed out the kitchen lamp, so the house and porch was black as the night. Couldn't hardly see my hand in front of my face, which was fine by me. I didn't cotton to being nobody's easy target, and from that fracas earlier I figured Yerby Watts was likely out there somewheres in the darkness, up to no good.

I uncorked the bottle and took a swig. Derned if I weren't fed up with all this tomfoolery. It was bad enough that the war had crawled on for four long years. That foolishness had cost everbody a heap, some more than others, mind you. I'd been agin it from the get-go. No-good highfalutin blowhard politicians, waving their flags and spouting their nonsense till patriotic fools rose up and went to killing their own countrymen. The war had took my best friend, and dern near took my brother. And for what? Ain't nobody had won a damn thing that I could see.

Now here it was, more'n three years later, and the dern hardheaded fools was still at it. Why couldn't they just let things be? Why couldn't the damn Federals just go back home and let us heal and get on with our lives? Weren't nothing but pure meanness and greed, way I seen it.

And why was some, like Yerb, so bent on revenge that they would do near anything to keep the misery going? Peace be damned at any cost. That was the law they lived by, never mind what grief and suffering it brung to others.

I went on wrangling with my thoughts till the whiskey was near gone, then carried the bottle and shotgun inside and sat down on the sofa. Left the front door open. Figured I'd be more likely to hear somebody snooping around from downstairs in the parlor than upstairs in the bedroom. The clock in the hallway went to chiming. Think I counted to ten, but I weren't sure. Might've been eleven. Anyways, I aimed to keep watch till daylight, then get some sleep. Figured that ought to be easy enough.

Next thing I knowed, somebody was slapping me and shaking me awake.

———◆———

Thought I'd never get that brother of mine to wake up. Even the whiskey bottle that clattered halfway across the room after I kicked it in the dark didn't stir him. I finally struck a match to make sure he was still amongst the living. Eli was sprawled across the sofa, his mouth slacked open, a dark spot staining the cushion where he'd drooled.

I lit a lamp, then grabbed the shotgun laying next to Eli and leaned it agin the wall. Didn't want him snapping awake of a sudden and shooting somebody.

"He's drunk as a mash-eating hog," I says to Gil Miller. "Help me get him up."

Me and Gil each grabbed a arm and pulled till we had Eli sitting upright. I kept a-hold of his collar and sent Gil to the kitchen to fetch a wet dishrag. Whilst Gil was working the pump I shook Eli and give him a few gentle slaps across the face.

"Wha... what the hell?" he says, coming to and pushing me away.

Just then Gil come back with the wet rag. I handed it to Eli. "It'll be light in a hour or so. You best sober up quick. There's trouble coming."

I went to the kitchen and put coffee on to boil, whilst Eli stumbled out to the porch to get some air and puke up the bellyful of whiskey he'd drank. When he come back inside we moved to the kitchen. Eli managed to hold some coffee down, and when he was full awake me and Gil commenced to tell him what we knowed of the situation.

"Luke and Yerb have both gone plumb crazy," I says. I told him about Matthew Long getting kilt by the Yanks, and Jed Hicks' close scrape with the cavalry on the Watts' farm.

"When Jed caught up with Luke and give him the news about his brother, Luke went loco," I says. "He rounded up his boys, then around midnight they rode for Bennet and shot it out with the Yankee garrison in town. Stirred up enough racket to raise the dead. Word is there's a passel of dead and wounded on both sides. I reckon you slept right through all that ruckus."

Eli put both hands on his head, leaned forward agin the table and groaned but didn't say nothing.

"Then Yerby Watts come by my place with some of Luke's gang," says Gil. "Yerb was so likkered-up he was near to falling out of the saddle."

Gil stopped a minute to pour hisself another cup of coffee. "Yerb kept threatening to burn us out, saying I had turned agin him up in Marianna. Me and Jim and our pa managed to talk him out of it, but only because we was all three packing iron and Yerb knowed we weren't bluffing.

"Yerb finally seen things our way and rode off," Gil says, and took another gulp of coffee. "But not before he said he knowed who it was that burnt him and his daddy out, and he aimed to do the same to them that done it. That's when I figured I'd best let you boys know what was up."

Eli held out his cup. He was pale as a ghost, and his hand shook when I poured his cup half-full. He held the cup in both hands to steady it and took a sip. Looked up at me. "You don't think Yerb would try it, do you?"

I shrugged. "Don't know what to think no more."

Gil set his cup on the table and stood up. "I got to piss," he says, walking out the kitchen door.

Gil weren't gone a minute when he come running back up the steps. Throwed open the screen door and stood there with the fear of God wrote all over his face.

"Come quick, the cabin's afire!"

FORTY ★ SIX

DANIEL FOLLOWED GIL OUT THE kitchen door while I run to the parlor, grabbed my shotgun and went on out the front door. I hurried around back, looking past the cornfield toward Danny's cabin. All I seen was dark, and that's when it struck me. A cold fist squeezed my belly. It weren't Danny's cabin at all—it was Uncle Nate's!

I caught up with the others and we lit out across the field towards the cabin. Yellow flames licked skyward past the roof. A shot rang out, then come a scream that sent chills crawling down my back. Aunt Nettie!

When we was maybe a hundred yards from the cabin, we seen riders coming up the road towards the house. Daniel throwed up a hand to stop us. "Eli, you go on to the cabin and see what you can do. We got to stop them riders." Then him and Gil run for the road to cut the riders off.

I lit out for the cabin running fast as I could, but ever step felt like my legs was made of rubber. Tears was blinding my eyes by the time I got close enough to tell what was up. Some feller was out back of the cabin, standing like a shadow agin the flames. A few feet away I seen what looked to be a log laying agin a stump near the winter garden plot. Least that's what my mind told me it was. But when I blinked back the tears I seen it weren't no log or stump at all. It was Aunt Nettie, sitting on the ground, holding Uncle Nate's head in her lap. He looked to be alive, leastways his eyes was open.

"Oh Lawd, they done shot my man," she screamed, rocking back and forth, "they done shot my man."

Well, sonny, things was mostly a blur after that. Reckon that's a merciful thing. Seemed like everthing slowed to a crawl in my mind. I run towards Uncle Nate and Aunt Nettie, aiming to see if I could help. Then I seen that feller raise his pistol and point it at me. Next thing I knowed he was flying backwards from the load of buckshot I put in his chest. Don't even recall aiming or pulling the trigger, but I done a fitting job of it.

Gunfire was popping like firecrackers down the road between the cabin and the house, but I barely heard it. Aunt Nettie was pointing at the cabin and screaming something to me, something about Jefferson. But it sounded all hollow-like and I couldn't make out just what it was she was saying. Reckon my mind was in a fog of sorts by then.

The sky was graying up, turning a mite red in the east. I headed for the front of the cabin, felt the heat of the fire near roasting the skin on my right side. Around front, I seen a lone horse standing under the big oak that shaded the porch in the evenings.

I walked on towards the horse, then froze. Something weren't right. Something in the tree didn't belong, a big broke limb or some such dangling where it ought not be. The wind gusted and the limb turned. Bile rumbled in my belly and spewed out my mouth. Weren't no broke limb hanging there, it was Jefferson!

Quick as I could I grabbed a-hold of Jeff's legs and lifted him up to take the weight off his neck, but it weren't no use. One look told me what I didn't want to know. Poor Jeff's eyes was bulging and his tongue was stuck out of his mouth like he'd been trying to lap up ever last drop of air. He was gone.

They had hung him too high for me to reach the rope with my jackknife, so I eased him down and turned loose of his legs gentle as I could. I stepped towards the horse. Figured I'd mount him and stand up in the stirrups to cut Jeff down. Before I reached the horse, Yerby Watts come hobbling out of the shadows behind, pistol in hand. His eyes was stone cold and there was a pure evil grin spread across his face.

"That nigger of yours won't be burning nobody else out," he said, "lest it's in Hell."

I'd knowed Yerby all my life, had even looked up to him like a big brother. But I aimed to kill him right then and there. I didn't say a word, just cocked back the left hammer, lifted the scattergun and squeezed the trigger.

Click!

Well, sonny, either I had fired off both barrels without realizing it when I'd kilt that scoundrel out back, or else the shotgun misfired somehow. Didn't much matter which. Yerb had me by the short hairs and he was fixing to yank hard.

He raised the pistol and limped a step or two closer. I heard the hammer cock back, stared down the barrel and waited for what was coming. Funny thing was, I weren't scared at all. Hamp was dead. My baby boy Adam was dead. And now Jeff. Figured joining 'em wouldn't be such a bad thing. But if Yerby Watts was going to send me to my maker, I wished he'd get on with it.

Of a sudden, I seen them mean eyes of his shift right.

"Drop it, Yerb!" somebody hollered, just as the pistol blasted.

———•———

We weren't no more than two hundred yards from Uncle Nate's cabin when I heard a gunshot, then spied riders coming up the road towards the big house. I stopped running and throwed up my hand. When Eli caught up, I told him to go on to the cabin, then me and Gil cut across the field towards the road. It was too late to save Uncle Nate's cabin, but we might be able to stop them fellers from burning the big house.

We struck the road well ahead of the riders and took cover, Gil on one side of the road and me on the other. I figured them boys would still be a mite blinded from the burning cabin, so that ought to help us get the drop on 'em.

"This ain't no social call," I says to Gil. "Shoot to kill."

Best I could tell there was four of 'em, riding in a double file. I felt the weight of the Colt's in my hand. Waiting was always the hardest part of battle, and this weren't no different. I heard the blast of a shotgun down by the cabin, then the riders was on us.

I cocked back the hammer, stood and fired. The lead rider on my side of the road pitched off his horse. Gil was blasting away with both his pistols. Muzzle flashes cut the dark. Balls struck the road and whizzed past my head. Before I knowed it, it was over. Three riders was laying in the road, dead or dying. The other had managed to turn tail and skedaddle.

The air was heavy with burnt powder. Through it I seen Gil bent over, holding his calf. I run over to him. "How bad is it?

"Missed the bone," he says. "I'll live. You check on Eli. I'll see to these boys."

I quick checked the Colt's chamber, then hotfooted it for the cabin. Only had one shot left, but it would have to do. Weren't no time to spare for reloading. I run down the road a ways, then cut across the field towards the cabin. The fire had died down a mite, and the sky behind the cabin was glowing red.

I was maybe fifty yards from the cabin when I spied two men that looked like shadows agin the flames. When I got closer I seen one was Eli. The other had his back to me, but I would've knowed that pegleg anywheres.

Eli lifted his shotgun and pointed it at Yerb, then lowered it. He stood there froze like a cornered rabbit whilst Yerb took a couple of steps towards him and raised his pistol. My gut went cold.

Just as I hollered for Yerb to drop it, his pistol belched flame and Eli fell in a heap. Yerb turned and stared at me with them dead eyes, then pointed his revolver and fired at the same time I dropped to the ground and rolled. I come up on my elbows, aimed in on his chest and squeezed off my last round.

The Colt's bucked in my hand. When the smoke cleared I seen Yerb laying flat on his back. His good leg kicked at the dirt a time or two, then went still. I got up and eased over to him, keeping my pistol at the ready, forgetting it was empty.

I stared down at Yerb. All the meanness was gone out of his eyes. I swore there was even a hint of a smile on his face. But my ball had caught him straight through the heart. Yerby Watts was dead.

———•———

Well, sonny, when that bullet hit me it felt like a mule wearing a red-hot shoe done kicked me in the ribs. My ears was ringing. I couldn't breathe, couldn't see clear from the flash of Yerb's gun. Figured I was a goner for sure, that's a fact.

It took a spell, but my head finally started to clear a mite and I was able to get a breath or two in me. My side still hurt like holy hell, but I figured then I might not be dying after all. I tried to get up, but somebody was holding me down, telling me not to move. Turns out it was Daniel, but I didn't recognize him right off.

The sun was peeking through the trees by then, and somewheres a rooster went to crowing. A passel of Aunt Nettie's chickens was scampering about the yard, chasing crickets and flies and such like it was any other morning. Daniel had took off his shirt and tore it in strips to use for bandages. Gentle as he could, he helped me sit up.

"Hold this agin your ribs here," he said, and put a thick fold of bandage to my side.

I done what he said while he took a long strip of his shirt and wrapped it around my chest, then pulled it tight agin the bandage to hold it in place.

"You are some lucky," he said. "Bullet just clipped your ribs, ain't hardly bleeding. Reckon when I hollered at Yerb it throwed his aim off."

That was true enough. Yerby Watts had been a crack shot all his life. It weren't often he missed what he was aiming for.

"Where is Yerb?" I said, wondering if he'd hightailed it when Daniel come to my rescue.

Daniel stopped his doctoring, looking near to tears. "Over yonder." He give a quick turn of his head behind him. "Dead."

If my ribs hadn't been aching so, I would've wrapped my arms around my brother and give him a hug. Figured he could use one right then. Him and Yerb growed up together, same as me and Hamp. The war ruint Yerb, but him and Daniel had been good friends near all their lives. I couldn't conjure up how it must feel to know you just kilt one of your best pards.

"I'm sorry it come to this," I said.

Daniel give a nod, said, "It's done."

Of a sudden, it struck me. "They hung Jeff," I said, my voice choking. I'd just then remembered, and felt shamed for it.

"I know. I cut him down. I'll see he's took care of."

Then I remembered Aunt Nettie, how she'd been holding Uncle Nate and crying. "Aunt Nettie's back of the cabin," I said, forgetting for a minute there weren't no longer a cabin there. "They shot Uncle Nate."

Daniel looked past me, said, "No sign of 'em. They must've gone up to the house. You rest here whilst I go fetch the wagon."

Daniel eased me down again, then mounted Yerb's horse and rode for the house. I tried to rest, but couldn't, my side ached so. Much as I dreaded to look, my eyes was drawn to the big oak. Yerby Watts lay sprawled on one side of the trunk, the pistol he shot me with still clutched in his hand. I was glad I couldn't see his face. On the other side of the tree, Jeff lay covered up with a blanket. Only his boots was showing.

I recollected the horror I'd felt when I looked up and seen poor Jeff's tormented face, and it all caved in on me. The tears come first, then I turned my head and heaved till there weren't nothing left to give.

After I seen Yerb was done for, I give Jefferson a quick look. Seen right off it was too late for him, so I hurried over to check on Eli. I looked him over and was mighty relieved to find he weren't hurt bad. The ball had just nicked him in the ribs on his left side. There was a nasty bruise, but the skin weren't cut too deep. Figured I'd give Eli a minute to clear his head and catch his breath whilst I took care of poor Jefferson.

I jumped up and grabbed a-hold of a limb and pulled myself up till I was straddling the limb the rope was tied to. Fished my knife out of my breeches, held tight to the rope and cut it. Jeff was a big feller, and it was all I could do to keep him from falling hard to the ground. Then I climbed down and cut the noose from around his neck.

Nearbout made me ill to look at the poor soul. He'd died hard, gospel truth. I drug him over to where he would be in full shade once the sun was up, then caught Yerb's horse. Untied the blanket from the back of the saddle and covered Jeff's body.

I tore up my shirt and used it to bandage Eli best I could, then told him to sit tight whilst I went to fetch the wagon. Walked over and stared at Yerb's lifeless face once more, not hardly believing he was dead. I said a little prayer, then mounted the horse and lit out for the house, tears stinging my eyes.

Calvin Hogue
December 1927

FINIS

I TIPTOED OUT OF DANIEL'S room and quietly shut the door. This last session had been difficult for the old Confederate. Even after six decades, he'd cried while recalling the death of his old friend, Yerby Watts.

Interviewing the Malburn brothers the past few months had been a rewarding, if at times trying, experience. I was both relieved and sad it was over. I'd certainly miss working with the old codgers, but dredging up and confronting old ghosts had been difficult for them.

Walking into the parlor, I caught the delicious aroma of fresh baking drifting from Alma's kitchen. In a moment she appeared, carrying a tray of sliced cake and fresh coffee that she placed on the table in front of the sofa.

"Help yourself to a piece of nut cake," said Alma, handing me a plate with a thick slice before I could help myself. "It's Grandma Malburn's own recipe, been in the family for years."

I took the plate and thanked her, my mouth watering.

"So, you're all finished with those old coots?" Alma said as she filled a cup with steaming coffee and handed it to me.

I nodded, hurrying to finish chewing. "Yes, but I was hoping you could help me with a brief epilogue. I would expect our readers will want to know what happened to Daniel and Elijah in their later years."

Alma laughed. "Well Sugar, that could fill up the rest of that notebook of yours. What is it in particular you wanting to know?"

I washed down another bite of cake with coffee. "Perhaps some information about the principals involved. What happened to them after the story ended. Marriage, children, when they passed away, that sort of thing."

Alma reached for the coffee pot and refilled my cup. "So, you wanting the family history in a nutshell." She flashed that big smile of hers. "Be glad to, Sugar. Now, don't you hesitate to hush me up if I get carried away."

———◆———

Uncle Nate recovered from his gunshot wound. He and Aunt Nettie moved into the big house and remained loyal servants and family to the Malburns until their passing sometime in the eighteen eighties. The widow Clara Malburn passed in eighteen and ninety-one.

Yerby Watts was laid to rest beside his parents in the small burial plot on the family farm. Although the property long ago passed from their hands, the Watts cemetery remains, protected by state law.

Luke Long survived the gunfight in Bennett and is believed to have moved to Texas shortly thereafter. Some say he continued to live by the gun, while others claim he settled down to become a respected and peaceful rancher. The truth may never be known.

Tom and Sara Gainer were blessed with three sons in the years following the birth of their daughter, Daniella. In eighteen seventy-two, Tom was elected to the Florida senate, in which he served for many years. Their youngest son, Benjamin, studied law and became a respected attorney and judge in Washington County, as well as the Malburn family historian. In nineteen seventeen, Tom Gainer succumbed to influenza. Sara Malburn Gainer survived her beloved Tom by two years.

In eighteen seventy-five, Ruth Malburn married the son of a northern veteran who had settled in St. Andrew after the war. A year later she followed her husband north to Pennsylvania when he left to oversee his grandfather's burgeoning iron mill. The couple had two children, both dying in early childhood during a tragic house fire. Devastated by her loss, Ruth's health began to fail. She passed from this life in eighteen ninety-five after a long struggle with consumption.

Twin sister Naomi became the wife of Reverend Joseph Porter in eighteen seventy-five. Eighteen at the time of her marriage, she served faithfully by Joe's side until his earthly ministry was completed. Joe and Naomi were blessed with six children. As of this writing, Naomi Malburn Porter is alive and well, enjoying the love and company of her and Joe's many grandchildren.

Joseph Porter ministered to the people of Econfina for more than half a century. He kept careful watch over the flock God had intrusted to him, marrying and burying scores throughout his long years of service. Try as he might, Joe was never quite able to shake the term *Lord A'mighty!* It was a failing that Daniel took delight in never letting him forget. Daniel's best pard passed away on a sunny June afternoon in nineteen twenty-one, shortly after performing the wedding ceremony for one of his and Naomi's many granddaughters.

In eighteen seventy, after a lengthy correspondence by mail, Daniel Malburn traveled to Tennessee, returning a few weeks later with his bride-to-be, Francine Waters. Daniel's best pard, Reverend Joeseph Porter, performed the honors. While Daniel continued to farm, Francine opened a dress and dry goods store in Bennet that she ran for many years. They were blessed with two sons and a daughter, all of whom grew to adulthood and produced "a heap" of grandchildren, sixteen, all told. Daniel's beloved Franny passed from this earth in nineteen sixteen.

Elijah and Annabelle's second son was born in January of eighteen sixty-nine. They christened him Hampton Jefferson Malburn. A daughter and another son followed in the ensuing ten years. Then in eighteen eighty-five, baby Alma came into the world. All the children survived to marry and beget "a passel" of little Malburns, insuring the family reunion would carry on for generations to come.

In nineteen eleven, while returning from a shopping trip in Bennet, a rattlesnake spooked Annie's horse, causing it to race away and overturn the carriage. Badly injured, she never fully regained her health. In nineteen twelve, Eli's sweet Annie closed her beautiful doe eyes for the last time and peacefully drifted into eternal rest.

———•———

By the time Alma finished her narrative, my hand was cramped from an hour of scribbling notes. I finished the last of the tepid coffee in my cup and checked my watch. Three o'clock. I'd have to hurry if I hoped to pick up Jenny on time. I thanked Alma for her hospitality and got up to leave.

"Now you come back and see us soon," Alma said as she brushed crumbs from her apron onto the service tray. "Just because that story of yours is done don't mean you can make yourself a stranger, you hear? And bring that pretty fiancé of yours along. I sure want to meet the young lady that snagged your heart."

I felt my face flush. I told Alma I had every intention of visiting in the future. "But it will be a while. Jenny and I are leaving for Pennsylvania next week to visit my family."

"Now don't you two go and get hitched up yonder," said Alma. "Lord, it's been a month of Sundays since I've been to a fancy wedding, and I wouldn't miss yours for the world."

I assured Alma she had nothing to fear. My future in-laws would disown both of us if we were to elope, I said. Our wedding was still planned for January at the First Baptist Church in Harrison. A sudden wave of sadness swept over me. "I sure wish my father was alive to meet Jenny and see us get married."

Alma squeezed my arm. "He'll be there in spirit, Sugar, you can count on it."

"Oh, I almost forgot." I pulled two envelopes from my coat pocket. "One of these is for Daniel, the other for Elijah."

"What is it?" Alma said, taking the envelopes.

"A check from the newspaper. Uncle Hawley felt the Malburn brothers deserved a stipend for their time and cooperation."

Alma stared at the envelopes with the *St. Andrew Pilot's* logo printed in the upper-left corner. "Now Calvin, you know that's not necessary."

"My uncle insisted. Since the story's been running, advertising revenue is up nearly fifteen percent. The paper has made money from it. Uncle Hawley's even thinking about offering bound copies for sale when the serial is finished."

Alma beamed. "Just to think, those two mule-headed rascals are almost famous in these parts, thanks to you." She patted my hand. "Well, you be sure and thank your uncle for me. I know Daddy and Uncle Dan will be tickled."

"I will," I said as I opened the front door. "I've got to run now. Thanks again for everything. And I'll see you when Jenny and I get back."

"You be sure and do that." Alma's eyes were watering. Suddenly she reached up to hug me and planted a kiss on my cheek. "The welcome mat is always out for you, Sugar. Here and at the reunion. You're family now."

I returned the hug and closed the door behind me.

CPSIA information can
Printed in the USA
LVOW12s0723270114

371111LV000